a novel
by

N. Wood LANE

The Bed
I
Made

The Bed I Made is a work of fiction. Names, characters, places and incidents are either products of the authors' imagination or are used fictitiously. Any resemblance to actual persons, living or dead, business establishments, events or locales is entirely coincidental.

The quotes used on the cover of this book appeared in the September 2011 Midwest Book Review for Warped Intentions, and a March 2013 review of Presumption of Paternity by OOSA Online Book Club.

ISBN-10: 193770520X
ISBN-13: 978-1-9377052-0-6
Also available in E-Book
ISBN-13: 978-1-9377052-1-3
Library of Congress Control Number: 2013935427
Printed in the United States of America

MavLit Publishing, LLC
www.maverick-books.com

P. O. Box 1103
Irmo, S.C. 29063
Cover Design: Maverick Literary

a novel
by

N. Wood LANE

The Bed
I
Made

Author's Note

There are times in life when we find ourselves having strayed off course. I can think of a couple of situations when I knowingly entered into them, and everything within me was saying don't do it. Stay away. But I did it anyway.

Over time, I sunk to depths I never imagined for myself. Each time I tried resisting and turning away was merely another opportunity for me to find an excuse why I should stay in them. I was powerless. It was as if I'd entered into a free fall and I accepted the fact at some point I would make impact with the ground.

A few precious people very close to me felt differently. They were responsible for shedding light to what I'd done wrong, and with some of them it has taken years to earn back even a fraction of their trust, which I don't take lightly.

If you cannot identify yourself with I've just shared, I'm sure you know someone who has strayed off course. Hopefully, you'll be able to identify with Sonia Buckner's character in *The Bed I Made*, which is the sequel to *Do It to My Mind*.

It wasn't by happenstance that Sonia's character emerged as the one whom I wanted to pick on the most. I believe we're all flawed individuals. Some are more tragically flawed than others. Some are more open than others about admitting to their flaws. And I think it's more realistic as an author to present characters like that.

The challenge is when we fall short, do we acknowledge that we were wrong? As the offender, are willing to humble ourselves, ask others to forgive us, and turn away from that behavior that got us into trouble? Are we willing to ask for divine help and allow the fragments of our lives be reconstituted to serve a greater purpose and meaning?

None of this guarantees the person(s) we offended will openly embrace us again. Sometimes the damage is too great. Time doesn't always heal all wounds. But perhaps time does enable the offended party to better mange them, serving as a reminder the decisions we make affects and alters the course of everyone's lives.

N. Wood Lane
nwoodlane@hotmail.com
2013

a novel
by

N. ‗Wood LANE

The Bed
I
Made

Chapter 1

This was the kind of message that Wharton Milner wanted to receive from Sonia Buckner. He had to read it a second time, ensuring that his eyes had not failed him:

> Wharton, I've been thinking about us a lot lately. I want to take our friendship to another level. Can we talk about it?

It was a good thing he was consumed with the lunch rush at The Groovy Soul, or he might have taken a moment to let out a loud whoop and possibly cut a jig.

All the time spent being attentive and lending a willing and sympathetic ear had paid off. All the patience he'd shown Sonia knowing she was a married woman and mother of a teenage son also appeared to have been rewarded.

And to think all this time knowing Sonia, he never bothered to remember that Trent was her husband's name. It didn't really matter. He'd seen him once, and that was all that he needed to remember.

> You've just made my day, Sonia. Mind, body, and
> soul . . . That's the way it's going to be!

Sonia showed no emotion when she sent Milner the text message from her Tracfone while on break from her job at United Care Plan in Columbia, South Carolina. She took a moment to reflect on the magnitude of her decision.

It came at a time after she'd recently turned forty. She felt that her marriage, although it was still in repair over the many disappointments that she blamed Trent for causing, would never get any better than its current state.

Trent had finally reached her sexually, but the enjoyment she desired was inconsistent. She felt she deserved better than what she'd been receiving at home, having now entered her peak years.

Her desire for Milner merely intensified over the past six months. Perhaps it was the anticipation of consummating something, which she strongly believed was justified, that made her even more confident about her decision.

Better yet, she may have convinced herself once and for all after he bought her a pair of diamond-studded earrings on her birthday while Trent forgotten about it all together. A couple of weeks later, they shared their first kiss while they were on another Saturday afternoon rendezvous in Augusta—a moment that Milner thought should have happened much sooner. Yet it worked out in its own time.

> When do you want to meet? I'll even make the time

for it (wink!)

When can we talk about it?

I'll figure something out and get back with you. :)

The idea came to her rather quickly.

"Palmetto Fidelity, this is Trent Buckner—"

"Are you always this friendly when people call you?" Sonia joked with him. "Wow, I could use someone like you on my team at work."

"Uh, noooo!"

"What's wrong? You wouldn't want me to be your supervisor?" Sonia reacted. "I've seen them pull strings allowing nepotism in contract services. Maybe I can get you to work on another team? Then it wouldn't be such a problem."

"Baby, I like what I'm doing, thank you very much," Trent said. "Well, isn't this a surprise. What did I do to deserve this personal call from you?" He checked the time on his computer and mentioned it was about 1:45 in the afternoon.

"I thought I'd do something different." Sonia rolled her eyes at her own comment. "Look here, I was thinking about stopping by that restaurant we went to in Cayce a few months ago. Do you remember it?"

"I can't say that I do. Give me a clue—"

Sonia was nearly moved to laughter; it was precisely her point. She could not believe how fast her husband was falling into this ditch—face first—that she was preparing for him.

"The restaurant that served that nice buffet home-cooked style—I think it's called The Groovy something. . . ."

"Oh yeah, that place! We talked about going back there. Were you thinking of us eating there tonight?"

"No, I was thinking about grabbing to-go plates for all three of us. I don't feel like cooking tonight, and I wanted something different."

"Sure. That will work. Just make sure it's something that I'll eat."

"And if it isn't," Sonia replied, leading him on in a seductive voice, "I'll make sure you'll have something that's always served at the right temperature, and no oven or microwave is ever needed—"

Trent was incredulous at his wife's boldness, which could be quite arousing whenever his mindset was full of mischief and raunch. "You know, I do have a taste for some of that—" He went as far as sucking his teeth and grinning.

"Baby, I've known you for sixteen years. I think I've got that one under control. See you later. Time for me to go back into the asylum."

* * *

Sonia noticed a few changes inside The Groovy Soul since the last time she visited. The first thing was a new paint scheme—predominantly white but with peach colored trimming. There were several live plants brought in for aesthetics, and there were various pictures representing a southern lifestyle.

She also noticed there was new help working the dining area and the cashier's counter to keep pace with the burgeoning crowd that appeared to be frequenting the place.

Although she did not immediately see Milner, she figured he was no doubt around somewhere.

"I see you didn't get any dessert containers," Sonia heard a familiar voice from behind. She turned slowly and acknowledged Milner by making eye contact with him. They had not seen each other in a little more than a week.

She replied, "You must have told the new help that you were taking care of me personally, hmmm?"

He walked to the other side of the buffet bar as if he made a casual inspection. "I don't miss a single thing whenever you walk in here. When did you get the new outfit?"

"You have been paying attention." She looked herself over, admiring the navy skirt suit she recently purchased.

"I'll be back with your dessert containers."

Sonia was finished with filling her main course containers just as Wharton returned. "Excuse me, sir. Are you going to take care of my order for me?"

He did not immediately respond. But then it dawned upon him what she meant. "Don't worry. That won't happen again. I'll be right back." He went back to his office and stuffed two twenty-dollar bills in an envelope.

When Milner returned into the dining area, Sonia had a small mountain of Styrofoam containers that she'd carried over to cashier's counter. He was there to offer his help.

"I figured a plastic bag would not work well for you, so I brought this box. Would you need help carrying this out?" He gave her a knowing stare.

"I really appreciate your service here, sir. Thank you."

"It's my pleasure. Thank you for visiting us!"

Milner was more than eager to escort Sonia out to her Infiniti M35, which was parked directly across the driveway.

He walked with great pride knowing that he and Sonia were soon to consummate their growing acquaintance.

"I've placed an envelope in this box addressing your order. Is there anything else I can do for you?" He looked over to his right at her.

"You can tell me what you have in mind for us—"

"I was thinking about us going in Charlotte next week, say, Tuesday. Would that work for you?"

"As long as I can plan three days ahead of time, that shouldn't be a problem. I'll text message you from work tomorrow confirming it."

They stopped at her car.

"Sonia, you look nice in your new outfit." He looked her up and down before licking his lips and nodding slowly for added effect. "A woman should have a nice set of legs like yours if she's going to wear business skirts."

She smiled back at him. "Thank you. I had you in mind when I picked it out."

"Did you really?" He gave her a side-eyed stare.

"I sure did. And I bet you'd like to see more than just my legs right now—"

He was moved to chortling. A few days' wait was not going to ruin it for him. "I better not make a scene. You know I would love to kiss you right here." He also entertained the thought of groping and fondling beneath her skirt.

"I don't know what I'm going to do with you, Wharton." She thought back to how soft his lips felt against hers, the way she felt light headed once their tongues entwined, and the way her body reacted to him pulling her body toward his—this visit was fast becoming more than what she'd anticipated.

"Just don't hold back on anything once you start with me," he answered. "That's all I ask."

Late that night, Sonia felt unusually mischievous and she could not suppress it. And what she had in mind did not involve Trent.

She first stopped by the other closet in their bedroom and retrieved the Tracfone she used to contact Milner. Then she tipped into the bathroom.

Peering into the mirror, Sonia inspected her face. It was still free of wrinkles and crow's feet. Next, she inspected her hair. Surprisingly, there was only a stray strand or two of graying amid her naturally auburn color; she dared not to look elsewhere on her body. She'd been considering of late to keep it bald rather than neatly cropped close so she wouldn't have to worry about it.

Next, she took a couple of steps back from the mirror, removed her silk kimono and the boy shorts that she wore to bed, and she inspected the rest of her body. She made a slow one-eighty in one direction and a slow one-eighty in the other, and she was quick to determine she was still firm in all the right places.

"I don't feel old," she whispered to herself. "I actually don't know how I am supposed to feel or act now that I'm forty. . . ."

She ran her hand over various areas of her body. It felt as if it was a fun and sensual thing to do. She reasoned the worldly view of what she was doing would applaud her for simply getting to know her body and loving herself. But this was something that was never taught or encouraged by anyone she knew of in the church.

Then she reached for the Tracfone. She began taking pictures of herself. Frontal view. Side view. Back view. She even went as far as sitting on the bathroom floor, spreading her legs far apart, and added a couple of pictures from that view.

Feeling aroused, she went as far as rubbing and stroking herself while fantasizing about Milner—it was a matter of moments before her body tensed and she struggled to remain silent while the pleasure produced a rippling effect throughout.

Afterward, she reviewed the photos that she'd taken of herself. She decided on sending Milner a photo that offered him a rear view of her along with the caption:

I was thinking of you tonight. Wouldn't you like to
know my thoughts?

Chapter 2

Milner could not get to his cell phone fast enough while he was in the process of opening the door to his home in Eastover, a community that bordered Richland and Sumter counties heading eastbound along Highways 76 and 378.

His hands were also full with a briefcase and a couple of boxes he brought back from The Groovy Soul. When he tried taking it out of his coat pocket, the phone slipped through his hand and made a thud on the porch.

"Argh!" he grimaced.

The phone buzzed on the cement and his improvised ringtone of "Everything Is Everything" by prolific Hammond B3 organist Booker T Jones was distorted by the vibrating.

"I hope the screen didn't crack," he mumbled aloud.

Milner went ahead with dropping off his stack of work onto a golf chair that he had situated behind his double-front door. Then he stooped back outside in the near-freezing temperature on this late-February night and retrieved his phone.

He smiled and nodded after inspecting it. No apparent dents or chips, and most importantly, the screen wasn't cracked. He dared not to think he could get away with that again. The screen on his other phone looked like a spider's web after the second time he dropped it. He was stubborn to keep using it until he could no longer dial or type any messages.

Checking the missed call, it came from his sister Willette, who along with her daughter Katrina helped him run The Groovy Soul.

"You caught me as I was trying to get inside my house," Milner told her.

"I'm sorry for calling you at this late of an hour," she said.

"But I needed your help."

"You know you can call me any time, sis—"

"Thanks."

"What's up?" He walked over to his comforter chair and plopped in it. He searched for his TV remote and clicked it on to the Weather Channel. "Has somebody already called in sick for tomorrow?"

Willette collected her thoughts before she responded. "No, nothing like that." She managed a weak chuckle. "It's only 11:45 tonight. We still have another nine, ten hours before first shift. Anything might happen before then."

"You're right." He exhaled loudly as if to catch his breath.

"I called you because MacArthur is at it again."

"What?" Milner sat up in his recliner; he was on alert, sensing it could only be trouble whenever his eldest sibling called family.

"Before you start killing the messenger, just hear me out first, okay?"

"Yeah, go ahead—"

"Mac says he's in trouble with back taxes and child support," Willette said. "He says he's been trying to do right. But he hasn't been able to keep a steady job, and he owes about thirty grand."

"And that's our problem?" Milner reacted.

"He is our brother."

Willette continued explaining MacArthur's dilemma, but Milner could only think about how much grief MacArthur had caused him, Willette, and their other sister, Constance, throughout the years.

After his family moved from Rogers, Arkansas to Compton in the South Central Los Angeles area, MacArthur was the only one among his siblings who found the temptations of gang life most appealing. He was expelled from two junior high schools and high schools each. His mother, Audrey, spent all she had trying to keep him out of jail. The most costly attempt occurred when MacArthur was seventeen and had already drop out of high school.

MacArthur faced time for participating in a rash of burglaries in neighborhoods on the west side of Los Angeles. The judge gave him a final chance at getting his life straight if he would make restitution, which totaled more than $4,000, and then enter into a job training program.

Audrey, who was protective of her children, got into more debt than she could handle by helping him. It resulted in her being evicted from the two-bedroom home that she rented.

With nowhere to turn, Audrey, Milner, and his sisters had to settle for living in a low-rent apartment complex that was a haven for rats, roaches, drug dealing, gang activity, and prostitution.

Meanwhile, MacArthur never participated in any job training program and he continued with gang banging. Along the way, he fathered four children before he was twenty years old. He also ended up on the wrong side of the law at age twenty-three when he was arrested for his role in killing a rival gang member. He was sentenced to seven years in prison, serving six.

Milner finally tuned back into the conversation. "Do I need to remind you how your brother has bled this family dry over the years?"

He went on to describe even after MacArthur got out of prison he continued fathering children and indulging into any get-rich-quick scam that came along. At fifty eight, MacArthur had eleven children; the youngest was a five-year old daughter whose mother was twenty-four, the same age as one of his children.

"I don't know what else to say." Willette's voice was full of distress. "He came crying to me. He really sounded scared. He told me he was too old to be going back to jail."

Milner was furious. Not at Willette for taking the call, but he fumed at MacArthur's scheme thinking if he could worry Willette, whose guilt was being as good natured as their mother was, then she'd panic and convince Milner into helping him.

"Let me do this, Willette," he proposed. "I'll call him and I'll see just where his head is."

"Thanks, Wharton. Let me know what happens tomorrow."

Grudgingly, Milner dialed the number that Willette had given him. Usually, it took him a while to come down from a day at The Groovy Soul, but this was not his idea of doing just that.

Milner had last seen MacArthur at their mother's funeral back in 1996, and they last spoken to each other in 2004. It was also the last time that Milner had helped MacArthur out of another of his tight spots by sending him $2,500.

"Yo!"

"You sure got a lot of gall with that attitude," Milner responded to MacArthur's greeting.

"Well, what am I supposed to say, fool?"

It took all of Milner not to curse out his brother and hang up. He got up from his comforter chair and began pacing the living room carpet.

"I'm calling to find out what your latest problem is—fool—since that's all you've been your entire life!"

"Humph, when you're all high and mighty, people like you are always gonna look down on folk like me who are struggling to make it another day."

"Don't give me that mess!" Milner screamed back at MacArthur. "I don't have to help you. And there's no guarantee that I will.

"So, if I were you, I suggest that you check yourself real fast and state your reason for needing any help from your family again—"

MacArthur, who's seven years older than Milner, once had similar rugged handsome features as his younger brother. But living a hard and troubled life had caught up with him. His thin hair was mostly gray. He had deep furrows in his brow from anger and stress. He'd lost several teeth due to his inability to care for himself financially. He was troubled by the bad news over the years with his own children—four of his seven sons were doing time in prison for crimes ranging from drug dealing, gang-related killings to armed robbery and murder.

"Man, these babies mamas are ganging up on me. Because times are hard, they think I can help them out when I can barely help myself," he said. "Then I tried filing taxes, and I got in trouble with both the judge and IRS."

Milner had already regretted calling MacArthur. "How in the world did you do that?"

"I claimed three of the youngest ones on my taxes just to come up with some money to take care of other things."

"Like what?" Milner did not bother to remind MacArthur that he could not file taxes on children who did not live with him.

"What's it to you?" he snorted before cursing back at Milner. "You're living the good life in South Carolina. Yeah, I hear you have a nice home, and that restaurant's making you money hand over fist. But you can't even think of helping out your own brother?"

"Why should I?" Milner retorted. "I don't trust you as far as I can throw you!"

"But you can help out Willette? Oh, I forgot. You two are just alike, anyway."

Milner responded with a profanity-driven diatribe that described MacArthur as every lazy, conniving, trifling bum known to mankind. Then he went on to remind MacArthur that he was helping out Willette because she was left with nothing after her husband died.

He did not mention to MacArthur that Charles Traynor refused to have any insurance on himself, claiming he did not want anyone to get rich off of him. Despite Milner's pleas, Willette refused to go against Charles by forging his signature on a policy application.

"You've had every opportunity given to you for help," Milner said. "But all you've ever done was get back into the same mess, if not worse—"

"Look, man, I'm too old to be going back to jail again! I know I won't ever be able to pay you back, but I've gotta do something."

In the background where MacArthur lived, a police helicopter hovered in the immediate area and police and fire sirens blared. Those were familiar, but forgettable sounds to

Milner, who sighed loudly into the phone.

Then he rolled his eyes. He thought about how he'd managed to do well for himself after leaving the Army. MacArthur could have done the same thing for himself.

First, Milner became an insurance agent and built up a large clientele base of individuals and families selling life, health, and annuities; he also did the same thing with businesses, offering group health insurance and other employer-based benefits before it became popular among agents in the late 1990s and early 2000s.

He parlayed some of his money into stocks and mutual funds, riding a wave of good fortune all the way through late 2007. He sold many of his mutual funds before the stock market plunged the following year. That provided him the investment capital to start The Groovy Soul—and part of that money's being used to supplement Willette and Katrina until the restaurant can sustain their salaries.

Opening The Groovy Soul fulfilled a life-long dream of his to own his own business; a significant portion of the restaurant's core menu was derived from recipes by his mother's family handed down to him.

"I know you're my brother, but there comes a time when tough love is necessary. And now's that time," Milner said. "You give me the name of where you're supposed to make your payments, and I'll write a check on your behalf for a portion of it. Then you're on your own!"

"How much are you going to help me with?"

"Beggars can't be choosy—fool!"

"Can't you at least tell me?"

"Okay, I'll tell you," he said, smacking his lips. "One thousand dollars."

"What? You drive a Mercedes. You have a house, and you own a business, and you can't do any better?"

"One more word and I'll write it for half, five hundred—"
MacArthur was silent.

"I thought you'd see it my way," Milner said. "And don't ask
me for any more!"

* * *

It was well after 1 a.m. Milner was engaged in phone calls
to MacArthur, Willette, and later Constance. He finally noticed the text message that was sent to him shortly before
midnight.

Immediately, he smiled. He had a greater reaction once he
opened the photo that accompanied Sonia's text message.
That was more of his idea of winding down from a long day,
although he had to tug at his slacks several times adjusting
himself.

He was more than convinced that Sonia was serious about
taking their acquaintance to another level. A woman as perceptive and careful as she was would not send him a nude
photo unless she had every intention on consummating what
she had going on with him.

Closing his eyes, he reflected on the way her body felt in
his embrace. Then he imagined what it would be like touch-
ing her flesh—and more. He reclined back and smiled at the
thought.

Chapter 3

An awkward feeling occurred once Sonia entered her cubicle and sat down at her desk.

Always a thinking person, Sonia had worried herself into a mini-frenzy over how Milner might react to the photo she sent him. Would he be like a high school boy or college-aged male and show off her picture? But at least nobody could put a face with it.

Would he think any less of her now that she'd made it clear she wanted to pursue a sexual relationship with him? Humph, they'd been secretly going out on dates over the better part of eight months.

Should she have sent him something that was even more provocative, like a frontal or genital shot? No, the rear-view shot was the safest one; her face was not in the picture. She pressed her palms together and rested her forehead on them as if she prayed for strength and direction. Something still didn't feel right about what she did, but she refused to acknowledge her actions as sin—even if adultery had long since been committed in her heart.

"Ms. Sonia, good morning. Can you help me with a call?" asked Alvantrae Benson, a phone rep who worked on Vicki Lawson's team; she was not scheduled to come in for another hour.

Sonia looked up. "Hold on." She rushed to put away her purse and turn on her computer. She also yawned.

"Long night for you?" Alvantrae inquired.

"No. Just had to get that out of me before I started."

She noticed something different about him: His hair was now in a ponytail rather than just combed to the back, his eyebrows were arched, and he wore a second left earring hole.

He smirked. "Well, it's okay if it were a long night."

"It's also okay that I'm not asking you if you've already referred to your resource directory." She awaited his response after mocking a question Vicki would have asked him.

He placed a hand on his thigh and rolled his neck while glaring back at her. "And I thank you so much that you didn't, Ms. Sonia."

"Okay, my screen's up. What's the problem?"

Alvantrae described that he had an inquiry from Hassiba on behalf of Midlands Palmetto Hospital.

"You're kidding me, right?" Sonia interrupted him.

He sucked his teeth. "I wish that I was."

Hassiba Mimoun-Garouj was least liked among most seasoned phone reps and all of the team supervisors. She was notorious for being relentless whenever she followed up on the progress and payment of medical claims filed by the facility.

If there was any discrepancy of information given to her, Hassiba would bombard the phone rep into submission with follow-up questions, resulting in phone calls that might last in upwards of a half-hour. A common tactic of hers included asking supervisors the same line of questions.

Hassiba was no more than four minutes into the conversa-tion with Alvantrae before she peppered him about an un-resolved $1.2 million claim that was filed fifty-four days ago. Claims usually took no more than thirty days to be resolved, if payment was approved and made by UCP.

"I explained to her that nothing had been denied, and it ap-peared that there was a notation about the claim being sent over for pricing verification. But that wasn't good enough for the little wench," Alvantrae said, rolling his eyes.

Sonia sighed loudly. "God, I don't want to speak with this woman!"

"Humph, you ain't the only one!" Alvantrae remarked. "My call-time average's going to be out of whack the rest of the day because of her—"

"All right, let's get this over with."

Sonia followed Alvantrae back to his desk. Along the way, she hoped this was not a harbinger of less-than-favorable things to come—the way of a sinner being hard—since she decided to move forward with Milner.

So, she dismissed it as being mere luck of the draw. There was always a one-in-eleven thousand chance on any given day that she might wind up speaking with someone of Has-siba's reputation. She resolved to herself that she would not allow one call dictate her entire day.

"I'm Sonia, Alvantrae's supervisor. How can I assist you this morning?"

Hassiba, a native of Algeria, spoke with a slight accent. "I want to know what is taking you so long with paying this claim? We've sent everything that you needed. I don't under-stand why this is taking nearly two months—"

"I've reviewed all the documentation that is currently avail-able, and there is nothing we can do on this one but wait,"

Sonia explained to her. "Claims of this dollar amount have a review-and-reconciliation process of its own. It must be approved and signed off by a panel of doctors and other officers of this insurance company."

"I don't agree with you at all. We know that what you people do is sit on the money and collect interest!"

"Hassiba, the claim has not yet been signed off for payment. And there is no way we can send an inquiry to those individuals to learn of its progress."

"Do you know whom I would need to speak with from this panel of individuals you're talking about?"

Sonia shook her head in disgust. She was more than certain she'd explained this process to her in the past. "Hassiba, we do not have that information."

"Who can I speak to who might have that information?"

Sonia looked up at the ceiling, as if she began counting backwards from ten. "I'll tell you what I'll do, Hassiba. Give me your phone extension, and I'll call you myself as soon as we know the claim will be released for payment."

After contemplating Sonia's offer at resolution, Hassiba relented but grudgingly. "You do know that I will be making a complaint about this—"

"You'll just have to do what you'll have to do. Thank you for calling."

Sonia dared not to ask if there was anything else Hassiba needed because that might result in the call time lasting in upwards of an hour. She was quick with putting Alvantrae back on the line with her.

Tanya Fuller's arrival at work was usually marked by loud conversation with another phone rep once she approached her work area. This day was no different. In fact, she was more than compelled to draw Sonia into it.

"Ms. Sonia, you know how my patience is with Shabu when they call here? So you know I'm already on high alert—"

Sonia often cringed whenever Tanya ranted about callers of Indian descent because she knew she would end up laughing along with everyone else.

Meanwhile, Tanya took Sonia's lack of response as a green light to continue.

"Well, I'm stopping off in the store on the way into work, and I must have ran into his first cousin or someone closely related . . . He's going to argue with me that I didn't give him enough money when I know I gave him a ten dollar bill."

Sonia's eyes widened with intrigue. She also knew a laugh line was in the making.

"I told him to keep the change, but I was going to walk out of his store with what I purchased. And I dared him to call the police on me!"

Tanya placed her purse on her desk, turned on her computer, and adjusted her chair's back position.

"The bad thing about it he always has the nerve trying to talk cool to me, saying, 'When are you going to give me your phone number?'" she said, attempting to mimic the store clerk's accent. "And the bad thing about it, I can't stand that music he plays in there—that belly dancing music has got to go!"

Two other phone reps along with Sonia could not hold back on their laughter.

"But that ain't all," Tanya said, laughing along with them. "Y'all saw me coming in here out of breath? That's because I got pulled over just as you leave Gaston. Ol' Barney had to make an example out of somebody, and it was me.

"Nobody ever goes fifty-five on [Highway] 321 once you're past the IGA store [driving into Columbia]!"

"Well, Tanya, I hope your day is better than it began," Sonia said. "At least you have not yet had to deal with Hassiba."

"Lawd, don't even mention that woman's name around me!" Tanya reacted. "I'd rather have ten straight calls from Shabu than to deal with her even once!"

Sonia glanced at the clock on her computer. It was 9:04. "Uh, Tanya, you need to log on your computer." She reminded Tanya that she could be counted as late if she was not logged in less than a minute.

Things finally quieted down once Tanya was settled in and began taking calls. There was the usual buzz of conversations in progress between phone reps and providers. That lasted until the first batch of e-mails were sent out by Phyllis Blake, director of contract services.

"This can't be so!" Tanya shrieked.

Sonia craned her neck so she could see what was wrong with Tanya.

"Ms. Sonia, did you see this e-mail that Phyllis just sent?" she asked.

"I've been working on reports. I haven't seen anything."

"These people are crazy around here!" Tanya began blinking her eyes at a fast rate.

"Hold on, I'll see what you're talking about."

Sonia figured two of the four e-mails may have had a direct effect on her phone reps: The first one was a request by Phyllis that phone reps on Sonia's team delay taking their breaks for lunch by thirty minutes. That would accommodate Vicki's team meeting to update phone reps about the contracts of select new employer groups coming on board at UCP.

The other one was an announcement about another hiring freeze in contract services. This would be the second time within the past twelve months: All employees could not apply for any UCP jobs outside of the department until it was determined there was sufficient staffing to absorb future turnover.

Contract services phone reps were already known to have the lowest morale out of all UCP employees, according to every company survey taken since 2008.

"Okay, which one are you talking about?" Sonia asked.

Tanya placed her call on hold She huffed before answering. "You know which one!"

"Let me guess, the hiring freeze?"

"Yes, that one!" Tanya's nostrils flared and her eyes were bulged.

"Ms. Sonia, I've been here seven years. I've been trying to get out of here for the past eighteen months, and every time there's finally something I'm interested in applying for these people want to clamp the ball and chains on you!"

Part mother. Part shrink. Part motivator. Part instructor. And part counselor. Those were some of the roles Sonia felt she performed when dealing with Tanya. And she suspected the roles would become even more diverse should she ever aspire to move up in management.

Initially, she tried calming Tanya's concerns. "I don't think they made that announcement just to keep you bound in this department. Think about it, a hiring freeze affects everyone. It means supervisors and managers can't move—"

"Yeah, the only way you're ever able to leave around here is if you're fired, you quit, or they're carrying you out of here dead on a stretcher!" Tanya ranted; she went on to remind Sonia that former phone rep Marla Thornton died sixteen months ago.

Ms Thornton had worked in contract services for eight years; she was persistent in her efforts to leave the department over the final three years.

The autopsy indicated a heart attack was the cause of Ms. Thornton's death; there was no evidence to suggest that stress being linked to her time in contract services contributed to her death.

"They know this job will kill you!" Tanya said. "And I bet just for kicks they decide that they'll stick it to those of us who they know really want out of here!"

Sonia merely stared at Tanya. Before she spoke, she made a pointing gesture at her computer.

"I know, I know! I need to get back to my call." She sucked the inside of her mouth. "You ain't no help!"

It's going to be one of those kinds of days…

Another twenty minutes passed before Tanya sought out Sonia again. These were the days she wished she were a unit manager because they worked in actual offices on the other side of the work floor.

"Ms. Sonia, guess what a billing collector just told me?"

She forced herself into showing much patience and tolerance.

"What, Tanya?" She went as far as smiling.

"This lady from McLaren Hospital in Florence asked me about Lance, claiming she missed chatting with him—"

"Wow, I hadn't heard that name around here in a while, and that might be a good thing," Sonia answered.

Lance Miles, a former phone rep, quietly left contract services less than two weeks after team supervisor Charlotte Dillingham and him had an open lover's spat in the workplace. Both were disciplined by Phyllis with strong verbal warnings.

Of greater significance to Sonia, Lance was the boyfriend of her older sister Shonna Chandler. They had not spoken to each other since Shonna refused to answer any questioning about her decision to date someone who was sixteen years her junior.

"You know what? I kinda missed him. He was all right,"

Tanya said. "I think Charlotte could have handled that better than what she did."

Sonia was careful with her words. "He did his job. He came to work on time. As a supervisor, that's all you can ask."

"After all this time, I never bothered to ask why did he leave? It was like one day he was here; the next day he wasn't sitting at his desk."

"From what I recalled," Sonia answered, "he e-mailed me that he had found work at another company. He didn't mentioned where he would be going or where he might be moving, either."

Lance's work area—directly across from Tanya—was cleared away the next business day, but nobody replaced him. Sonia suspected with the recent hiring freeze she'd likely to be assigned a replacement from among the pool of temporary phone reps being considered for permanent status.

That was the least of Tanya's interests. She was emphatic to recall watching Charlotte follow Lance in hot pursuit to his desk and then calling him out about them having sex on the third floor of the UCP building—and that she had the best seat in the building while eating popcorn.

"I had to pull that girl away, or it might have gotten real nasty." She then lowered her voice. "Charlotte and I are still somewhat close, but not as close since that day."

She went on to say Charlotte had neither mentioned Lance's name since the incident nor had she divulged anything else whenever she was asked about him.

"I guess I would, too, if I'd put our business out there for everyone to know," she added.

Both returned to doing their work after Tanya's last comment. But the mere mentioning of Lance gave Sonia a greater reason for reflection: It had been more than seven months since Shonna hung up on her. This was not the first time that

that she and Shonna were on non-speaking terms.

Although Sonia held out in hope that all was well with them, she still believed that Shonna should have made a better choice in men.

Chapter 4

Milner gave Sonia instructions to meet him between 9:45 a.m. and ten o'clock in the parking lot of a Hyatt Place hotel near downtown Charlotte. That was only after they went back and forth about him wanting to meet her at a location in Columbia and then they'd drive there in his Mercedes.

"I should be comfortable with us going on a date in the same car," she said, "but I'm not yet there."

"What's wrong? You think I would leave you stranded in Charlotte if things didn't go well?"

"That's always a possibility, you know—"

Milner chortled at her reasoning. "Sonia, I know where you're going with that. I've already come to accept you're just going to fight me tooth-and-nail when it comes to certain things."

"That is true. I can't wait to see you, but I do want to be careful."

Since she knew Milner liked looking at her legs, Sonia picked out a sapphire color floral print dress with a matching Bolero shrug along with some black pumps to wear while in Charlotte. She also figured that she would wear her hair down just to send a message that she was not at all uptight about their tryst.

Sonia had already planned that she would leave home shortly before 8 a.m., placing her in the midst of the morning rushhour traffic into Columbia on I-20. And the drive up to Charlotte would take her just over ninety minutes.

It turned out that she and Milner were on their cell phones from when she drove past Ridgeway on I-77 northbound until she reached the outskirts of Rock Hill, a span of about forty-five minutes' driving time.

"It was your choice that you wanted to drive up here in your own car," he teased her. "We could have had this same conversation with you as my passenger."

"I know. Maybe next time," she answered. "I also like driving. It gives me a chance to see things that I haven't seen in who knows how long."

Without giving much thought, she casually mentioned that she'd almost forgotten what it was like to be wanted by another man. Very few had captivated her over the years dating back to her first liking of boys in junior high school.

"Funny," she mused aloud. "My sister called me a prude not long ago."

"I know that's your sister. What gives her the right to call you one?" Milner went on to say he found it hard to believe that Shonna would say anything along those lines about her. He ascribed to the theory that there was a little freak in everyone.

"Hey, that could be a function of their life experiences and how much they're willing to try something different, erotic, and sensual . . . That's just a nice way of saying only they know."

Sonia then thought about her own marriage. As best as she recalled, Trent never accused her of being boring and conservative in the bedroom; she thought they were border-line freaky when things were going well for them.

"Okay, well based on what you've seen and know about me, what makes you think that I'm not a prude?" she asked him.

"I guess we'll find out soon enough, hmmm?"

"Good answer!"

Milner then asked Sonia where she was on I-77. She told him that she was approaching the Carowinds theme park exit right at the North Carolina-South Carolina border—less than ten minutes away from their meeting place.

As if he needed any more motivation, Milner browsed through his cell phone's picture gallery and opened the one that Sonia recently sent him. He smirked and rubbed his crotch. Attractive women came into The Groovy Soul every day, but she was at the top of his list.

He zoomed in the picture slightly, enabling him to focus more on her cheeks. They were so shapely and full—the kind that left lasting impressions and memories. He let out a modest grunt in admiration. But then an incoming call chimed on the car's speaker system.

"If you look to your right . . ."

Sonia cast an alluring stare at him and smiled. She then hung up and turned off her engine. After putting away her Tracfone and gathering her purse, she joined him inside his car.

"Good morning," she greeted him; her fragrance quickly filled his cabin.

The words never left Milner's mouth. He leaned against his door panel and shook his head. He appeared to be caught up in a rapture of a different kind.

Sonia knew she looked good, and his inability to speak merely confirmed it.

"You look like royalty," he finally said. "You are the total package!"

"Thank you, Wharton." The tone in her voice hardly resembled the formal one she was known for using at UCP. It was soft, pliable and seductive, hinting at something similar to the nude picture of her in his cell phone.

There was also a gleam in her eye and glow upon her face. It was as if she was eager to board a cruise ship to a tropical vacation spot.

Milner leaned over and kissed her on the cheek. "I've been waiting for this day."

"So have I," she replied; his cologne was mesmerizing to her. "I'm looking forward to having a good time."

Being more than an hour—and nearly twice the distance—away from Columbia placed Sonia in a different comfort zone. She did not put up any argument with Milner after he announced that they would drive around Charlotte in his car rather than them using separate vehicles.

Besides, he argued, if they were going to take it to another level they might as well look and act the part.

"Have you eaten today?" he asked.

She looked over at him. "I'm not really a breakfast person." Then she glanced downward; her stomach just growled. "On second thought, I'll take you up on that offer."

Milner, while backing out of his parking space, announced they would find a place to eat and then hang out at the South Park Mall a for while.

They were barely thirty seconds into driving on Tyvola

Road when Milner's phone chimed. Sonia decided to close her eyes and recline in her seat.

"Wharton, when you said that you would handle this issue with MacArthur I didn't know that it meant he would be put in jail again!" Willette's voice was highly agitated, causing him to grimace.

"Can we talk about this another time? I told you that I was taking a day off." He rubbed his forehead with his left hand.

There was the shuffling of dishes and other culinary items in the background. It sounded as if the crew was well into preparing for the lunch rush.

"I'm really disappointed in you," she said. "He's making it sound as if you didn't do anything at all."

"I did do something. I sent him a grand, and that was all that I was going to send him!"

"How much does he owe?"

"Thirty grand. At least that's what he told me." Milner's expression was fast changing from pleasant to annoyance. "Willette, I'm tired of bailing our brother out of trouble, and then all he does is go back to the same thing.

"My initials are WPM, not ATM!"

Willette remain persistent with Milner. "So you are going to let him just stay in jail, if that's what the judge decides?

"If I were in a position to help, I would. But I see where this is going. I'll talk to you when you get back. Hopefully, you will have thought about it."

Milner then looked over at Sonia and apologized for the interruption. He gave a brief explanation about MacArthur's latest brush with the law, emphasizing that what got him in the most trouble was claiming non-custodial children on his IRS return. That further compounded the trouble he already had with the child support system.

"I'm not a cold-blooded person, Sonia. What people don't

understand in life is that they've got to do some things for themselves," he said.

"My brother always wants to throw in my face that I should be obligated to help him out because I own a business and I've managed to accumulate a few things. But I don't have to do anything if I don't want to!"

Sonia turned and looked at Milner. A vein was beginning to show in his temple. This was a part of his demeanor she had neither seen nor encountered.

It was equally intriguing to find out just how he might react to the softness of a woman's voice in the midst of a heated situation. Would his anger diffuse and subside? Or would it be incensed?

"What type of relationship do you have with your brother and sister?" she asked.

"Actually, it's brother and sisters," he corrected her; it was as if he flipped another switch and his voice returned to the calm, suave tone that she was more familiar with.

"Oh, yes. That's right. You did mention you have two sisters."

He looked straight ahead while apprising her about his family.

"Willette and I are really close. We were like partners in crime while growing up. We would fight each other. And if someone messed with us, we'd turn and fight them. Then we'd finish our fight. I'll listen to her when I won't listen to anyone else," he said.

"My sister Constance and I, well, we get along. But she's five years older than me. She was closer to my brother while growing up. Then she got married and she's been into her own little world, and I have no problem with it."

Milner then inhaled deeply through his nostrils as he began forming thoughts about MacArthur.

"As for my brother . . . the best thing I can say about him is I really think he would want to do what's right in life, but he has no idea or concept of how to accomplish that. It's as if the only things he knows how to do is procreate—he has eleven children—and get into trouble."

Sonia could not resist prodding him for a deeper response.

"May I ask you this question?"

"Sure."

"Okay," she commented, while folding her arms. "Do you think your brother would help you if the situation was reversed?"

"No." He reached out for her hand, to which she gave him her left hand to grasp. She tucked their hands into her lap and began stroking his.

"Sonia, we can talk about my brother another time. This is our day together, okay?"

* * *

As if the director ordered a soft wipe for transitioning, Milner went into another mode. He pressed the media button and then reached out for Sonia's hand again. His touch was even softer.

He began bobbing his head in sync with the beat. First, he blurted out good morning. She almost replied good morning to him; she also recognized he could carry a note rather capably.

Next he said aloud having her near him was amazing.

Then he looked at her saying it was outrageous and emphasized her smile. Then he smiled back at her, noting their moment was getting personal.

She now found herself bobbing her head along to the song as well.

"Who do you think you are?" she asked.

He chortled. "Don't you like this song?"

"Yeah, I do. Who is he?"

"Anthony Hamilton. He's actually from Charlotte."

"I've never heard of him until now." The mere thought prompted her to consider what had she been doing lately with her life. "I need to get out more, don't I?"

"That can be arranged if you stick with me—"

She was incredulous and could not hold back her laughter that he was pulling out all the stops to set the mood for her—and it was working.

When they got out the car at the SouthPark Mall, Milner walked over to her side and offered her his hand. They first entered the mall holding hands, but that quickly changed to them browsing the place arm-in-arm.

She looked up at him periodically. He appeared to be exceptionally proud of who was at his side. His chest was puffed out and he had a coolness about him that suggested he was in complete control of everything.

The moment seemed almost too good to be true. She clung to him tighter as if to get his attention and perhaps bring him back into reality.

"Wharton, I'm not naïve about doing this," she mentioned to him.

He shrugged his shoulders. "I know. But you've got to admit we do look good together, don't we?" She glanced at their reflection on one of the shop windows.

"I agree that we do. But I'm just curious. You're such a handsome man. Did you ever think it was easier to have sex with a married woman?"

He slowed down their pace and directed her into Neiman Marcus. For a moment, he recounted to himself all the times he considered it sinister yet appealing about being the solution to a married woman's romantic frustrations.

But then a much more reasonable thought came to mind. "Sonia, there are some things that are still the same no matter how you look at it—"

"Looking at what?" she countered; they had stopped just shy of the women's section.

He turned to her. "You just happened to be legally aligned with another man, and you may also have certain financial and family responsibilities with him. But after that, you're still a woman.

"You have needs, desires, and wants; I understand that. I've also been married. Think of it this way: What if you were single and you had a boyfriend?"

They resumed browsing the women's section. Sonia was divided in thought, contemplating Milner's reasoning and resisting the temptation of wanting to buy something from Neiman Marcus.

"Did I say something wrong?" he asked.

Sonia felt nervous for the first time during their date. It was her conscience, but she was determined to suppress that reminder of righteousness—God would just have to understand how she longed to be desired and wanted, and He would have to understand the extent of the void she felt was being filled by Milner's company.

"What if I told you that I was in the mood right now?" she said.

Milner felt something grab him in the gut. Her body language spoke loudly, inviting him to partake in the drawing of her soul unto his, and his unto hers.

Since they were near a rack of dresses, he smiled back at her and playfully ran his hand across her backside, stopping to squeeze her cheeks.

Mmmph!

They were just as firm and full as he imagined. She then positioned herself as if she was checking out dresses, but she actually rubbed up against him.

"You're a very perceptive man," she said. "I like that. A woman can feel very secure around you."

A black jewel-neck cocktail dress caught Sonia's attention. She held it up and stared at it with much admiration. But then she placed it back on the rack.

"Obviously, you like it," Milner commented. "Why don't you get it?"

Sonia looked him up and down as if to suggest he had to be kidding her.

"I'm serious." He reached into his coat pocket, making sure that his wallet was there.

"Wharton, I like it," she said, shaking her head, "but I'm not feeling this dress that much."

"Okay, then what are you feeling?"

She glanced down at him and bit her bottom lip. Then she looked up.

"I get it, but can we do just one thing first?"

"Okay—"

He locked arms again with her and they headed out of the store. He recalled seeing a flower kiosk not far from Neiman Marcus. There, he requested a single red rose; the gesture alone nearly brought Sonia to tears.

Yes, it was getting personal just as he crooned en route to the mall.

She stood on her tip-toes and kissed him on the cheek. She also offered him a stare that suggested even more; he felt his blood rushing downward.

"Now we can head back to the hotel," he said. "I have a surprise already set up there for you."

It was about two o'clock in the afternoon. While she went

to the ladies' room earlier, he called ahead and instructed the hotel to have some champagne chilling on ice and a fruit-and-cheese basket in the room. Everything had gone about as well as he anticipated.

On their way back, Milner broached a different kind of conversation.

"Can you tell me now what you were thinking the night you sent me that picture?"

She licked her top lip and grinned. Next, she hiked her dress up revealing more of her legs; he winked and nodded at her.

"I wanted you that night and I needed to do something about it. If I felt the way I do now, I would have asked to come over to your place and have you take care of it—"

"Mmmm, you're welcome any time you want to come over there."

"I like that you recognized that I'm in the mood." She paused and inhaled the rose's fragrance. "That really turned me on. You just don't know how much it did." She went as far as running her hands over her stomach and down to her thighs while looking at him the entire time. He leaned back in his seat, stealing looks at her and savoring the sight of her sensuality in action. "The first time I saw you, I can't explain it; I just felt there was something there."

"You saw something I certainly didn't see." She brought his right hand up to her lips. "But here we are."

First, she kissed it. Then she sucked his ring finger, tugging on it with her tongue and bridge of her mouth. She also arched an eyebrow to emphasize the gesture.

Message received.

And her sister said she was a prude?

He spoke in a low, sultry tone to her. "We're almost back to the hotel. I can't wait to feel and taste all of you—"

In the next breath, he returned to the Anthony Hamilton

song that he serenaded her en route to the SouthPark Mall. He told her again that having her near him was amazing—and it was more than personal.

* * *

There were no words spoken once Sonia and Milner entered the hotel room. She was quick to turn around and drape her arms onto his shoulders. He reached down and slipped his hands under her dress, taking full advantage of her flesh, and they engaged in a long, searching tongue kiss.

In one motion as Milner raised his hands, he pulled Sonia's dress over her head, revealing her white chocolate flesh. She took a step toward him and he engulfed her with a tight embrace.

They entered into another long, deep kiss. This time, he scooped her up, causing her to clasp her legs around his waist. He felt the warmth and wetness from her body as she rubbed up against him.

"Wharton, you've definitely reached my mind, body, and soul just as you said you would." She proceeded to kiss him fully on his lips before uncoiling her legs.

Upon separating, Sonia tugged at his slacks, unzipping them and then unbuckling his belt. He helped himself by unbuttoning his shirt—they removed the rest of their clothing in a matter of moments.

Milner then led Sonia by the hand over to the bed where he sat down and had her to stand in front of him. She sucked air through her teeth as soon as she felt his soft lips upon her flesh. Her knees buckled once he tantalized her with his tongue. Sensing the moment was right, Milner led Sonia to lie back onto the bed. Their bodies complemented each other in rhythm and motion.

Then they made it a moment worth savoring.

"Mind, body, and soul means giving you my best, baby," he whispered into her ear; he grunted at the sensation her body gave him.

"Can you handle that?"

She stroked his back and clung onto him.

"Yes, I can . . . Mmmm, you feel so good. I could not have ever fantasize anything like this—"

Then she matched him stroke-for-stroke. Along the way, she was far more verbal and demonstrative with him than she'd ever been with Trent.

There was no guessing whether Milner reached Sonia. Her body shuddered and convulsed in his embrace.

"How old did you say you were?" Sonia asked him while catching her breath.

He chortled at her soft stroking of his ego. "It's only a number. What matters is if we're good for each other—"

She placed her head onto Milner's chest; he had an exceptionally strong heartbeat. Moments later, she gazed upward into his brown eyes; he gave her a soft kiss on the lips. Upon pulling away, she studied his face; it was void of wrinkles and crow's feet. She also noticed he had only a few flecks of graying in the midst of his neatly-cut style.

"For a man who says he's fifty-one, you certainly look good. I'm sure you've seen plenty of fellas half your age who haven't taken care of themselves as you have."

"I guess being in the military helped instill some kind of discipline in me." He maneuvered himself so that he could stretch his legs, although he was more interested in getting back inside her.

"Does that also explain for your stamina?" she inquired. "Because it's obvious you can go a while."

He chose a philosophical response. "When you're with

one and you click with that person, all you want to do is please that individual. It's never about being caught up in yourself."

"Stop teasing me, Wharton! You knew I was ready, it had been a while since I last had one, and it wouldn't take long for me to get mine. That's all there was to it. But we'll see what you have to say this next time—"

And with that, Sonia turned over onto all fours, wiggling her backside at him.

"Whatcha got, ol' man?" she said. "I'm ready again!"

Milner was more than eager to position himself behind Sonia and enjoy the access she'd given him. Especially since she afforded him the visual pleasure of her cheeks jiggling and bouncing against his flesh.

Clutching onto her hips, Milner closed his eyes while he groaned and grunted with each stroke. Sonia added to the rhythm they'd created by making slow, sensual gyrations along with matching him stroke-for-stroke.

"This is what I'm talkin' 'bout!" he hissed before leaning forward onto her.

"Is it really?" She now maneuvered herself to a more upright position and placed her hands atop his while he cupped her breasts. He then kissed her along her neck.

"That picture you sent me did you no justice," he whispered into her ear. "There's nothing like having the real thing."

She reached back, keeping his head pressed into her flesh. "Guess what I'm thinking about now?"

"You don't have to tell me. I can feel it all in the way you're giving it back to me—"

* * *

Sonia and Milner were reclined on the bed sipping from the same glass of champagne and feeding each other grapes, pineapple chunks, strawberries and cheese squares. She felt she could do it again with Milner but she noticed he was more flaccid than erect. Maybe he was human after all. There was only so much a man eleven years her senior could do, yet he'd already done enough.

This was the kind of romancing that she wished Trent could have conjured up over the years.

Too bad for him, she snorted.

"What's on your mind?" Milner inquired.

She leaned back against his chest. "A lot of things." Then she turned and faced him. "I feel so complete being with you. I . . . I can't explain it!"

"I think we have great chemistry together," he tried summing it up for her. "That's something that can't be created. It's either there, or it isn't."

"Agreed. Maybe that was what I was trying to explain for myself."

She lurched over to her right and noticed it was fast closing in on five o'clock. "I need to start getting ready."

"I understand," he replied, sighing. "I would like if you'd come out to my place one day. I think you'd like it."

She kissed him on his cheek and eased out of the bed. Meanwhile, he licked his lips and kept his eyes affixed on her backside as she strode toward the bathroom.

While showering, Sonia closed her eyes and contemplated just how her heavenly relationship might be affected. Numbness came over her. She did not feel as if she had the will to ask Him to forgive her simply because at that moment, the last thing she wanted to do was turn away from seeing Milner again.

I have tried doing right as best as I can all these years, but for once something I did felt so right. It's just not fair that it might be seen as wrong.

She proceeded scrubbing away as best as she could the

the scent of what more than two hours of sex had produced. She then closed her eyes again, angled herself under the shower head, and allowed the water to rinse away the residue.

Perhaps out of all this, she hoped, she would be allowed to take with her the memories of being with Milner and they remain vividly intact for as long as she chose to embrace them.

On their way out of the hotel room, Milner tugged at Sonia for another hug and kiss. She obliged him, but her mind was on the reality that awaited her roughly one hundred miles away in Chapin.

"I hope my husband doesn't get any funny ideas tonight," she mused aloud. "I don't think I'll be in the mood for it."

"Quite frankly, I wouldn't be surprised if he had them. I know I would if you were my wife."

"It's easy for you to say that. You're a divorced man."

"Ah, but you forget that I was married for ten years."

"No, I haven't. It's just that I had to shoo him away this morning, and I didn't want to spoil anything for you."

"Well, I thank you very much for that."

They headed out into the parking lot holding hands. He suggested that she followed him to a nearby gas station so that he could top off her tank.

"It's the least I can do—"

"Thank you, but you've already done so much today."

"Next time, maybe my place?" he asked her again.

She smiled at the thought. "Maybe."

He allowed her to ease into her car. After closing her door, he hovered over the driver's side window even as she started her car and placed it into reverse.

"Yes, Mr. Wharton Paul Milner. May I help you with anything else?"

"I'm glad that we've taken this to another level," he confided in her. "You know where I am. You don't have to look any further."

She puckered her lips to him and then backed out slowly. He stood there with his arms folded and nodded with great approval.

Chapter 5

Ten minutes had passed since the last time Shonna told Lance that she would be ready. She still had not emerged from the bathroom.

"Hey, what's taking you so long in there?" Lance yelled from the hallway.

"I'm almost done!"

Shonna couldn't decide on anything. All the while, she went back and forth wondering whether she should wear her hair up or down, with bangs or without; she thought she'd given herself enough time to prepare and be ready.

Finally, she went ahead with simply combing her hair down without doing anything special to it. Her hair was naturally long, anyway. Besides, they talked about taking in a movie. It was not as if they were going anywhere among socialites and other noteworthy people.

"All right, are you satisfied?" she said, appearing before him in the living room of her northeast Columbia home.

He smirked and jerked his head back. "It took you long enough!"

Shonna placed her hands on her hips, cutting a mean glare at him. "Okay, I'm not the most punctual person!"

"Come on, let's go."

Shonna's job as general manager of WNPW-FM required her to make several public appearances each month, and Lance accompanied her to most of them since they became an item. But both were homebodies at heart. They preferred spending time with each other at either his apartment in West Columbia or at her home. They might hit a happy hour or two a month. Or in this case, a movie.

An avid fan of wrestler-turned-actor Dwayne "Rock" Johnson, Shonna needled Lance about seeing Johnson's latest movie titled *Snitch*. They had already missed the 8:25 p.m. showing. The next one began at 9:05.

They got no farther than reaching Killian Road when Shonna realized she'd forgotten something.

"Can we turn around?" she asked Lance, who reacted by shaking his head.

"What's wrong?"

"I forgot to unplug my curling iron, and I left the iron on in my room."

"How can you forget to do something like that?"

"Because you were rushing me to get ready!"

Lance faced Shonna while placing a hand on his thigh. "How can you blame me for you being so slow with getting ready?"

"I just did. Now can you take me back?"

He merely looked at Shonna again.

"Yes, and what are you looking at?" She leaned back in her seat and folded her arms.

"You. That's what."

Back at her place, Shonna rushed to her bedroom and checked on the curling iron on the bathroom sink counter. She let out a loud sigh in relief once she recognized that she'd actually turned it off. And she had also unplugged the iron and placed it on a night stand.

She was in no hurry returning to the living room where Lance waited for her.

"See, you rushed me out of here and I panicked over nothing!"

Lance glanced over at the wall clock. It was fast closing in on nine o'clock. "Are you ready to go now?" He began walking toward the front door.

"I was thinking, Lance, maybe we can just stop and get something to eat."

"Really?" He looked at her with surprise. "You're thinking you'd rather get something to eat?"

She now stood next to him at the door. "Yeah, I'm really thinking about that now."

"Whoa, all that talk about wanting to see this movie, uh, what was it . . . *Snitch*? You spend all that time in the bathroom getting ready—"

"Hey, I'm entitled to change my mind, aren't I?" she countered.

He hunched his shoulders. Being indecisive was not a characteristic of his. "So, let's get it straight. What is it you really want to do?"

Shonna looked back into the living room and then at him; she repeated looking. "I really would like to see the movie."

"Well, we're about to miss another showing. I'm not sure what time is the next one."

"But you know what?" Shonna said, pausing.

"What?" He began toying with his car keys.

"I don't feel like going anywhere. Let's just get a couple of

DVDs and hang out here."

Lance looked down and slapped his forehead while Shonna erupted into laughter. It was a comical moment to her because she felt comfortable with showing an indecisive side of herself.

Guardedly, Lance moved to open the front door. He then looked back at her before he stepped outside. "Are you sure this is what you want to do?"

"Yes. I am sure."

He rolled his eyes and smirked. "Finally!"

"You're not getting impatient with me?" She smacked him on the backside. "I might have to do something about that if you were."

"Don't push your luck, woman—"

Beyond an occasional difference of opinions, no dramatic episodes had arisen since Lance's incident with Charlotte while he was employed at UCP. Nor had he made contact with anyone at UCP since he left.

He'd shown no hints of being bored with Shonna despite their age difference and her being rather set in her ways. When they were seen together in public, he was tactful in the way he checked out other women so that it did not raise any suspicion—she was at least under the impression that he was solely interested in her, and her only.

Although he'd collected other women's phone numbers on occasion, he had yet to stray from Shonna. There was something about her maturity, sophistication, and bedroom prowess that kept him coming back for more.

"I was thinking," he mentioned to her in passing on their way back from a Red Box kiosk at a nearby Dollar General, "It's been almost eight months that we started this relationship."

He reached out for her hand, which she obliged; she then stroked his.

"I can't say that I've been keeping up with the days and hours. Why would you bring it up?" she asked.

He shrugged his shoulders. "I don't know. Just something that came to me."

"Come on," she reacted, turning to face him. "A person doesn't think about things like that unless they're bored and uninterested or they're a numbers freak.

"Which one is it?"

"None of the above."

Shonna still had concerns about the way others perceived her and Lance. She was aware of the curious stares she received whenever they were together in public. Some of it may have been out of admiration for his matinee idol features. But she suspected it had more to do with the obvious.

She repeated her comment to him and pressed for a more specific answer.

"I'm telling you, it's none of the above." He spoke more forcefully to her. "It just dawned upon me that we met each other for the first time about this time a year ago. Do you not recall that?"

"Lance, one thing you'll find out about me is that I don't take trips down memory lane."

"Okay . . ."

"I think people who spend their time recalling the past never get anywhere. It's too easy to think you may have missed out on something back there." She withheld adding she felt it was her way of keeping a fresh perspective about life. "I'm always thinking ahead."

Shonna was more than aware she sounded a bit direct, even snippy with him. But he should know that she was a woman who would tell him exactly what was on her mind.

Thus, it was moments like these that posed a bigger threat to her tolerance and patience. Lance could be mistakenly viewed the same way as her nephew Taylor, who recently turned fourteen.

Although Lance was not one who was led around by her—he was actually the one who made many of the suggestions where they might go or what they might do—she reminded herself that if he wanted to remain in a relationship with her, he had to deal with both the good and bad.

The silence between them lasted for only a few moments. Lance glanced over at her, asking, "What's on your mind now?"

She touched her neck and then stroked it. She once heard it being one of the places that gives away a woman's aging along with weight gain, breasts sagging, and the stomach.

Then she looked over at him, a picture of someone being in the absolute prime of life.

"I was thinking about you meeting my parents," she said. "I've not seen them since the holidays."

Lance swallowed fast and hard. "You actually want to introduce me to them?" This was even bigger than him meeting Sonia.

"Why not? It's not like I've been keeping any secrets from them—"

She was quick to clarify herself.

"What I mean is that I think you're a special man in my life. I've introduced you to everyone else except for them. So why not?"

She made a mental note that she would contact her father, Tillman, in the morning since they talked nearly every day. He reached out for her hand again while they were waiting at a stoplight. Then he leaned over and kissed her on the cheek.

"Light's green," she alerted him.

"I know!" He pointed out to her there was nobody in back of them. Then he stomped on the accelerator in retaliation.

"Hey, I'm not going anywhere, so you don't have to rush," she retorted. "The goodies will still be there."

He smirked. "I'm going to remind you of that once we're back!"

* * *

While they were cuddled up in bed together, Lance mulled the seriousness of his involvement with Shonna. There were times during sex he felt the words "I love you" welling up within him especially in the midst of something passionate and intense. But that was as far as it went. He managed to suppress the inclination that she might interpret him telling her that he loved her, or that he was in love with her, as a sign of weakness, inexperience, and that she'd managed to blow his mind.

She needs to be the first one to say it, not me.

"Hey, why you're just now deciding on introducing me to your parents?" he queried just as she turned to her side, inviting him to spoon up to her.

She reached back for his hand, guiding it onto her breast. "You know I could ask you the same question, as in why haven't you introduced me to your family?"

"First of all, my family is in Washington, D.C." He thought he had an iron-clad response for her.

"That may be true. But we can drive, ride a train, or fly up there."

"I've not been back since coming to this state," he said. "And I've only spoken to one of my sisters."

Shonna wiggled her hips against him. She liked enticing him into achieving an erection. It was her warped way of her knowing she still had his attention.

"I'll cut you a little slack since I can only speak for the time we've been in this relationship," she said. "But to answer your question about my parents, I just feel the timing is right."

"How do you think they'll react to meeting me?" He clung to her tighter and pressed his flesh upon hers as if they were about to engage in another romantic dance beneath the sheets.

"I think my father will only be concerned about me being happy. He'll look you over and he won't say much. But he's a pretty good judge of character. As for my mother, well, she might tell you exactly what's on her mind. And if she's anything like Sonia, which she is," she paused, while taking a deep breath, "just be ready for a quick departure from there."

"Hey, I've been wanting to ask you about that," he reacted. "Why don't you bring up Sonia's name any more?"

Several moments passed before Shonna found the nerve to respond. The mere mentioning of Sonia had her fuming. It almost took her out of the mood being with Lance, who was quick to pick up on the tension throughout her body.

"My sister needs to learn how to talk to people. That's all I'm going to say about it."

As tempting as it was for Lance to press further for answers, he waited a while before continuing their conversation.

"My gut tells me that Sonia doesn't like us dating." He spoke barely above a whisper.

She was terse with him. "Like I said, my sister needs to learn how to talk to people. She doesn't know everything."

"I'll just follow your lead whenever we go meet your parents, okay?"

"Thank you."

She turned over and kissed him. Her body finally softened within his embrace. This time, she was the one who initiated sex by pulling him atop of her. It was as if she had to make an open statement that she could do whatever made her feel happy with her life.

Chapter 6

Wanda Odom could not believe that Trent passed her over after interviewing for the St. Andrews branch loan officer position.

The job went to Amy Cardiff, who previously worked at Brighton Credit Union, which was also based in Columbia. She replaced Cortez Anderson, who was fired after his much-publicized involvement with a customer. Details of his relationship went viral on the Internet and social networks.

It should have been merely a formality that Trent hired Ms. Wanda, she thought. She'd been with Palmetto Fidelity since 1995, in her current capacity as lead teller since 2005, and her record and reputation at Palmetto Fidelity was impeccable.

Although Ms. Wanda was a highly respected colleague, she rarely socialized with the rest of the tellers. She had a small circle of people whom she felt understood the extent of her dismay.

"I never thought he was like that," she complained to Cortez, calling from her cell phone during her lunch break. "I really didn't."

Cortez, who found work as a finance and insurance manager at Midlands Ford, a car dealership in the Columbia area, also started a mortgage brokerage company on the side, which he operated from his home.

Six weeks after his dismissal, he reached out to Ms. Wanda and he enlisted her help with his wrongful termination case against Palmetto Fidelity. An arbitration hearing was set for the eighteenth of May at the Palmetto Fidelity building in downtown Columbia.

"I hate to tell you, but I told you to watch out for him," he said.

"Are you trying to say that I'm hard-headed?"

He was slow to respond. What he was inclined to tell her was that she was rather set in her ways. But he dismissed it as something to be expected, considering she was in her mid-fifties.

"I'm not saying that you are hard-headed. But it's obvious you've forgotten the terms in which I left," he said. "I really think when people's jobs are on the line you'll quickly find out where their loyalty is."

"Listen, I went into that process trusting nobody. But I also knew that I met and exceeded every qualification they were looking for in that position."

"Do you know who else applied for the job?"

Ms. Wanda mentioned fellow St. Andrews branch teller Maytreka Blanding was interviewed, and she was told through her contacts at the corporate office in downtown Columbia that three candidates from other Palmetto Fidelity branches were also selected for interviews.

"Who knows, maybe he did this out of retaliation," she said, sighing.

"Why would you suspect retaliation?" He began walking to the other side of the service department so that he would not worry about any eavesdroppers.

"Because I told him that you and I were were having an affair at one time."

"You did what!" Cortez was quick to look around and make sure nobody was watching him.

Ms. Wanda maintained an extramarital affair with Cortez for the better part of a year between 2009 and 2010. She confided in Trent that Cortez's immaturity and recklessness was her reason for breaking up with him. But she ended it after an acquaintance saw her with Cortez coming out of Shekinah's, a once-popular spot for happy hour on Wednesday and Friday evenings near the Columbia Mall. The acquaintance told her husband, Oscar, about them. He confronted her, but she vehemently denied it.

"She's been like the devil, a liar from the beginning, never beholding the truth!" Ms. Wanda decried the acquaintance.

Cortez and Ms. Wanda best fit the description as strange bedfellows. Her professional persona was along the lines of a conservative, church going woman. She was seen as maternal, always offering godly insight and wisdom, whenever she interacted with anyone at the branch. Cortez, for all his professional talent, was an unabashed womanizer and free spirit. One of the biggest complaints about him was the steady flow of women that visited him at the bank.

When they were together, Ms. Wanda and Cortez were both excitable and passionate. They had a tendency to insult each other until anger was provoked; they also rarely apologized to each other.

"Why would you tell him anything like that?" Cortez continued ranting. "That was not a smart thing that you did!"

"Hey, I had to make sure nothing might happen to me—I still need my job, dummy!"

"Dummy? Nobody knew anything about us, *dummy!* So it was not necessary that you ran to him asking questions about company policy . . ."

Cortez caught himself—this time. He reminded himself about his need for additional information. He needed Ms. Wanda more than she needed him even if the sex was great between them—their clashing personalities also produced many memorable moments in the bedroom.

Thus, he figured Ms. Wanda's disappointment was good news. Perhaps she might be motivated to work harder providing him any inside information that might improve his case.

Along those lines, he planned to first challenge the bank's code of ethics since that was the basis of him being fired. H.R. generalist Neal Scanlan said he breached "the spirit" of them after admitting to having a relationship with a bank customer, who confronted him on the job after he'd broken up with her. Deloria Lovett brandished a pistol in his office, but she was shot and killed by police.

The bank had yet to respond to his formal requests for a copy of the code of ethics.

Secondly, there were known rumors of corruption at Palmetto Fidelity. He believed if he could establish there was a culture of corruption that existed at the time of his dismissal the bank would viewed as questionable to fire anyone unless the offense was as egregious as stealing.

Finally, he was curious to learn of the outcome of local businessman Primas Lovett's lawsuit. He was called into questioning by the bank while it prepared to respond to Lovett's attorney A. Mitchell Duffner. Palmetto Fidelity was accused of gross negligence, which resulted in his wife's death.

"Wanda, I shouldn't have reacted that way."

"I'm glad you came to your senses," she said, leaning back in her car seat. "You're a lot smarter than you lead people on to believe about you."

"I'm going to act as if I didn't hear that." In the next breath, he then went on to explain, "I guess I was surprised you'd even mention anything about us."

Ms. Wanda mentioned to Cortez she had maybe twenty minutes before she had to return to the bank. She'd been so miffed by the news that she hadn't eaten all day—although she called him from the parking lot of a Wendy's down the street from the St. Andrews branch.

"What does that have to do with me?" he bantered with her.

"It has everything to do with you," she retorted. "I called you because some how in your warped thinking, you might convince me to go do something for myself."

He shook his head. "You're not making any sense."

"Oh, I'm making plenty of sense."

She went on to say that she'd been on a fitness program since the start of the year, and she credited him with giving her the motivation.

She'd lost twenty-five pounds and was able to wear clothes she once wore twenty years ago. She felt she had more energy. Her skin was much more vibrant, but she had not yet figured out a way to overcome the dark circles that were forming beneath her eyes.

"You know what? You're not complaining whenever you're on top or in back humping me," she reminded him.

Humph, if she only knew . . .

"You aren't complaining, either. Obviously, I know how to get the job done with you."

"I lose another ten pounds and we'll see who's bragging the

most."

"Hey, I'm ready to prove myself anytime, any place!"

Chapter 7

After their Charlotte rendezvous, Sonia started a new habit of calling Milner early in the morning rather than waiting until the afternoon. It made perfect sense to her.

Milner usually didn't leave home until 8:30, so he did not have to contend with any interruptions at The Groovy Soul. Sonia was either at home alone at that hour when Taylor was at school or she would be calling him while she was en route to work.

"I find myself doing things I never thought I'd ever do," she confessed to him. "Do you find that happening to you?"

It was not something that Milner spent his time considering—he was silent for several seconds before he came up a plausible response for her ears.

"I guess if there's anything different for me it was taking time out to see you like for our date in Charlotte," he answered. "Before then, it was on a Saturday; that's not our busiest day of the week."

Sonia was taken aback by Milner's response. The first thing that came to mind was the mere fact he was the one who pursued her. And like most men, he said and did all the right things that eventually piqued her interest in him.

"If my memory serves me correct, Mr. Milner, you told me the first time we met on a date that you would always make time for me," she said.

"I certainly did say that. And I think I've been a man of my word," he responded; it then dawned upon him that he backed himself in a corner.

"Let me try this again after taking my size twelve's out of my mouth—"

"Please proceed, mister." She looked around her bedroom while awaiting his response.

"Nothing's changed here. I want to see you as much as possible, Sonia. I also understand that it may not happen always when I want or you want," he said. "For us to see each other like we did . . . Like I said, I'll always make time for you. Bottom line!"

Not that she tried rationalizing her affair with Milner through scripture, she had already come to realize that she would have to take more things into consideration, including how she might better deal with her desire for Milner; the newness of pleasurable sex was fast getting the best of her.

It was as if another person was being introduced to her, and the person was Sonia Buckner herself.

"Just so you know, Wharton, you won't ever have to feel like you're being pressured into doing anything for me," she said. "I'm not one of those needy, high-maintenance women who have no real concept about life."

"I've never doubted that about you. So I'm not sure why you brought that up."

"I figured if we're to continue seeing each other we might as well lay out some boundaries."

Milner excused himself to yawn and stretch. He'd been sitting in his comforter in the living room. Now he got up and strode into the kitchen where he began preparing himself some bacon, frozen waffles, and apple juice.

"And what might they be?" he asked. "I thought we pretty much understood each other already—"

"Are you being sarcastic with me?"

He was moved to laughing. "Sarcastic about what? Let me ask you this—do you miss me already?" His voice was cool and seductive using a favorite line of his, and he beamed that his moves were still smooth and effective both in and out of the bedroom.

Meanwhile, the question caught Sonia off guard. She'd spent most of this call trying to find out whether Milner's attitude about them had changed, if any, and he fired a shot at her soul that hit its target.

"If I answer that question, what are you going to do about it?" She did not give him any time or room to respond before she finished the sentence. "You don't have to answer it right now."

"But I asked the question first!"

"Yeah, you did, didn't you?"

Milner mulled aloud that maybe he did need to schedule some regular time away from The Groovy Soul. He'd spent the better part of the past year working six days a week, but that was what he expected.

Then another thought came to him. He sought Sonia's opinion about having WNPW broadcast live from The Groovy Soul like it did last year. The event would coincide with the restaurant's second anniversary.

"I'm flattered that you would ask me before anyone else,"

she replied, but that was as far as she wanted to go with it.

First, she had no intention of being a part of any coming out event like it was with Shonna and Lance. Secondly, she had no desire of sucker punching Trent by going anywhere near The Groovy Soul with him.

"But I think maybe you need to discuss that with your sister and niece."

"Hey, it was just something spur-of-the-moment. By the way, how is your sister?"

She closed her eyes and shook her head. Shonna was a name that had all but escaped her vocabulary. "She's been busy lately, so we haven't had a chance to speak to each other."

"Well, give her my regards. I'm sure if I, uh, we decide on going to them for another promotion I'll be speaking with her, anyway."

* * *

Sonia was just a few strides away from entering the contract services workplace when she noticed Vicki crossing the hallway, heading into the break area that contained a refrigerator, coffee pot, and drink machine.

"Psst, come over here!" Vicki said, motioning for her.

"I don't have much time for gossip this morning." Sonia had spent most of her free time on the phone with Milner and she rushed to arrive at work on time.

"I'm glad I saw you out here in the hallway. I've got some good news to share with you."

Usually if it was gossip, Vicki would have shown a mischievous grin. This time she appeared to be genuinely excited. She looked around, ensuring nobody was nearby before she shared the news with Sonia.

"I got an interview!" Vicki whispered before she inserted

five quarters and a dime into the drink machine.

Initially, Sonia thought it was strange that she landed an interview anywhere at UCP during a department's hiring freeze. Applications were deleted if it's known to be one from that employee's department.

"Where did you apply?"

"Not here!" she snapped back at Sonia. "It's a place called GSI out past Irmo. They do a lot of background checks for businesses and government agencies."

Sonia smirked. "You, working at a place like that? They might have found the right person because you know about everyone's business off in contract services."

"Well, I thought I'd share the good news with you. It worked out that I'll interview with them the day after tomorrow." Then the mischief that Sonia was so accustomed to from Vicki finally emerged. "And afterward, I'll have some time for myself." She swayed her arms and wiggled her hips.

"Well, aren't you going to ask?" she needled Sonia.

"Why should I? You're doing a pretty good job so far—"

Vicki was even giddier to volunteer that she met a man at a jazz club two weekends ago in Atlanta, and one thing quickly led to another. They've since seen each other on three other occasions in Columbia, spending parts of each time in a hotel room.

"Girl, I loved every moment having my back blown out . . . Mmmph, there's nothing like it!"

Then her expression changed. "But now I'm having a bit of withdrawal. He's been out of town on business. We've only talked and text messaged. I'm wondering how I'm going to act when I see him again. It will be the first time in over a week."

Sonia felt obligated to voice her values and opinion with Vicki. Anything less might be perceived as her having compromised them. But she tried easing out of the conversation by taking a step toward the hallway; Vicki took a step in the same direction with her.

"What do you think I need to do?" Vicki queried.

"First of all, what guarantee is there you're going to see him again? You met him in a jazz club and both of you got a room the same night—haven't you seen enough drama around here to remind you things like that shouldn't be done so fast?"

Vicki, who took a sip from her Pepsi, stared at Sonia in disbelief. She knew that Sonia could be rather judgmental, but she still valued her insight.

"I forget you're too virtuous of a woman to understand how passion and chemistry works," she said. "Maybe I shouldn't have shared that with you, anyway."

"Wait a minute. You came to me with your juicy news. I didn't come to you. And what do you know about him?"

"He also works for GSI. He's a project manager. He was in Atlanta on business when we met. The IRS is one of his company's clients. He's separated—"

"You mean he's married?" Sonia rolled her eyes in derision. She then took another set of steps toward the contract services workplace.

"I saw the papers. He's got papers showing he's filed for separation, and he's waiting for his divorce to be finalized."

"Why would someone carry around papers like that?"

"He showed them to me the second time we saw each other. He felt it was important that I knew everything up front, which is more than I can say for most men that I've met."

Sonia shifted her purse from her right shoulder over to her left shoulder. She made sure that she spoke loud enough that only Vicki heard her should someone walked past them.

"Does he know that you're married?"

"Of course he does." She waved off the thought. "Most men

don't care if a woman's married. That's just a technicality to them."

"Have you ever tried working things out with Jermichael?" she inquired. "All I've ever heard you say about him is that you're always entertaining offers. Why did you marry him in the first place?"

"Because I needed the benefits! He had them at the time. But things change. People change."

Vicki went into a diatribe about being married to someone who had shown no interest in her after their honeymoon. Although he worked long hours at the dealership, they rarely spent any time together. It's been a loveless and sexless marriage.

Over time, Vicki said she spent too much time sitting in front of a television set eating chocolate ice cream and cherry cheese cakes as a way of dealing with the boredom and being rejected by her husband. She realized that was the fastest way of making herself unappealing to most men, and she was determined to remain marketable.

She then paused to search her purse for Gerald Conway's business card with his photo on it. "You see that?" She held it in Sonia's face.

"Do you think I'm not going to entertain my options when someone like him comes along?"

Sonia first darted her eyes away, refusing to look at Conway's card. Along those lines, she was quick to make the association that he offered her a job at GSI as an inducement with many strings attached to it.

"How many times I've had to help you with all the broken pieces after another disappointment? You've been married three times, and dare I say you'd jump at being married a fourth time if the right one came along.

"I think what's more important is you finding out who you

are and you first loving yourself. I think it's time that you re-ally consider that."

Vicki sucked her teeth. "I do love me. And if it weren't for the fact we've got to get inside there for work, I'd show you just how much I love me."

Chapter 8

Pointing at the second house on the right, Shonna directed Lance to turn into the driveway. It was the only home on the block with both a red brick exterior and cedar wood siding.

"This is where it all began for me," she said with some resignation in her voice. "Are you ready?"

"I'm ready if you are," he replied. "But are you sure you want to go through with this?"

Lance appeared to be calm and laid back about meeting Shonna's parents for the first time. In fact, he seemed all the more intrigued.

"What can your parents do to me?" he asked Shonna. "Kick me out of their home? They can't forbid me to continue dating you; I'm a grown man."

He shrugged his shoulders at the thought.

"My biggest concern is people have a way of making others people feel out of place," Shonna countered. "I don't know if that's ever happened to you; it's not a good feeling. I hope that won't happen here."

Lance looked over at Shonna again while she pressed her head back against the headrest and stared up at the roof. Then she folded her arms, recounting to herself the last man she introduced to her parents.

That was in 1998. She and DeMorris Pierre were both twenty-nine. At the time, he was separated from his wife. She did not want a divorce, but it did not stop her from finding another man. He struggled with guilt and shame because he expected better of himself—he cursed both the day that he met her and their wedding day—and he felt as if he let his family down.

He impressed Shonna's parents and even her maternal grandmother Esther, who was still living at the time. Sonia was not as judgmental back then about her sister's choice of men being that she was infatuated with Trent. But he also carried a truckload of post-marital baggage after his divorce was finalized. He went through stretches of wavering with his commitment to Shonna. This went on for the better part of three years before he broke up with her once and for all, leaving her heartbroken.

"It's not often I've done this, Lance. I guess that's why I'm feeling the way I do." She let out a loud sighing. "It would be nice if they're supportive, but I guess it really doesn't matter."

In the next breath, Shonna unhooked her seat belt and opened the door. Lance joined her walking to her parents' door holding hands.

"How do I look?" she asked.

He cut a side-eyed glare at her. "You probably should have asked me that back in the car."

"I'm going to take that as you saying I look all right for my parents—"

He nodded and sneaked a playful pat on her backside, to which she shooed his hand away.

"This is the wrong place for that!"

* * *

Prentiss Chandler gave little reaction when Shonna told her the night before that she'd be coming by with a male friend. Shonna barely helped her own cause by providing few details about Lance—other than he's not married, gay, bisexual, or had a jail record, as best as she knew.

The best thing that came from her phone conversation with her mother was Sonia appeared having kept her word that she wouldn't tell their parents anything about Lance.

When Prentiss opened the front door, her eyes never widened but rather she shifted them to her left at Lance and then to her right at Shonna. It didn't matter that he was tall and handsome. What caught her attention was Lance's obvious youth.

No, her eyes had not deceived her.

She did not say hello to them. Instead, she backed away and walked off to her left toward the kitchen, leaving Shonna and Lance to let themselves inside.

"Are you sure you're ready for this?" Shonna mumbled to Lance.

Hey, I'm along for the drive, he thought to himself. This was something you wanted to do . . .

She grasped Lance by the hand and led him directly ahead into the living room. She motioned for him to sit on one of the sofas while she caught up with her mother in the kitchen. Meanwhile, Prentiss went ahead with preparing dinner for her and Tillman.

"Your father's out in the back working on the fence. One of

the trees fell down and knocked out an entire section," she said, never looking up at Shonna.

"You could have at least said 'hello.'" Shonna spoke loud enough that only Prentiss heard her. "I'd expect something like that from Sonia, not you—"

Prentiss finished cutting up the steak meat and adding green and red peppers into the skillet. Then she looked over her shoulder. "What did you expect from me, young lady?"

"Mom, that was not nice. I told you that I'd be bringing someone over, so you shouldn't have been surprised."

"You know why I reacted the way I did. At first I asked my-self did you have any children that your father and I weren't aware of. But that would be cutting it real close." She placed hands on her waist and stared at Shonna.

Looking down first at the floor tiles, Shonna acknowledged the obvious age difference between Lance and her; that was all she was conceding to Prentiss.

"Lance is someone who makes me really happy. He's got his priorities straight, and he's doing good things for himself," she said. "The least you can do is come out there for a couple of minutes."

"Nope. This is your home. That's your guest."

"If that's the case, Lance and I could have stayed home [at the family's other house on Hard Scrabble Road.]" Shonna then folded her arms and leaned against the door sill.

Prentiss reacted with a smirk; she did not make any further elaboration.

"I'll be back, Mrs. Chandler—"

"You go right ahead. I've got this food to finish. I'm not go-ing anywhere."

Back in the living room, Lance sat with his hands folded behind his head staring at the pictures over the fire place and on the wall.

"Things didn't go over well with your mother, huh?" He straightened his posture, anticipating Shonna would sit next to him.

"I shouldn't be disappointed, but I am. I guess I was naïve to think differently." She leaned over and kissed him on the cheek while he grasped her hand.

"I guess I'll go back in there and let her know we're leaving. I know she won't tell my father that we came by."

She did not make any noise once she returned to the kitchen, but Prentiss noticed her.

"What does his mother have to say about him dating you?" Prentiss queried.

"I haven't met her."

"Well, you talk to me once you have." Prentiss glanced out of the kitchen window. "You might want to tell your father that you're here."

Shonna followed the sounds of a hammer making contact with nails and wood in the backyard. Not far from where Tillman worked replacing boards was a pine tree cut into large sections that could be used for heating in the winter. A large roll of wiring was also nearby. It was to be used for decorating the fence.

She waited until Tillman took a break before she greeted him. He was slow at straightening up; he also arched his back as if to work out the stiffness.

"Hey, Dad," she said, smiling; she then looked back toward the house. "Mom said you'd be out here."

He looked over at the pine tree stump. "It's supposed to rain again tomorrow, and I figured I better get this done." He then shook his head. "I know I'm not going to feel like doing anything tomorrow."

Shonna came over and gave Tillman a hug and a peck on his cheek.

"Hey, little girl. What brings you here today?"

"I guess Mom didn't tell you that I was bringing over a male friend of mine."

He shook his head. "She didn't, but you could have told me, too."

"I know." She was too far committed talking to him to avoid mentioning Lance. "He's in the living room right now. Can you at least say hi to him?"

Tillman balked at the request. "What did your mother have to say about him?"

"She didn't say anything. She wouldn't even talk to him—"

"That's not like your mother. There must be something else to it," he said, maintaining eye-to-eye contact with her.

"There is. Lance is twenty-eight."

He removed his glasses and wiped the sweat from his brow and nose bridge. "We talk almost every day and you never mentioned anything about a boyfriend to me—"

"Yes, sir. I know."

"Well if you knew that much, I think you better do what your mother says first before I say anything to him."

Shonna was quick to discern from Tillman's expression—a furrowed brow and a scowl—that he was not approving of someone twenty-eight years old dating her.

"That means meeting his family. I don't know if that might ever happen!" she replied.

"Well, he'll do it, if he's serious about you. Just watch and wait."

He then arched his back again and grunted, complaining now about him not being forty-four like her; he was seven weeks shy of his sixty-ninth birthday.

"I should pay someone to do this kind of work, but I still feel that I can do it myself. And it's good exercise."

Shonna held out her arms to hug Tillman. "Dad, don't overdo it out here. I'll let Lance know that you couldn't stop what you were doing to visit with him."

"Okay, little girl. Remember what I said." He winked his eye at her.

"I will."

On their way out to Lance's car, Shonna noticed Tillman walking across the front yard. He still had a lean, angular build, and his stride was still rather long.

"Is that your father?" Lance queried.

Shonna turned around and smiled. "Yes, that's him!" She waved in his direction.

"Bye!"

He stopped just shy of the front steps and waved back at them.

* * *

Shonna confided in Lance she spent a sleepless night over nothing. All that time browsing the Internet for articles that might help her deal with family members who may be opposed to her dating a much younger man was merely information gathered and not used.

"Sometimes we make a big deal out of nothing," she said, looking out the passenger side window. "My mother is going to have her opinion. I can either respect it or ignore it."

She related to him one of the articles that gave her some encouragement came from a seventy-one year old woman who had been involved with a man fifteen years her junior for nearly three decades.

The article refuted any notion that an older woman should be viewed as a cougar or even worse, a barracuda.

"Why would you think of yourself as a predator?" Lance reasoned with her.

"I guess that's the mindset of most people. A woman in my situation is viewed as someone looking to rip a man into shreds."

He chortled at her comment. "I only expect for you to rip one of my shirts to shreds when you really want me."

"Come on, Lance. I'm serious. The longer we're involved with each other, the more of this we're going to encounter."

"You're right. But I'm okay with it."

Tell me that six months from now, she thought.

Another article she considered relating to him discussed the inevitability that she may find herself making time references to things that may be more relevant to her. For example, she's old enough to remember visiting record shops which sold vinyl records that were played on stereo turntables. Where as once Lance was old enough to understand music, CDs was the predominant medium. And now there's mp3s, music played from flash drives, iPads, and other digital sources.

Sighing, she lamented, "I guess my friend was right. At some point I may have to consider a different crowd of people to go around—apart from even my own family."

She mentioned the friend was Dana Foreman whom she attended college with barely twenty years ago. "Oops!" She placed her hand over her mouth realizing that Lance was probably in the second grade when she finished college.

"I'm sorry. I guess I'm not having a good day."

Lance was slow to figure out what Shonna meant. Saving face, he reminded her that he was the one who made the first move by asking her out for lunch. He went on to say he was even more nervous the first time they had sex, which prompted her raising eyebrows at him.

"Yes, I was," he said, nodding his head for emphasis. "You knew what you wanted and how you wanted it done. I was guessing the entire time, hoping like crazy I wouldn't do or say anything stupid."

She shook her head. "Lance, you can't always fall back on sex."

"I know. But it was the first thing that came to mind."

Chapter 9

Sonia couldn't get comfortable holding a conventional phone while lying in her bed talking to Prentiss.

"Mom, can I call you right back?"

"Are you trying to get rid of me?"

"No. I don't even know why we even keep one of these phones. All of us use cell phones around here. I'm going to call you right back."

Prentiss was quick to reminisce of another era. "They didn't have all these cell phones, smart phones, and whatever kind of other phones they have out there now when you were in high school.

"You had to use a regular telephone just like the one I'm calling you with—"

"Okay, I'll call you right back!"

Sonia figured she might as well be in her own element—using her smart phone with ear phones—since Prentiss was likely to keep her on for a while. A conversation lasting more than an hour was commonplace with them.

"All right, Mom. Now what were we talking about?"

"I almost forgot that fast." Then it came back to her. "Oh, yeah. Your sister. She came by today."

Sonia rolled her eyes in derision. "She did? How is she?" She placed a pillow under her head. This had to be worth listening out for the punch line.

"Uh-huh, she came by here, all right," Prentiss answered, sighing. "I know she has a mind of her own, but I don't quite get it this time around."

"What's wrong?"

"I'll just say this much. I just hope she comes to her senses before it's too late."

"Mom, I don't understand—"

"Shonna came by with a man who's almost young enough to be her son. Her nose is so wide open it's a crying shame. I had nothing to say to her or him."

Despite her acrimony with Shonna, Sonia felt vindicated for voicing her concerns when she did; her mother merely confirmed them.

Besides, most logically thinking people would probably agree with her, anyway.

"Was his name Lance?" The moment was almost déjà vu for her.

"How did you know that?" Prentiss then realized Sonia baited her into divulging first. "Wait a minute, how long have you known about this?"

Sonia breathed through her nostrils loudly into her phone. "I've known for quite a while now. I figured at some point she would try introducing him to you and Dad, and I knew it wouldn't go over well with either of you."

"What did Dad have to say about it?"

"Nothing, as far as I know . . . She went in the backyard and

spoke with him while he was working on the fence. Then she
left with that young fella, whatever his name was—"

"Lance."

"I don't care what his name is. I told her when she finds out
what his mother has to say about dating her son then she can
come back and talk to me about him!"

Prentiss was on a roll, and she cut Sonia off right after the
first syllable.

"Back in my day, they talked about rocking someone's
world and it being all about the motion of the ocean. He could
be the baddest ship out there, for all I care. Sonia is forty-four
years old. She can't be that desperate—"

Trent had entered the bedroom. She pulled back the covers
expecting him to join her in a few moments.

"Mom, did I mention already that Taylor had four A's and
three B's on his latest progress report?"

"You don't say?"

He mouthed to Sonia to give his regards to her parents.

"Mom, Trent said hello to you and Dad!"

Prentiss did not bother to respond. She did not despise
Trent, but tolerated him. His winning over her mother, Esther, had been his saving grace, and she'd remained respectful
of her mother's sentiment toward him.

"Mom said hello to you, Trent!" Sonia volunteered telling
him, to which he nodded back at her.

"Well, I'm going to get off the phone now. Let's hope that
she comes to her senses."

Prentiss refused to end their conversation without getting
in the last word. "I know what you did there. But someone
needs to talk some sense into your sister. Maybe you can
reach her . . . Bye!"

If she only knew, Sonia mumbled silently to herself.

Trent was settled in the bed with Sonia barely a couple of

minutes before she brought up a favorite subject of hers.

"Are we going to have some God time tonight?" she asked. "It's been nearly a week, and you can't say that I've been pestering you."

"Okay, why not?" he replied, shrugging his shoulders.

Sonia sat up next to him. "Hey, you should be the last person making such a casual response about spending time with God.

"You should be thanking and praising God every chance you have that you're still married."

Trent, who held back from cursing, simply stared at Sonia while she continued lecturing to him. All he saw were her lips moving.

"Sometimes we all need to stop and acknowledge how good God is to us," she continued. "Don't you think He's pleased when we're sharing His word as husband and wife?"

She faced him, expecting a response. But he remained silent. He'd since come to compare God time with Sonia as merely her next bully pulpit opportunity.

"I don't understand your being quiet, Trent. As the husband, you need to be spending time with God to find out what He has for this family." She then looked at him again, with raised eyebrows.

He clasped his hands behind his head and stared at the ceiling. "Sonia, we'll have some God time tonight. But let me ask you this: Do you get your kicks when you try portraying me as a heathen?

"I guess you're trying to set yourself up for the next great testimony you'll give in church sharing just how good da Lawd's been good to you, hmmm?"

"See, Trent, that's exactly why I've been quiet lately." She shook her head as if she expressed disappointment with him. "You're not serious with God. Because if you were, you wouldn't be talking like that.

"It speaks of you can find out the state of a man's heart by what proceeds from his mouth; it also speaks of what you treasure the most is where your heart is—"

Trent chortled. Hard, in fact. "Sonia, if I were you, I'd stop right there. You don't want to hear [about] what I think is coming from your heart."

He went into a brief discourse about striving toward the mark of a higher calling. First, however, an individual must forget about the things that were in the past. But before that, the individual must take self-inventory. Then goals are set after careful analysis.

"You want God time?" he said, mimicking her with raised eyebrows. "I'll give you some God time.

"Now, you want to know why I said we've got to take self-inventory? The writer had already done that when he said he counted himself as not having attained or, depending on the translation, apprehended."

Trent explained the verb count in the Greek was similar to the words calculate or account. "That's right, some kind of analysis had taken place. An honest one. Now, can you say that for yourself?"

He looked at her with arms folded—and more than ready to delve further. But she turned over onto her side, pulling the sheets over her head.

"We don't have to have any God time tonight, Trent. It was only a suggestion."

Her displeasure was tempered by what she had already planned for the following afternoon: Meeting Milner at his home in Eastover. She mused silently any time spent with him would more than make up for any time lost with Trent.

* * *

Sonia felt invigorated knowing there was someone different and exciting in her life. She was no longer a frustrated married woman, but someone who had taken control of her life in a way she once objected.

Each time she'd seen Milner it was as if she'd stretched herself to do something more different than the last time. Visiting his home in Eastover was undeniably something she never fathomed doing.

The drive there didn't seem to be a bad idea after all, she reasoned. The route taken—I-26 eastbound over to I-77 northbound and then ending up on Highway 76/378—allowed her to purge away any thoughts from her workday at UCP and suppress any feelings of guilt.

According to his instructions, she was to turn right on Antioch Zion Church Road. The landmark was a church building next to a burned-out building on her left. Then she'd drive about two miles and look for his home on the left.

"Are you there waiting for me?" she called from her cell phone.

"I certainly am."

"Well, I should be showing up at your place very soon."

"Just look for my Mercedes in the front yard. It's the only one you'll see on your way coming in."

Milner was more than casual awaiting Sonia's arrival. He wore black athletic pants and a matching Polo shirt. Once she drove into his yard, he opened his front door and stood on the porch—she waved as soon as she recognized him.

"Did you have any problems finding my place?" he asked. "We have a running joke out here that you're in the real suburbs of Richland County when you come to Eastover."

"I've lived in Columbia all my life, and this is really my first time coming out this way."

"There's a first time for everything. Come on in. "

Milner compared living in Eastover to when his family was in northwest Arkansas during his early childhood. The neighbors all seem to know each other. A resident must drive about twenty minutes to the nearest supermarket. And there's hardly any crime in the area.

"I guess you can say the country boy never left me." He then held out his hands toward her. "Come here."

Sonia was more than eager to hug and kiss Milner, who groped and squeezed her buttocks along with running his hands up and down her back.

A warm, tingly feeling also came over her while she offered more of her tongue to him. She also responded with pressing her breasts harder upon his body each time he groped and squeezed her.

"I don't know what I'm going to do with myself," she whispered after coming up for air. "I can't stop thinking about you, Wharton."

"What you're going to do is allow me give you a tour of my place, and then we'll see what we'll do afterward." He held out his hand for her.

The first thing Sonia noticed about Milner was that he was big into electronics—he was proud of his surround sound and home theater system for the living room; everything worked via a remote or through a Wi-Fi streaming player he kept on the coffee table.

His house was slightly larger than her home in Chapin, which had four bedrooms and two and a half bathrooms; his home had five bedrooms and three baths. He led her out on the backyard deck through the dining room. She was quick to notice his yard was lined with a privacy fence, although she found it odd that he'd have something like that in a still rural area of Richland County. Then she looked off to the left: He had a swimming pool and a yard that was large enough to host a party for maybe a hundred people.

She mused aloud she could probably stroll naked throughout his place or even go skinny dipping once it got warmer—it was to reach a high of sixty-seven on this mid-March afternoon.

Milner laughed heartily. "That is very much possible even today—the water's heated."

"You would say that," she said, looking over her shoulder at him. "How many other women you've treated to such a 'friendly' environment?"

"A few. I'm divorced. I never said I lived like a hermit." He held his hand out for her again. They walked back inside the house.

"Well, at least you're honest—I guess."

"More than you could imagine."

She fired another question at him. "When was the last woman you had visit here?"

"Today."

Sonia stopped in mid-stride, yanking her hand away from him.

"The last woman was you." He revealed a wide, inviting grin. "And I expect the next woman will also be you."

She shook her head. "You're really smooth with your words, Mr. Milner."

"Wharton," he corrected her. His reply was accompanied by a kiss.

"I've got a little surprise for you in the bedroom."

She glanced downward at him, biting her bottom lip. "I wouldn't call that a small thing—"

"Seriously, I do have something for you in there." He led her by the hand again.

They walked farther down the hallway stopping at the last bedroom on the right. "Go ahead, open the door." She gave him a suspicious glare. He motioned with his head. "Go ahead."

Cautiously, she turned the knob and pushed the door. She brought her hand up to her mouth after taking a step inside.

"What's that at the foot of the bed?"

He walked past her and brought the small box with a ribbon to her.

"Open it."

The box was about the size of a watch. After removing the ribbon and taking off the lid, she brought her hand up to her mouth again. Her eyes also spoke volumes about Milner's latest gift: a fourteen karat gold bracelet with her name engraved into it. "Wharton, what am I going to do with this? I can't take this home with me—"

"You can wear it when you're around me. Or you can keep it here."

She turned to him and rubbed her body against his, looking upward.

"You are an incredible man, Wharton; I certainly didn't know what I was getting into when I decided to get involved with you . . . I . . . I'm overwhelmed by your kindness and attentiveness."

He smiled at her. It was as if she was a customer of his at The Groovy Soul but on a more personal level. "Just say thank you," he replied.

"I'll do more than that. Thank you, and . . . after I freshen up . . . I'll show you my gratitude even more."

"The bathroom's over there." He made a head gesture to his right. "The towels and soap are in plain view."

She sashayed past him toward the front door, prompting him to lick his lips. "I need to go out to my car and bring my bag."

Minutes later, Sonia returned wearing only a bath towel,

prompting an incredulous expression from Milner.

Additionally, he did little to hide his arousal for her: there was a significant bulge in his athletic pants that he was more than willing to expose to her.

"Are you trying to remind me of what I've been missing since our last time together?" she said, casting an alluring stare at him.

"I could have sent you a picture. But I knew you were coming here today."

She caressed and fondled him while they entered into another deep kiss. But Milner was ready to indulge her. She obliged by allowing the bath towel to drop to the floor. In one motion, he scooped her from her feet and led her onto his king-size bed. Then he removed his athletic pants while she helped remove his shirt.

Within moments, the bedroom was filled with them moaning and kissing and sucking sounds—literally and through their teeth.

"Mmmm, Milner. That's my spot!" she hissed, reaching back to press his head into her body. "Yes, right there!"

She was also determined to reciprocate the same feeling to him.

"All the way up and down, baby. Mmmm," he moaned, "that feels soooo good—"

They were so in tuned to each other that Sonia simply followed Milner's lead when he nudged her to dismount. She beckoned him with outstretched arms and legs, to which he eagerly assumed his place atop her.

It was not long before the room was filled with flesh slapping against flesh and them breathing heavily between kisses and strokes. Once he rose up, she dug her nails first into his back and then into his chest. He also reached beneath her and squeezed her cheeks.

"Milner, baby . . . I want to get on top—"

"Okay."

Sonia realized she had never felt as assertive with any man until Milner. But now was not the time to analyze. She balanced herself by placing her hands on his chest while riding him up and down and gyrating her hips, provoking him to utter passionate obscenities.

"Whoever called you a prude lied," he said. "They outright freakin' lied!"

"I know they did! But as long as you know I'm your freak, that's all that matters!"

"Mmmm, yeah . . . My freak that ain't missin' a single beat!" He then sucked air through his teeth. "So sexy . . . Keep riding it, baby . . . Keep riding it!"

She closed her eyes, arched her neck, and continued with her sensual gyrations while Milner fondled and pulled at her nipples. Suddenly, she grunted and dug her nails deep into his chest. Then she collapsed forward onto him.

"You're going to make me say things I've been trying to keep inside of me," she whispered to him. "And if I do say them, I'm not sure how I'll be able to handle it."

She more than stroked his ego. He kissed her on the forehead, and they resumed their lustful dance atop the sheets.

* * *

Milner suggested they drive over to Sumter and dine at a Japanese hibachi restaurant. Initially, Sonia balked at the idea of making the half-hour trip.

"I'm content with staying here," she said.

"Come on, we're going to Sumter, not Columbia."

"I understand that. I would rather not take a chance that someone might see us together."

"Sonia, we've gone to Augusta and we've gone to Charlotte. And not once you've told me about any issues so far. Don't you realize that Sumter is about the same distance from Columbia as Columbia is to Augusta?"

She pondered his logic. A drive from Columbia to Sumter would take nearly an hour—and that's if she made all the stop lights and didn't see any police along the way.

"And where [did] you say we're going?"

"The restaurant is just before you pass Walmart. The mall is farther down the road."

"I guess we can do that. You think we'll be back here in time so that I can be home before seven o'clock?"

"I promise that I'll have you back in plenty of time. That means I won't try any hanky-panky while we're in Sumter."

"Don't you think we've done enough in here?" She kissed him on the chest and stroked him softly.

* * *

Later that evening while Taylor was goofing off on Twitter with his cell phone, Da'Mitri Bynum, a friend and classmate of his, tweeted something directed at him.

@TayBuck: I saw your mom in Sumter today

That message didn't seem right. He knew his mother worked in Columbia just off the I-20 freeway before heading into the downtown area. So he sent Da'Mitri a direct message for clarification.

Where did you see her?

I was in Sumter to see my uncle who is in the Air

Force ... I saw her in the parking lot at a restaurant

If you saw her in a parking lot what was she doing?

You don't want to know

What was she doing?

Your mom's a bop

I bet you won't say that in my face

You'll find out tomorrow in school

I'm ready . . . I'm waiting

Taylor dismissed Da'Mitri's message because that hardly sounded like anything his mother would be associated with. He logged out of Twitter and spent the rest of his time listening to music that corresponded with his mood—fuming.

Chapter 10

The question that Taylor asked Trent caused him to cringe. It was seemingly innocent, yet also inevitable.

"Dad, when do you think you'll let me drive to school?"

"When you have your own car to drive," Trent answered, looking straight ahead while driving him to school.

"If I'll be driving my own car, when are you and Mom going to get me one?"

"What makes you think we're going to get you one?"

Taylor had already thought this through about him joining the population of student drivers at his high school. He told Trent once he turned fifteen next year, either he or Sonia would need to take him to apply for his learner's permit. Next, he'd need to complete an Alive at 25 course so that he would be eligible for a school parking permit. Finally, one of his parents would have to enroll him into a driver's training course.

"Then you can get a discount on my insurance and I'll be all set," he said, looking over at his father smiling.

Trent merely cut a glare in his direction. "Whoa, wait a minute—"

"Dad, you're always telling me I need to plan ahead. So that's what I'm doing."

"Yeah, that's really planning ahead," Trent said, nodding. "I hope you also plan to keep your grades up and make some kind of contribution to the cost of you driving."

Taylor leaned back in his seat, puffing out his chest. "I've also been planning for that, too."

Then he became quiet and looked out the passenger window. Trent waited a few moments expecting Taylor to continue with his bright ideas.

He didn't.

"Care to talk about what's on your mind now?" Trent inquired.

"I've got three tests today in classes that I hate—English, math, and Spanish," he said. "Nobody likes any of my teachers. They're pushy and lazy.

"I even have a friend and her brother had my English teacher, like, four years ago. We're being taught the same, boring dumb stuff. She's irrelevant!"

So much trying to relate to a teenager. The paternal instincts took over this conversation.

"You just do what you need to do and get out of there with the best grade you can get. Then she'll be irrelevant forever."

"I've got a ninety-one in the class, but yes, Dad." Taylor now sat up in his seat. "Hey, can I have some lunch money?"

Trent shook his head. It seemed as if it cost him something usually in the form of money each time he spoke to his own son.

"Oh, and by the way, I was thinking about going to the varsity soccer game today. So can you give me something extra for that?"

"Didn't your mother give you any money before she left?"

"I wanted to ask her but she'd already left for work."

Trent mused to himself it sounded as if Sonia wanted to keep her money and put the tab squarely on him this time around.

* * *

Da'Mitri strode into History class thinking all night about what he would say to Taylor. Where he sat in class meant everything because Taylor's desk was two ahead of his, so he had the option of whispering or passing a note to him.

When they made eye contact, Taylor lowered his head and looked away. Da'Mitri merely smirked. He stopped next to Taylor, whispering, "That ain't gonna help you. I'm ready and I'm waiting, too." He then went to his desk.

This was not going to be an easy day, Taylor sensed. He'd been teased by classmates and friends, but they never said anything about his mother.

The lights were turned off about halfway into the class' ninety-minute session for a video. Da'Mitri's went as far as switching seats with Nicholas Barton so that Taylor would not miss what he said.

"Hey, Taylor, I hear your mom's a bop," he whispered to him.

The spoken word always had more of a negative effect than words seen on Twitter.

Taylor turned around, replying, "You better stop that—"

Da'Mitri laughed in his face. "I told you I'm ready, too. So you better shut up!"

Their teacher, Sam Kirchner, caught both of them talking.

"Uh, gentlemen. Would you rather finish that conversation at your vice principal's office?" Then he directed his chiding at Da'Mitri. "You need to go back to your assigned seat, or both you and Nicholas will be serving an in-school suspension!"

Nicholas wanted no part of any suspensions and demanded that he and Da'Mitri switched seats.

Da'Mitri and Taylor had a math class together, but there was no exchange that occurred. They had a test that took nearly an hour to complete. Secondly, they sat on opposite ends of the classroom. But those dynamics changed once they were in Spanish.

There were more students who were friends with Da'Mitri than Taylor, which would only intensify the needling. Also, this class overlapped lunch, and that might attract a bigger audience.

"So, Taylor . . . Your mom bops for that old guy. What about for me?" Da'Mitri said after finishing his test.

Taylor dipped his head and tried counting backwards from ten, but that wasn't working. So he reached into his bag and retrieved his cell phone, sending Da'Mitri a text message:

> **If I get up from this desk I'm gonna stomp your eyes out of your skull**

Da'Mitri didn't text back to him, but replied, "I ain't got no time for that—" So he lunged to his right and whispered to another friend, Ryshane Lowery, about what he saw in Sumter.

Ryshane's eyes lit up, and he took over where Da'Mitri stopped.

"Hey, Taylor, are you next to go bop?"

He turned around and looked first at Ryshane and then at Da'Mitri. Their shoulders were heaving up and down and their mouths were covered, hiding their laughter.

"Lunch is in a few minutes."

"Like whatcha gonna do then? You ain't done nothing yet?" Da'Mitri retorted.

Taylor turned around and fumed. None of this made any sense to him. Usually, jokes about a student's mother were benign. This went too far describing Sonia as going from one man to another. Making it worse were comments that she was seen in Sumter.

When the lunch bell rang, Da'Mitri told Ryshane and two others to put the word out that something might happen. He spotted Taylor returning from the cafeteria with a tray and was about to sit down next to Dawn Mattox, a close female friend of his.

That was all he needed to see. With Ryshane and a few others nearby him, they all crashed in on his quiet time with Dawn by sitting at the same table.

"Taylor, can you justify one, good solid reason why your mom was in Sumter yesterday?" Da'Mitri sneered.

"I told you to stop with that mess, Da'Mitri."

Da'Mitri and his crowd all erupted in laughter.

"So your mom's gonna bop for the rest of the crew?" Ryshane said, looking to his left and right.

Taylor bunched his lips and began rocking back and forth. Dawn looked at him bewildered.

"Hey, Taylor, do you know if they offer online degrees for bopping?" one of the other students asked, prompting Da'Mitri to nearly spit back into his drink.

That was all Taylor could stand. Immediately, he darted to the other side of the bench and unleashed a flurry of punches on Da'Mitri's head and back; he never got a chance to stand up or was able to get his hands up and effectively block the barrage.

Meanwhile, a loud roar and oohs and ahs filled the cafeteria area, and a throng of students ran over to view the one-sided brawl.

"I told you to shut your mouth but you didn't!" Taylor yelled between punches.

"I can't help your mom's a bop!"

Before he could rear back with his hardest punch yet, a teacher grabbed him from behind along with a security officer and whisked him away.

Another teacher came by and escorted Da'Mitri away since he was the other principal in the ruckus.

* * *

Minutes later, Taylor sat across from Arlene Hinton, who was vice principal over ninth graders. Both stared at each other for several seconds. Taylor still breathed heavily from the energy he expended in his fight, but also out of rage.

The silence was broken by the crackling of her walkie-talkie.

"Ms. Hinton, as far as I know this fight broke out in the cafeteria area," an instructor chatted with her.

"Well, we're going to find out exactly what happen very shortly. Thanks for your help."

"No problem."

She folded her hands and placed them on her desk. "Taylor, we have a zero tolerance for fighting at this school. You was told that in orientation."

"I remember. But I didn't start this!"

"Then what happened?"

"It started last night on Twitter," he explained. "Da'Mitri said he saw my mother somewhere and he called her a 'bop.' And he kept teasing me today!"

She leaned back in her chair. "Why didn't you go to a teacher about it?"

"Would you go to a teacher when someone's calling your mother a bop?"

"Before we go any further, what is a bop?"

He sighed and glanced upward. "It's kind of hard to explain."

He began shifting in the seat. "It's like someone is going from one person to another."

"That's not any reason to get mad and fight someone."

"Okay, let me call your mother a bop in front of everyone and see how you'd act!" He then leaned forward in the chair. "I'm not going to let anyone talk about my mother like that!"

Ms. Hinton clasped her hands and rested her chin on them. She then told Taylor to sit quietly for a few moments while she left the room.

The first person she attempted to call was Sonia, but she was unable to reach her. The only number given was her cell phone.

The next person she attempted to contact was Trent. He provided both his cell phone and office number.

"Mr. Buckner?"

"This is Trent Buckner, how can I help you?"

"This is Arlene Hinton, vice principal at Taylor's school. We've had a situation involving him—"

Trent leaned forward at his desk. His eyes narrowed and his forehead furrowed. "What's wrong? Is he all right?"

"Physically, he's fine. But he's in my office for fighting. Apparently, some students were teasing him and the next thing that happened was Taylor being pulled away from hitting the student."

"I'll be right over there!"

When Ms. Hinton returned, she had Taylor to sit in a meeting room a few doors away from her office. She did not mention that she'd contacted his father and he was on his way.

Trent tried calling Sonia's cell phone while he hurried over to Taylor's school, but she didn't answer. He'd forgotten that she rarely answered her cell phone at her desk. So he text messaged her, but he received no immediate response.

> **Taylor is in some trouble at school and I'm on my way there. I'll fill you in later.**

Intermittently, Trent checked his cell phone while driving in traffic for any response from Sonia. He dismissed it as her being at lunch or besieged by a high call volume along with the problems that often came with it.

Once Trent arrived at the school a few minutes later, he text messaged Sonia a final time before he went inside the building.

> **I'm about to find out what's going on with Taylor. Hope it isn't too bad. Text me when you get this message.**

The school's main office was the first door to his right. After signing in, he was told Ms. Hinton would be with him shortly—Taylor was still unaware that his father was outside the room where he sat.

Trent never bothered to sit down. He noticed people walking in and out of the main office and down the corridor where he suspected Taylor was. Eventually, a lady wearing a red and white floral dress walked slowly in his direction.

"Are you Mr. Buckner?"

Trent unfolded his arms. "I'm Trent Buckner."

She smiled briefly. "I'm so glad you came here. It's so rare to see a child's father come to school particularly for students like Taylor." She then winked at him.

Trent acknowledged what Ms. Hinton meant. But he persisted, asking, "Where is he?"

She walked over to a door nearby him.

"What happened?" Trent asked.

Upon opening the door, Taylor, whose head was on the table appearing as if he'd fallen asleep, jerked to sit up straight in the chair.

"Dad, I didn't start this!"

Trent did not immediately comment, but he sat next to Taylor while Ms. Hinton sat across from them.

"Mr. Buckner, as I told Taylor, the school district has a very strict policy about fighting," she said.

Trent replied, "What I want to know first is what happened?"

"Well, since you're here, why don't we ask Taylor?" She looked over at him.

Taylor slammed his back into the backrest, sighing demonstratively. He recounted all of what he'd already told his vice principal, adding that Sonia was seen in Sumter.

"I didn't believe Da'Mitri at all. But he's been teasing me about it since last night—him and a few others were calling her a bop!"

Trent glanced over at Taylor and studied his expression and demeanor. Taylor had a tendency to fidget whenever he lied to him. He also checked for whether Taylor was being evasive while he talked. He then turned his attention to Ms. Hinton.

"I'm sure you know that Taylor is not a problem child. This is his first time being in trouble. He'll be the first person to tell you that he doesn't like it if I'm ever involved in situations like these."

Ms. Hinton folded her hands and placed them on the desk. "The school district's policy is to expel the child since fighting is not tolerated."

"We're not talking about him using any weapons. It sounds like to me a good ol' whuppin' occurred." A part of Trent wanted to puff his chest out in pride since Taylor was the aggressor and clearly won the fight. But the part that Ms. Hinton saw was a parent stressing to her that his child was not a troublemaker.

"Mr. Buckner, while sorting all this out, I did speak to the other child involved in this, and it appears that the fight occurred over what Taylor had told you. But we cannot let this go unpunished."

Ms. Hinton went on to tell Trent that Taylor would be suspended a total of six days. The first three would be served at home and the next three would be served in-school. The mitigating factor was Taylor's prior good behavior.

She then asked Taylor to step out of the room and go to her office.

"Mr. Buckner," she said, lowering her voice, "the fact you came up here also helped. It really did. I've seen it done, and I've done it myself a number of times, where by the child's presumed to be trouble just waiting to happen because there's no parent there to show any concern for, or to defend the child."

He shook his head. "I can understand school policies have changed but it sounds like to me you people just don't want to deal with much of anything. These children are just statistics for you; they can either help you get a better job or whatever kind of raises you get around here." He looked around the room for emphasis.

Ms. Hinton stood up. "I'm sorry you feel that way. Some of us do care about the children."

"So you call kicking a child out for three days caring about them?" He also stood up and folded his arms.

"I'll go get Taylor."

She left the room.

While waiting for Taylor, Trent attempted piecing a few facts together. He recalled Taylor's preoccupation while they drove to school, but he went along with him attributing it to having three tests.

The most puzzling tidbit was Taylor fighting over Sonia being seen in Sumter by one of his classmates—and especially since she worked less than ten minutes away from the St. Andrews branch.

Chapter 11

On their way home, Trent told Taylor that he was not outraged by him getting into a fight.

"Tell you the truth," he confessed, "I got into a few of them over my mother when I was a kid in Louisiana."

He explained his mother once suggested that he shouldn't be so quick to get mad whenever other kids said something bad about her. She placed the onus back on him asking whether he was ashamed of her.

"Then if you're not ashamed of me, why get all bent out of shape?" she challenged him.

Trent reminded Taylor, "You know you can't do anything like that again as long as you're in high school—"

He nodded. Next, he searched his school bag and pulled out his cell phone. He then tweeted:

Don't mess with me or my mom! #shots been fired

He coolly put away his cell phone and reclined back in the passenger seat.

In the driveway, a thought suddenly came to Trent: Sonia pontificated a couple of nights ago about him participating in some God time with her. But the next day, Taylor's being teased by his classmates that she was seen in Sumter. Now he's dropping Taylor off at home after he was suspended from school. As much as he tried keeping an open mind, it wasn't working.

More thoughts of her giving him grief for an array of reasons, including her confronting him about a supposed tryst he had with Brazilian businesswoman Alcione de Oliveria, began swirling in his mind.

His patience was now razor thin considering the way the day had already unfolded. He stopped off in his work office and text messaged Sonia once again.

> Taylor got into a fight today. He was suspended 6 days. Three days at home, three in-school. You haven't answered any of my texts. You don't care about your own son?

He leaned back in his chair, closed his eyes, and clasped his hands behind his head. He suspected kids simply don't post things like that on Twitter just to be cruel. And based on his adulterous past, anything was possible—the tightest of games could unravel in the least likely of places and situations.

A scenario he always recounted to himself was the story of a local pastor who took his mistress on a cruise to Jamaica. While eating, two members from his church came over and spoke to him—of all the things that could have happened.

The pastor, without any means of escape with his mistress, acknowledged the church members and continued with his meal. Upon returning from the getaway, he nearly lost his church and marriage; he'd since saved and restored both, but the marriage took the longest.

His train of thought and growing rage was interrupted by a soft knocking on the door.

"Dad, I just want to tell you I'm sorry for getting into trouble today," Taylor said as he took a couple of steps inside.

Trent swung around his chair. "You don't have to apologize for setting someone straight about your mother. Just remember next time you have to handle it better. You can't try settling everything by fighting."

He stood up and offered Taylor a hug.

Taylor smiled at him. "Thanks. You're the best."

Before returning to work, Trent checked his cell phone. The message icon was lit.

> **What is all this about Taylor getting into a fight and being suspended?**

He smirked at Sonia's text reply.

> **Why are you nowhere to be found today? That's not all we need to talk about...**

Sonia searched for her Tracfone in her purse so she could send Milner a message.

> **I might not have a chance catching up with you later today. Keep me in your thoughts :0**

She then composed herself and sent a quick reply to Trent with her regular cell phone.

> You know I'm not able to respond to text messages
> as quick as you'd like. Is Taylor okay? Do you know
> why he got into a fight?

> I've already addressed Taylor's suspension with
> him. Why don't you answer why nobody's been
> able to catch you at all today?

Sonia had always been accessible whenever Taylor became sick or had any problems at school. Now she was unsure whether she should cry, pray, or both after sensing the sharpness of Trent's text messages.

When she checked her messages, she noticed Trent sent them while she was at lunch. But she spent most of her break talking to Milner—she left her regular cell phone back at her desk.

Then she was in meetings after lunch. They did not end until a few minutes before she received Trent's latest text message, which questioned whether she cared about Taylor's welfare at school.

She recognized that she was fast slipping into compromise just to maintain her contact with Milner; she couldn't blame him for her actions. But this was nearly a year in the making. It happened to have gained added momentum since their date in Charlotte.

Since she'd already taken time off once this week, it was to her advantage not to leave work so suddenly. Team supervisors were subjected to the same scrutiny as phone reps when it came to attendance.

> I saw where you text me but I've been in meetings
> most of today. Can we talk about this later?

> We better talk about this.

Trent was back at the bank no more than forty-five minutes when his cell phone buzzed and vibrated as if it were his electric clippers.

A series of text messages were forwarded to him from Taylor, who was enraged by an act of retaliation by Da'Mitri.

> I told you that I saw your mother in Sumter

> Since you didn't believe me . . . Maybe you'll believe this

The next text message was a picture of Sonia who appeared to be looking back at a building while she entered a car. The picture was taken in a hurry. Part of the door to a silver car, which could not be easily identified, was also captured in the shot.

Trent first reacted by leaning back in his chair and taking a deep breath. Another text message came in before he could reply. This one was an image of a tweet from Taylor's Twitter feed.

> I don't lie #boppin

Now Trent was incensed. He was inclined to driving over to Sonia's job and demand that she talked to him. That would have been a likely thing she'd done if he were between her crosshairs.

After giving it additional thought, he sent Sonia another text message.

> What time do you get off work?

> At 5:30. Why do you need to know?

> I can't ask? You were gone this morning before Taylor went to school.

> What's wrong with you, Trent?

> Nothing's wrong with me. Maybe the problem is YOU!

* * *

The day had unfolded rather suspiciously, Sonia thought to herself, but she was convinced that Trent was too clueless to suspect anything about her and Milner. There was no way he could trace any phone calls to her because she'd been using a Tracfone. All but one date she had with Milner was inside the state of South Carolina.

As best as she knew, she managed to maintain the same demeanor and personality around him.

She sensed his problem with her was his inability to speak to her while all hell broke loss at Taylor's school. He should understand that things happen. Then it dawned upon her that she had not contacted Taylor. Maybe he was upset that he had not heard from her all day.

> Taylor, I've been busy all day today. I was in a meeting when your school called me. I know you were suspended for fighting. I'd like to know why.

Sonia returned to her work, but she wasn't accomplishing much. Taylor had not replied as fast he usually would. And the end of her shift couldn't come fast enough.

"Ms. Sonia, can you help me with this caller?" Tanya blurted out.

She was slow to lurch over to her right and make eye contact with Tanya. That was also sufficient for Tanya to continue with her question.

"This new Health Care Reform stuff has me confused," she
said.

Sonia answered, "It has me confused, too; there's been so
many updates to it."

"Just please explain whether shots for shingles are covered
under this?"

"How old is the patient?"

"She's sixty-two."

"Yes, so long as they meet the age requirement. Tell your
caller to visit the government's website. It's all there." She
told Tanya to put her caller on hold while she confirmed the
information. "According to the website, it is recommended
for adults age sixty and older."

Tanya nodded emphatically. "Well, that's good enough for
me!"

"I hope it is, because I'm outta here in about six minutes!"
Sonia mumbled to herself.

To ensure that nobody approached her with another question, she gathered her purse and went to the bathroom. She
also took both cell phones with her.

> I got into a fight. No big deal now. When are you
> coming home?

Sonia exhaled in relief that Taylor replied to her. She was
quick to text back to him she expected to be home around
six o'clock.

While she was in the bathroom, she saw where Milner had
already replied to the one she sent earlier.

You're always in my thoughts. Can't wait to hold
you in my arms again!

That brought a smile to her. At least someone cared to send
her something positive.

If you're a good boy, I might surprise you with
something to think about until we see each other
again :)

Sonia had every intention of leaving UCP without bothering to look into her rear-view mirror. She walked at a brisk
pace out to her car, which was parked nearby a tree off to the
left of the building.

She was so tunnel vision with leaving she did not notice an
Acura TL approaching from her left. She flinched at the sound
of the horn.

"So this is the only way I can speak to my wife, hmmm?"

"Trent, what are you doing here?" Her heart began pound-
ing hard and fast.

He parked his car in front of hers and got out. "Maybe I
should ask what were you doing in Sumter?" He took a couple of steps toward her, placing his hands at his waist.

"I don't know what you're talking about." She went ahead
with getting inside her car.

"I don't know what I'm talking about? I'm not going to
make a scene out here. Open that damn door!"

Sonia was too stunned to resist. As soon as Trent slammed
the door shut, he hurled obscenities at her with such inten-
sity that it took her several moments to collect her thoughts.
This was by far the last thing she expected.

He put his finger barely millimeters away from her face.

"I've had it with your bull! You go around acting like nothing stinks on you, but it's stinking to high heaven right now!

"Your son got into a fight today because kids were calling you someone who bounces around from one man to another, and you were seen in Sumter with another man!"

She now regained her nerve to refute him. "Trent, you should be the last person to come yelling at me about being seen with someone!" She pointed in the direction of the Shell gas station not far from the UCP parking lot.

"I saw you just last summer with that foreign hussy who begged me to forgive both you and her. You think I've forgotten about that?"

He lunged at her. His eyes were bulged and his hands were in a choking position.

"I don't give a flying you-know-what who you were seen with. What bothers me is when my son gets suspended because he thought someone was lying about his mother!"

"Wait a minute! I work hard every single, doggone day at that building over there. I put up with the stupid people they hire, the stupid people who call, and the stupid people above me who make the decisions. And I'll be damned if you're going to come at me like a lunatic with something unfounded as me being seen in Sumter!

"Trent, I've put up with your cheating on me—I don't know whether to say thank God or just consider it His grace that I've not caught anything from you. I'm just waiting for the day a woman comes knocking on the front door about you fathering a child outside of our marriage—"

In the back of Sonia's mind, she couldn't believe being caught in Sumter could have happened. The one time she let her guards down with Milner by going against her better judgment has produced the worst day of her marriage.

"I don't have a problem with you calling me a whore or a

liar, but I do have a problem when you're going to say that your son's lying—I knew something like this might happen, so I came prepared."

He reached into his shirt pocket and scrolled through his cell phone. He held up the cell phone picture of her entering Milner's car.

"Now, are you going to call your son a liar?" He then went silent, staring intently at her.

Sonia lowered her head. It took all of her to keep from bursting into tears. She closed her eyes. She was too decimated to even offer up a plea to heaven.

"And what makes it so flippin' bad is when I do the math, you had the audacity to try beating me over the head with your sanctimonious God talk a few days ago. Then the very next day you're spending time with someone in Sumter—of all the places!

"I'm not from South Carolina, and even I know there's nothing much that goes on in Sumter."

She still hadn't composed herself to respond; Trent lit into her further.

"Okay, I take it your silence is an admission of your guilt— you were messing with another man," he yelled, nodding his head as if he'd figured it all out.

"Ms. Holier Than Thou. The Righteous One of Columbia. Always pointing out where the other person has fallen or has faults. And she has a telephone pole stuck in both eye sockets . . . Ha!"

Trent finally struck below the waist with his words. She took her frustrations out by pelting him with repeated punches on his shoulder and back. Her ability to do what she really wanted was hindered by the vehicle's center console.

Also, she accidently stepped on the accelerator a couple of times, causing the engine to race.

It still didn't matter in the heat of the moment . . .

"You know what it's like being married to a clueless cheat for a husband? Do you know?" she said between punches. "I'll tell you . . . it's been pure hell!

"And I'm glad that I did it! At least someone shows a sincere interest in me. At least someone remembers what's important and what makes me happy. At least I have a smile on my face when I think of that person—and he can do it better!"

Suddenly, Trent reached up and grabbed Sonia by the wrist. Then he improved his leverage by grabbing her other hand despite fighting him. He leaned over into her side of the console.

"I could easily knock you into next week, woman . . . Do you not realize that?" he yelled at her; he was also aware that some passerby might call the police if they were seen fighting inside her car.

"In fact, you'd deserve it if I were to beat the living mess out of you! And to think you could get away messing around with someone in Sumter. Obviously, you're not much of a pro at it—"

"Humph, that's what you think!" She still struggled to free herself from his grip.

"You eff'd up. That's all there is to it, and you're going to have to deal with it. Don't think about coming to 19 Schillingford Court tonight!"

Trent pushed her back in the driver's seat, hastily opened the passenger door, and slammed it so hard that he hoped it fell off the hinges. He walked off mumbling and cursing to himself.

"Whatever . . . I don't need to, anyway!" she yelled.

Her words had no impact. He'd already slammed his door shut and peeled out of the parking lot. But the enormity of all that had transpired finally caught up with her. She placed her head on the steering wheel and wept bitterly.

Chapter 12

Okay, Trent had his moment of rage, Sonia acknowledged after crying for nearly twenty-five minutes. Maybe it was justified—but to what extent?

It still didn't seem right to her that she was now on the wrong side of the marital infidelity coin.

While driving home to Chapin, she often said the word humility and that it was needed at this moment. She figured if she went there as the prodigal wife she might be able to salvage everything. Surely Trent would show compassion. And mercy might be obtained for the merciful. At least that was what she felt she showed him so many times in the past.

She took a couple of deep breaths as she turned into the neighborhood. And she reminded herself again about showing humility once she turned into the driveway, parking behind his car.

But her best-made plans were immediately tested. Trent came out to meet her at the walkway in front of the steps.

"Uh-uh, you're not coming in this house!" The visage of anger that she last seen of him hadn't changed. "Don't even think about it!"

"Just who in the world you think you are?"

"The same person who's put up with your self-righteous mind games all this time. That's who."

Annoyed, she tried walking past him as if he never stood there. She got barely a step past him before he grabbed her by the arm and spun her around.

"I told you back at your job don't think of coming here tonight, didn't I?"

She jerked her arm away from him, but he stood directly in her path.

"Trent, get out of my way. That's my house, too!"

"See, what you failed to realize is that it's not just me who knows about your activity," he said, pointing toward their home. "You have a son in there who's trying to make sense of all this. He doesn't deserve that!"

"Hah! Look who's donning a breastplate of righteousness? The whore himself!"

She folded her arms and sucked her teeth, but he was not moved by her comment.

"Obviously, you have selective retention. But I'm going to help you out here." He turned around and went back inside the house, slamming the door behind him. She was left stunned and embarrassed in front of the neighbors.

Rather than making a bigger scene out of it, she quietly returned to her car and drove to a nearby shopping plaza—she was also in desperate need of using a bathroom.

Let him blow off some steam, she thought. *I'll come back by in the morning.*

She was already tired of fighting and crying. And in the greater scheme of things, she didn't think it seemed fair that

God didn't give her the same length of rope as others whom she felt had done things far worse than her. Nor was this the way she envisioned her day would unfold when she rushed out of the house so she could have her morning conversation with Milner.

Now she was faced with having to find a place to rest her head for the night.

"Hello?"

At least she answered the phone . . .

"Shonna, this is Sonia."

Humility was not the word that came to mind with her sister. It was more like bracing herself for humiliation.

She cleared her throat and spoke slowly and softly, forcing herself to consider words she had hardly entertained over the past several months.

"I . . . I know the last time we talked didn't end well . . ."

"You got that right!"

Sonia sensed from the harshness of Shonna's voice that she was on the brink of hanging up.

"Please, will you let me say this—"

There was no response or breathing into the phone by Shonna on the other end.

"I . . . I had no right talking to you the way I did the last time. It was one thing to disagree with you, but I went too far with it." To her, the moment was like a known bigot coming to the only person who could help her, whose orientation and/or race had been targeted by her vitriol. But she also had to get to her point—fast.

"Shonna, I should have called you much sooner and apologized for the things I said. Unfortunately, some things have happened today and I really need your help."

She didn't say another word.

The silence between them lasted for several moments. If

there was to be any hanging up, it was going to be Shonna, who previously deleted Sonia's number from her cell phone.

"Why do you need me?" Shonna reacted with sarcasm. "Obviously, things were going well for you; I guess there's some truth to what it says about taking heed where one stands unless he falls."

A part of Sonia wanted to lash out at Shonna. That was her pride kicking and screaming. Another part of her tried applying not allowing anything to be done through selfish ambition or deceit. That was humility crying out.

"All these months, I have kept things to myself. I felt that I had no choice based on the decisions that I made," she told Shonna. "I really need your help. That's the best way I can sum it up to you."

"Wait a minute. You want me to help you, but you can't tell me why? It sounds like to me all you want are things on your own terms. You don't need my help!"

Shonna smirked at her own comment.

That was all that Sonia could stand. "Fine. I don't need your help. You're not the only one I can call on!"

She hung up.

The moment was all too comical for Shonna. "Sucka didn't want no help, sucka won't get no help!"

* * *

Although it may not have been the easiest of phone calls under the circumstances, Sonia felt she had a more favorable chance with her parents.

"Mother dear, how are you?"

Prentiss was set on alert. "I'm fine, but I know you're not."

Sonia dropped her guard almost immediately. "How did you know?"

"That was the way you'd speak to me when you were in tight spots as a teenager and in college."

"Nothing ever gets past you, does it?" Sonia spoke in admiration and concession.

"I thank Him above from whence cometh my help, and who gives me a spirit of power and love and a sound mind—"

Sonia went into a discourse about her and Trent getting into an argument over her rumored to have been seen in Sumter the day before with another man. She did not mention the source of it all stemmed from a fight that Taylor had with a classmate.

"He came up to my job this afternoon and made a big scene in the parking lot. I'm sure someone saw us." She hissed at the notion she might be a conversation piece among UCP employees.

"Then he stormed off peeling rubber and all. I eventually went home, but he wouldn't allow me inside. He really went off on the deep end about this."

Sonia guessed the trip from the Food Lion parking lot in Ballentine where she called her mother to their home off Farrow Road should take roughly a half hour. Thus, she took another route that would enable her to reach the I-26 freeway heading eastbound much sooner.

"I was calling ahead to let you know that I need a place to rest my head for the night."

"I see." Then Prentiss went silent, contemplating their brief exchange.

"Mom, are you there?"

"I'm here."

"Have you fixed anything to eat? I'm also hungry. I hadn't eaten anything since this morning."

"Yeah, I've already cooked. I made stew meat, green beans and potatoes."

"Sounds good."

Prentiss felt pressed to delve deeper with Sonia. "Let me ask you this."

"Sure."

"Was it true that you were in Sumter and you were with another man?" she asked.

Sonia felt as if her heart dropped to her stomach. Confessions like these were never easy. "Yes, Mom. It's true. I was in Sumter and I was with another man."

Her response was also all that Prentiss needed to hear. She recounted to Sonia various proclamations she made during her childhood years.

"You remember when you and Shonna were kids I said I wouldn't take care of nobody's kids? Thank God, both of you have been good about that."

Then she reminded Sonia about the diminished role she'd have in her life after Trent married her.

"I told you that there were things that only you'll be able to solve with your husband, and I'll never be blamed for you two getting divorce, God forbid. But one thing you should know is I've always tried to teach you and Shonna in the way you should go.

"That also includes not being associated with any form of unrighteousness."

Prentiss explained she would be harboring sin if she allowed Shonna to stay at their home for the night. "I can't help you until you take the first step: You have to renounce the things of dishonesty, both that which is obvious and hidden."

Is this some form of holiness that I've not heard of?

She reminded Prentiss that Trent had all but kicked her out of her home because she made a mistake in judgment.

"I thought I could turn to my own parents for help, but you're talking to me like I'm a serial criminal. You know, you've always had a self-righteous aura about you—it's you're always right," she ranted, "and God help the poor soul who doesn't agree.

"Sometimes, I wonder just how Dad puts up with you. I bet what he does is tune you out!"

Prentiss was not moved by Sonia's argument. In fact, she remained as calm as when she answered the phone.

"You're my daughter; I put you in this world. But I didn't raise you to be cheating on your husband. Nothing good comes out of that kind of behavior," she said. "You know the ways of a sinner is hard."

Sonia had now made it onto I-26, but she was not sure whether it would be worth her while. "What else are you going to say? That you don't mix with the ungodly? As if you've never done anything that would be considered ungodly!"

"This home is just as much your home," Prentiss retorted, hoping also to reason with Sonia. "But I've not heard any hint of repentance, or anything of the sort.

"So why should I let you stay when there's a chance you'll go see someone who isn't your husband?

"You're asking me to look the other way with sin."

Sonia's eyes were bugged out; she also was heavy on the accelerator.

"Mom, I just got kicked out of my home, which I hope will only be for the night. I've not had any chance to sit down and think about anything. How can you be so quick to judge?"

"How am I judging you?" Prentiss reacted. "I'm doing my best to speak to you in truth and in love—"

That would be subject to debate, Sonia fumed. She recognized she was not making any progress with her mother.

"Oh, forget it! Don't be the one who strains the gnat but swallows the camel. I'm sorry that I bothered you."

She hung up again on a family member.

Now feeling desperate, Sonia felt she had no choice. She was determined to find help in her moment of need.

"Shonna, it's me again. Please don't hang up on me." Her voice was noticeably troubled.

"Okay, I won't. But you must be a glutton for punishment."

"Please, sis. I really need your help. I just got off the phone with your mother—"

"Oh, she's *my* mother now?"

"Anyway, I need a place to stay for the night. Trent's ticked off to high heaven at me."

Shonna was on the brink of gloating. This was too good to pass up hearing. "I can't imagine him being that way with you."

"Well, he is. Maybe he has a reason."

"Why does he?"

"Apparently, someone saw me in Sumter yesterday with another man." She was quick to keep control of the conversation.

"And before you open your mouth and judge me like your mother, yes, it is true. I've been seeing him for almost as long as we haven't spoken to each other—at least eight months."

Shonna placed her hand over her mouth as if this was the biggest news of the year. Of all people, Sonia Chandler-Buckner had fallen; she was now among the downtrodden and captives. Who could set her free?

"I-I hadn't said anything. I'm just listening."

"Thanks. I appreciate it," Sonia responded.

Shonna went ahead with informing Sonia that she and Lance were still dating, and she was expecting him to come over and spend the night with her.

"I'm sure your mother probably told you that this place is just as much yours, which it is. But I do want to warn you that Lance and I will probably be getting our groove on tonight. So if you hear the headboard banging against the wall, maybe even some loud moaning or screaming, don't be shocked and don't come knocking on my door!"

She then told Sonia that they would discuss her problem with Trent early in the morning.

Chapter 13

Shonna looked over at Lance who was still sleeping. She was proud that she'd satisfied him the night before with such passion. It felt so right doing it with him, and she felt even better being a satisfied woman both emotionally and sexually. It was an enviable place to be at this stage in her life.

She didn't mind exploring things sexually with him that maybe at one point in the past she might have frowned upon, turned up her nose at, or even deemed solely as something that was reserved for the man she'd married.

Humph.

Time was not running out, but times sure had changed.

She eased out of bed and put on a garnet and white football jersey of her alma mater—she attended the big university located in downtown Columbia—and headed for the kitchen after visiting the bathroom. She wasn't a coffee drinker, but she still had an affinity for junk food. A Mountain Dew sounded just right.

That was another enviable thing about Shonna. She was only a size larger than she was in college. And she liked it even more when Lance raved about her body still looking so fit and sexy.

"Good morning," she greeted Sonia, who appeared in the kitchen maybe ten minutes later.

Shonna gave Sonia a knowing stare, prompting her to chortle. "I warned you before you came over what was going to happen."

"Yeah, I know. But it couldn't have been that good—"

Sonia excused herself on that note. Apparently, it was similarly good for Charlotte, who went ballistic on him after he decided he wanted Shonna over her. Joining her at the kitchen table, she mused silently to herself about having a Milner moment of her own.

"Do you have anything I could wear for work?" she asked. "I was hoping that I'd be able to drive back home, take a shower in my own bathroom, get some clothes . . . You know how that goes?"

Shonna reclined back in her chair after taking a sip from her glass of soda.

"I do, but think about it: Are you going to drive all the way back on the other side of town—it's almost seven o'clock now—and deal with all that traffic?"

"Yeah, thanks for reminding me," she said. "Okay, what kind of outfit you think I might be able to wear?"

Shonna looked Sonia over, bringing her hand up to her chin. Sonia was slightly shorter and shapelier.

"It might be a stretch, but I do think I have something that will work."

"And where do you think you're going with that?"

"Nowhere," Shonna retorted, tipping her head toward Sonia.

"And if I were you, I'd check myself."

Sonia raised her hand slightly. "Okay, I get it. I'll only speak when recognized." She then gestured with zipping her lips shut.

"Good. While you're at it, give me all the details about you and Trent. Don't hold back anything—"

Sonia leaned forward and partially hid her face from Shonna's view.

"Aren't you going to tell me who he is?" Shonna interrupted her.

Sonia merely stared. The last thing she wanted to do was disclose she'd been with Milner. She'd never hear the end of it.

"Well, I'm waiting—"

The Chandler sisters were reasonably close when they were on better terms, but Sonia felt this was the very thing that had already led them to not being on speaking terms. It was Shonna who insisted on meeting with her last year at The Groovy Soul and divulging whom she was dating, which she discovered was Lance.

"Can we not go there?" Sonia begged.

"You know I'm going to keep asking. I wouldn't be your sister if I didn't."

"Here's what I'll tell you. We've seen a lot of each other. We started out real slow, and it's kind of built up to where it is now.

"Humph, we didn't start having sex until recently."

Now placing her chin in her hand, Sonia also described how she took time off work and visited her "male friend's" home in Eastover.

"Is that right?" Shonna got up and headed toward the refrigerator for a refill of her Mountain Dew. She gestured to Sonia, "Want any?"

"Puh-lease! You're about as bad as your nephew wanting to drink that stuff in the morning. Isn't Mountain Dew bad for your teeth?"

Shonna joined her back at the table. Just for spite, she took a long sip. "You might want to use that line with someone else. I'll have you to know that I've never had a cavity after all these years.

"But continue with your story—"

"This is sort of complicated. I still haven't learned of all the details. Trent says Taylor got into a fight with a classmate who said he saw me in Sumter with my friend."

Taking a deep breath before responding, Shonna said, "That is a problem. And how in the world someone saw you in Sumter, anyway? There's nothing there!"

"Tell me about it. That's the only reason why I agreed to go. We'd met for dates in Augusta and Charlotte, so I figured who in their right mind would be in Sumter seeing us together?

"Obviously, I guessed wrong. What made it even worse, I tried denying it to Trent. But then he was ready for me. He showed me a cell phone picture that was taken."

"Busted, hmmm?"

"Big time." She mulled aloud the one time she ever considered going through with cheating on her husband resulted in her being caught.

"I mean, I've been careful. I've even used a Tracfone so nothing can be traced back to me."

In the midst of their conversation, Lance came rambling into the kitchen. Shonna's eyes lit up and she broke out with a silly grin, prompting Sonia to turn around.

"Sonia—"

"Hi, Lance." She dared not to ask him how was he. Shonna's eyes had already said it all. "How's the new job going?"

"Fine," he answered. "I can't be any happier where I am."

He then stopped by Shonna, touched her on the shoulder, and made romantic telepathy with her—to which she blushed in everyone's presence.

Oddly enough, Sonia noticed Lance seemed to be right in his element being around her sister, although she still believed time and their age difference would outweigh all the good chemistry and sex they seemed to enjoy.

She waited until he left the kitchen before continuing, "Do you think you have feelings for him?" She figured that was as safe as any question to ask.

"What do you think?" she answered, arching her eyebrows for emphasis; a familiar twitching sensation between her thighs was also a nice reminder.

She was quick to return the conversation back to Sonia. "It's easy to say you have to decide what you're going to do. One thing I do know about when married people cheat it's usually out of selfishness."

Although the passage about not allowing anything to be done through selfish ambition and deceit briefly crossed her mind, Sonia went on the offensive.

"I know I've never said much about the bad things that have happened in my marriage with Trent, but there's been a lot of them. Sometimes, a person can only take so much and then they react maybe in ways that some would consider unacceptable."

Shonna reminded Sonia about being the "other woman" in her relationship with DeMorris Pierre until his divorce was final.

"After all the emotional support I gave him, he still went his separate ways. You remember how broken hearted I was?"

She nodded. "But how is my situation similar to yours? I've gone through a lot with Trent. He's been so clueless for so long. Now he wants to act like he's blameless. That's what really ticks me off!"

"I know I've been the one who's applauded women for getting what they're not getting at home, but is it really the right thing to do?" Shonna then hunched her shoulders.

Sonia had to catch herself from forming Milner's name on her lips.

"My friend once met Trent and read him like a book. And the sad thing about it, I thought Trent would at least pick up on another man trying to hit on his wife. But he was so caught up in himself. It was embarrassing."

"Let me ask you this," Shonna countered as she leaned back and crossed her leg. "Is Trent a bad husband? Is he a bad father? Has he been your worst friend?"

Sonia stared at Shonna, processing her question. How could someone who's never been close to being married have the audacity to ask such a weighty series of questions?

"I'll answer it this way. Sort of, no, and not really."

"That's my point," Shonna answered. "Your reasons for being with your 'male friend' are all selfish."

She then brought up her relationship with DeMorris Pierre once again. "I thought it would be cool being that 'Clean Up Woman' since according to him, wifey had no desire to take care of home." She shook her head. "And I had the nerve to bring him around the family, you remember?"

Sonia rocked her head from side to side, as if she did not want to acknowledge ever meeting him. But the mere thought of her actions was getting the best of her again.

She excused herself and went to the bathroom. Upon her return, she noticed it was almost 7:30. Her shift was to begin in an hour.

"I need to get ready. What was that outfit you were telling me about?"

Not to mention, she was experiencing withdrawal from not being in a position to contact Milner. But what would she tell him, anyway?

She'd gone this far not divulging anything pertaining to Trent. Maybe she could continue keeping her domestic problems separate.

Before Shonna got up from the table, she was quick to remind Sonia of another important item. "Just so you know, you're welcome to borrow my clothes. But this doesn't change anything between you and me.

"You've still got a long way to go before I would consider us on speaking terms once again."

Chapter 14

Trent went through his checklist of do's and mostly don'ts with Taylor before leaving for the bank.

"I want to make it very clear with you, NO girls!"

"Dad, I'm in the ninth grade. All the girls I know don't have a driver's license."

Trent folded his arms and leaned against the doorsill of Taylor's bedroom. "You may have a point there, but they do have older brothers, sisters, and friends who do drive and can drop them off over here and then come and pick them up." So he emphasized again with him no female company.

"Also," he added, "don't open the door for anyone; I don't think I need to explain that any further."

There was only so much more that a fourteen-year-old could take listening to his father. Taylor, now sitting at the edge of his bed, began staring at the ceiling and mimicking Trent's voice and diction.

"*I don't think I need to explain that with you, Taylor . . . No friends, no girls, no visitors!*"

Trent was hardly amused. "Okay, now that we understand each other, make sure you start on your classwork. You've got all this time to yourself and no interruptions!"

"Yes, Dad. Anything else?"

"Ah, yes. They're in the kitchen," he whispered to himself about his car keys; he then turned his attention back to Taylor.

"No, I think that should do it. Why don't you come lock the door for me—"

Time away from school should have been a welcomed occasion for Taylor, but it was far from that with him. He slept sporadically throughout the night, and he'd been up non-stop since 3:35 a.m.

Although he had his social networks as an outlet, few of his friends, if any, could relate to what he'd been brooding over since being suspended.

"Dad," he said, catching Trent's attention just as he opened the front door, "what is wrong with you and Mom? Just when I think things are back to normal, now this with her. I don't get it."

Trent looked over his shoulder at him. "This is not the best time to ask that question." He sighed, but then he closed the door and led him back into the living room where they both sat down on the sofa.

"This stuff is really bothering me," Taylor said. "I don't think it's fair to me at all."

"You're right. It isn't fair."

"What are you going to do about it?"

"Good question," Trent answered, bringing his hand up to his mouth. "I'm still trying to figure it out, too."

There was also no way that he could relate anything to Taylor from his own childhood. His parents were separated and divorced before he reached the fourth grade.

As much as it pained Trent to see his son full of confusion, anger and already lacking sleep, he had not made any effort at reaching out to Sonia. His sentiment was good riddance, if she felt being with another man was necessary. And his conscience was clear, he felt, because he had for the most part kept his word to her. No better example was his dramatic gamble last summer proving to her that he had not done anything improper with Alcione.

"Please do something, Dad," Taylor whined. "I don't know how much more of this I can take."

"I'll try."

"Can you start by asking Mom to come back home?"

Trent wondered to himself whether he asked Sonia anything similar while he was banished from their residence for more than a month—and then reconcile less than a week before he was to appear in divorce court.

"Your mother has to want to return home." He did not elaborate that meant her admitting to her wrong behavior for starters.

The mere thought of all this provoked him to sighing. "All of us will have to deal with this. It's easy suggesting that we pray. But that is what you, me, and your mother need to do. We can ask for His will to be done. His desire is that we're all here in this house together and you do not have to see these kinds of things," he said. "My prayer is for you to have peace of mind."

And with that, he took a deep breath and held out his arms for Taylor. They stood up and hugged. He reminded Taylor that he would be calling to check on him periodically, so keep his cell phone nearby.

These days, Ms. Wanda smirked and hissed at any thought

or mentioning of Trent Buckner. She lost any remaining respect that she had for him after he passed her over for Cortez's old job. If anyone asked her, she was quick to say he was
nothing more than a spineless buffoon.

Now, she had too much time invested at Palmetto Fidelity
to consider leaving. At fifty-six, she would be eligible to retire
with twenty-five years of service in a less than seven years;
she would also be eligible to apply for Social Security.

Since the bank's intranet posted openings that were not yet
available to the public, she arrived at the St. Andrews branch
about twenty minutes early. Trent was not there, which
made it even better.

She discovered the main downtown branch had a loan officer's opening. This time, she was determined to ensure herself
an inside track to be hired.

"This is Rena. How can I help you?"

"Girl, what you been up to lately?" she reacted.

Rena, whose husband was local businessman and Columbia city councilman Fred Avery, was a human resources
manager at Palmetto Fidelity's downtown office; they'd been
friends for more than a decade. She was an affable woman in
her late forties.

They also attended the same church, Grace Redemption,
which had a prominent television ministry in the Columbia
market.

"I'm always about my Father's business. That's what I'm up
to," Rena answered.

"Listen, there's s a loan officer's opening that I'm really interested in applying for."

"You know how it goes, Wanda. You apply online and the
process starts that way."

"This opening was posted yesterday. Do you know how
long it will remain open?"

"Openings at this branch do not stay open for long, so I'd recommend that you act on it fast."

"I'll do that. Thanks."

Ms. Wanda was also aware that all calls both internally and externally at Palmetto Fidelity were recorded. She mused that's why cell phones were made for moments like these.

"Hey, now I can talk the way I really want," Ms. Wanda said. "I can sure use a sister's help with this opening—"

Rena first warned Ms. Wanda about her connection may not be reliable from her location on the tenth floor. Then she said, "You know I'll help you as best as I can."

"Thanks. Do you know what it's like being around someone you simply don't like?"

"Don't we all have one or two like that?"

"For the life of me, I still don't know why I was passed over for this branch's loan officer opening. I thought since this boss of mine had seen me every day as someone he could count on it would have been a no-brainer."

Rena mentioned that she had a fairly good relationship with branch manager Agnes Lindler, who had taken up on a couple of hiring recommendations she'd given her in recent years; there was still no guarantee that she could influence her decision.

"I hate to tell you, sister, I hear stories like that all the time," she said. "But that reminds me of something."

"What?"

"Our generalist left recently, and what I hear it was a big stink about him basically being a loyal employee who got jacked around by Cut Throat—uh, I mean, his boss, our boss, Lois Driscoll."

"I don't get it. What does a generalist," she said, pronouncing the position slowly because she was not familiar with it, "have to do with me? I'm just looking to get out of what I see is a bad situation."

Rena asked Ms. Wanda for patience. There was simply too much to break down. "Here's what I know, and it came straight from the horse's mouth on his way out the door:

"He was given the choice of being fired or resign himself after being asked to fire someone that cost the bank a lot of money."

"How much money?"

"About $750,000 just to shut up a customer because he threatened to sue the bank."

Ms. Wanda was running short on patience and time. The bank was scheduled to open in less than five minutes. "You need to hurry up. It's almost nine o'clock."

"Okay, that was the background to everything else. He mentioned that he was asked to fire a loan officer who got the bank in the news for all the wrong reasons. I think you can put some of the pieces together."

"You mean politics?"

"Amen, sister."

This was not as bad a day after all even if Trent showed up. She was now eager for Rena to give her the punch line, if there was one.

"Okay, so you're saying my boss had no choice but to bring in someone from the outside because he was told to do so?"

"Unfortunately, there's a lot of hush-hush stuff behind all this. You know how you have to watch and pray in these situations—"

"I better get going. Can I call you later?" Ms. Wanda asked.

"Of course you can. Hopefully, I might have more to tell you."

Cortez immediately came to mind after Ms. Wanda's conversation with Rena. She wished that she had more time to call him. This just might be the kind of stuff that he'd been wanting, and it might come at a price that would be mutually beneficial.

No sooner when Ms. Wanda put away her cell phone, she saw Trent rushing inside the bank. He waved in her direction as soon as they made eye contact, but she did not wave back at him.

Chapter 15

There was nothing like entering her own home, Sonia said to herself after she pushed open the mahogany wood front door. She looked around in the living room and noticed nothing was out of place. She dropped her Coach bag on a metal stand nearby her and headed toward the kitchen.

"I'm gone just one day and they're already leaving dishes in the sink!" she mumbled aloud. "I should have known that."

Instinctively, she placed the plates, cereal bowl, and silverware in the dishwasher. It was still a labor of love. Then she strode down the hallway toward the bedrooms. Along the way she heard a television and music playing. The singing voice was, well, familiar but it needed help.

"Taylor? Is that you?"

There was no response.

She knocked on the door of the last bedroom on the left before reaching the hallway bathroom.

"Taylor!"

"Who is that? Mom?" She heard him scrambling out of the bed rushing to open the door. "What are doing here?"

She replied, "I should ask what are doing here?"

"I'm suspended three days at home. I also have three days' in-school suspension. You do know that, don't you?"

Taylor turned around and proceeded to sit back on his bed. He was not overly excited about seeing Sonia, who followed him inside his room. She looked around. His room was an absolute disaster. Books and papers were strewn across his bed. He had pants and shirts hanging on his closet door. He had two cups, a plate, and a bag of tortilla chips with salsa in a container on the dresser. The carpet also needed vacuuming.

"Hey, when are you going to clean up this room?" she queried him.

"I'll get around to it today."

"I hope it's sooner than later."

"Whatever."

She placed her hands on her waist. "And what's with the attitude?"

Taylor merely stared at her. She had some nerve, he thought to himself. She's the reason why he was home at 1:15 in the afternoon.

"I asked you a question," she said.

"No, why don't you answer why were you in Sumter, and why one of my classmates saw you there?" he yelled back at her.

This all sounded rather familiar to her in his demeanor and the tenor and pitch of his voice. Then it quickly dawned upon her that Taylor never learned about her catching Trent driving around with Alcione, which he claimed to be at a business dinner with a bank customer. She merely explained to him that his parents had a big argument over something his father had hurt and disappointed her. He moved out, and she said there was the possibility that he may not come back at all.

She did not have any righteous cause or argument this time around. He was the one who first learned of her being seen with another man.

"Taylor, baby, I'm sorry to have disappointed you."

"No you're not! You're not sorry that I had to beat up somebody because he called you a bop!"

His words were piercing to her conscience. She wanted to reach out and hug him; the tension in the room was too thick.

"Taylor, as long as I can remember, I always wanted to have children. And I always prayed that I would be the best mother a mother could be to her children. I . . . I—"

"I don't want to hear it!" Taylor yelled, stuffing his earphone back in his ears; he also leaned back against his head board scowling at her.

She took a step toward him. "Baby, mothers make mistakes, too. We're not perfect." The pain in her voice was unmistakable. Her eyes began welling.

"Mom, can you just leave me alone?" He reached for his cell phone and began browsing his social networks.

She dropped her head, turned around, and strode quietly to her bedroom. There would be no quick solution to this. It was far more complicated.

While in the bedroom, she gathered several changes of clothes, some personal items and her cell phone chargers, packing them in a suitcase and one of Trent's duffel bags he once used while he was a world-class track athlete.

She paused from packing and looked around. The first thing that she stared at was her wedding pictures. Her favorite one captured her and Trent kissing before Pastor Edwin George Middleton. There was another picture capturing the same moment, but a six-year-old Taylor, who served as the ring bearer, was in the background hiding his face.

Next, she sat down on her side of their bed. She held up her left hand and toyed with her wedding and engagement rings, but she never removed them—she had yet to do that even when she'd been with Milner. She sighed loudly.

Then she glanced over at the clock. It was almost 1:30 p.m. She apprised Phyllis that she'd be taking an extended lunch, but that she would return before two o'clock. Out of habit, she straightened up the bed before leaving. She was more than sure that Trent would recognize that she'd been there.

She stopped by Taylor's room on her way out, knocking first on his door.

"Yeah, what do you want?" he reacted; she dismissed his yelling because he had on headphones.

"I'm about to leave."

"Okay, bye." He returned to watching a Netflix movie from his iPad.

She was reduced to making a silent procession out of the house, unsure of where she might be hanging out for a second night.

* * *

Sonia liked Shonna's choice of clothing, a grey double-breasted skirt suit that fit her in all the right places. A few of her phone reps even gave her admiring stares and wanted to know where she got the suit.

She'd managed to suppress thoughts of Milner for most of the morning, but the habit that she'd formed took over. She could not recall the last time she had not spoken to him or viewed any text messages or e-mails that he'd sent her usually before she went on her break. She had the length of her driving time—usually fifteen to twenty minutes—to contact him.

"Where have you been? I missed talking to you this morning. I was wondering if you had changed your mind and felt that I'd been a bad boy."

Sonia could tell Milner was in his office because it only muffled the sound of dishes, pots, pans, and water used for washing.

"Come on," she reacted, chortling. "Where did you come up with that idea?"

"Hey, I waited the rest of yesterday for that something-something you were sending me and I never saw it."

She was slow to respond.

"Sonia, are you all right?"

"I guess I am. It's been a long couple of days."

"Are you sick?"

"No, nothing like that." She was listless with her response to him.

"Well, if it helps any, I'm glad to hear your voice. It's always the highlight of my day."

Milner's smooth words brought a smile to her. But she didn't feel comfortable talking any further.

"Can I call you once I'm off work today?" she asked.

"Sure. I'll be here probably working on the dinner menu like I usually do. I'll look for your call. I'll carry my phone on my hip."

"Thanks."

In the parking lot at UCP, Sonia checked her regular phone for any text messages. She snorted and smirked once she recognized the one from Trent. She had a hunch about the kind of message he sent her.

> Taylor text me that you just left the house. I told
> you don't think of going there. You had no business

showing up!

She had less than five minutes before she was expected back. Replying to him, if at all, had to wait.

Back at her cubicle, she had barely turned on her computer and accessed screens she needed to monitor the phone reps' time spent on their calls when an unlikely visitor helped herself to sitting in the chair adjacent to her desk.

"I like that skirt suit you're wearing today. I think something like that would look quite sexy on me," Charlotte said, looking herself over.

Since her meltdown with Lance, Charlotte made few interactions with Sonia, and for that matter most other people inside contract services. Vicki went as far as joking that Charlotte had gone stealth on everyone.

"Thank you. I'm really flattered."

"You've got to tell me where you got it from. I'll probably go by the same place right after work and see if they have anything like that in my size."

Sonia leaned back and folded her hands, placing them in her lap.

"I'm sorry, I can't tell you anything about this suit. My sister let me borrow it."

"Well, tell her that I like it. And if you remember, find out where she got it from." Charlotte then got up and pranced back to her cubicle.

While it was still on her mind, Sonia went ahead with sending a quick text response to Trent. But he had already sent a follow-up to the previous one he sent. She was not surprised by the tone of it:

> I would appreciate if you did not show up unannounced at my place.

She brought her hand up to her forehead, but placed it down almost immediately. She did not need to draw any unwanted attention to herself.

> Trent, I understand you're angry at me. But that is still my place. I needed to get some clothes. Do you remember I allowed you to do the same thing?

> Like I said, I would appreciate if you didn't show up unannounced.

Trent was being unreasonable, she hissed. She could not resist retaliating.

> What's wrong? You kick me out and the next day you're already planning to bring women there? That is still MY place, too, and I would appreciate if you didn't bring your jump-offs around MY SON!

> Go #$%@ yourself ! ! !

She smirked at his reply.

* * *

Instead of driving directly to Shonna's after work, Sonia went in the opposite direction. She figured it was better to follow up on her hunch sooner than possibly later.

The first thing she looked for once she turned into the parking lot was an older, greenish Ford Ranger with a black shell covering the bed. She smiled once she spotted it.

It was a different feeling walking inside The Groovy Soul thinking that she was more than merely a customer. Milner was more than stunned by her appearance.

"Mmmph! Good evening to you!" He walked over closer, envisioning her without anything on beneath her attire.

"Yes, good evening."

"I thought you would be calling me?" He looked down at his hip, tugging at his holster. "I told you I'd be carrying my phone."

"I changed my mind," she replied, then casting a knowing stare at him. "I am allowed to change my mind, aren't I?"

"Oh, absolutely." He asked her to wait briefly while he greeted the dinner party of four that came in right after her.

She figured she had some leverage with Milner, so why not use it to her advantage? When he returned, he handed her a menu to browse over and camouflage their conversation.

"You look good today," he said, nodding approvingly.

"Thank you. But I don't feel that way."

He reared back in his stance and folded his arms. "You didn't sound well earlier. What's wrong?"

"Hubby found out about us."

He was both silent and stoic.

"Even showed me a cell phone picture that was taken of me getting inside your Mercedes."

"Where?"

"In Sumter."

Milner inhaled slowly and deeply through his nostrils. In his next breath, he went ahead with leading her to a table closer to the back of the restaurant.

"What did you tell him?"

"Nothing. Really. Nothing other than some choice words. I spent last night at my sister's place."

"That's not good. Have you since spoken to him?"

"Only by text message, and that wasn't nice, either. He cursed me out."

Milner alerted her that he'd be back to continue their conversation. Meanwhile, she went ahead with visiting the buffet bar. She hadn't eaten anything all day.

A glass of iced tea already awaited her once she returned.
Milner's attentiveness was spot-on. She doubted Trent would
have been as considerate. Perhaps it was hunger. Maybe it
was also the combination of a great selection. A green salad
loaded with fruit, cucumbers, cherry tomatoes, diced ham
and turkey, with Italian dressing had never tasted so good.

"I'm really surprised something like this happened. I don't
think that either of us have been reckless," he said, stopping
by her table.

She hunched her shoulders. "I don't know what to say."

"Is he already talking about divorcing you?"

"Nope. I'm not really concerned about him. I'm more so
concerned about my son. He's really upset about it."

"I'm sorry to hear that."

She sat up in her chair and acknowledged with a nod. "As
for me, I really hadn't decided what I'm going to do. I just
don't know yet."

"I'll be right back—"

While Milner attended to other patrons, she tried text
messaging Taylor since she'd already mentioned him.

> **Are you all right? The last thing I would ever think
> of doing in life is hurt you.**

She received a quick reply from him.

> **Mom, leave me alone ! ! !**

Taylor was old enough to form his own thoughts, which
had the impact of a dagger piercing her heart. She leaned for-

ward with her forehead into her hand.

"I can tell something just upset you," Milner said, passing by her table again.

She nodded.

"Wharton, can you get me a to-go plate for this?" She looked down at her smothered chicken steak, rice, and corn.

"I'll be right back."

At least she knew that she could eat for free at The Groovy Soul. But there were other things she contemplated in that short time.

When Milner returned, he offered to walk her out to her car. She was impressed once again by the way he handled himself: She was more than confident his employees, Willette, Katrina, or any of the patrons would not suspect them having an affair.

"Wharton," she said as soon as they stepped outside, "I was thinking if I could stay at your place until I can find one on my own."

She then looked at him—he was agape at her suggestion. They slowed their pace of walking.

"Sonia, I don't know what to say. I mean, my sister and niece do come over to my place quite often—"

He wanted to tell her that he'd not mentioned anything about them to Willette, although he was not obligated by any means.

"I asked my parents, but they won't let me stay at their place. And I'm not really comfortable staying at my sister's. She and her boyfriend... Let's just say are rather active whenever they're together, you know what I mean?"

"Of course I do. I don't think I'd want to hear my sister calling out God and her boyfriend's name in the same sentence."

"Exactly."

Sonia had the money to find an apartment despite knowing

the cost of a decent one in the Columbia area was as much as buying a home. Along those lines, she did not want to spend that kind of money especially if she and Trent reconciled sooner than later.

They now stopped at her car.

"Wow, you sound like you're really into me now that things have hit the fan," she said.

Milner returned a confused stare.

She retorted, "You had no problem buying me jewelry, offering to put gas in my car before I went home after our dates, or wanting to buy me $750 dress.

"What's wrong with you offering me a place to stay until I can get one on my own?"

She noticed he was agitated for the first time.

"Sonia, I hope you're not trying to blame me for this, because it won't work!"

"No, I'm not blaming you. But maybe I'm now finding out what the real Wharton P. Milner is like since you've been grunting and moaning in my ears—"

She placed her hand on her waist, expecting an answer from him. He looked around and sighed. Had the roles been reversed, he was of the opinion a married man could not get away with approaching a single woman about offering him her place to stay right after their affair was discovered by his wife.

More than likely, the man would be on his own whether he had the means or not—and she might dump him on the spot.

"Here's what I'll do," he offered, "I'll put you up in a hotel for a few days."

He then told her to meet him back at The Groovy Soul shortly before closing.

Chapter 16

In the quietness of the early morning, Sonia tossed and turned in the hotel bed she'd been sleeping on the past four nights.

The mattress was too soft for her liking. She missed the convenience and ambience of home. She was running low on clothes to wear. She missed family life.

It was far from perfect, but it was hers.

Staring upward at the ceiling, it had been even more difficult for her to pray lately. She'd never felt so separated spiritually.

As much as she tried quieting herself that she might hear that still, small voice she depended on to guide her so many times in the past, it seemed as if the confusion from within distorted any connection.

It's really scary, she began praying. *I feel as if I'm by myself. I've never been this way before.*

I always had Trent and Taylor. I had my sister. I had my parents. But

I have nobody right now—and I can't consider Wharton in all of this. I have You, but look at what I've done. You hide Your face from sin and iniquity.

I'm in this because I was tired of being disappointed, and I felt someone actually showed me more consideration and attentiveness. I don't consider myself high maintenance. But you begin thinking that you're entitled to do this when you feel the other person doesn't make any effort.

I'm sorry for falling for the lust and desires of my heart—I guess I didn't know I had it in me. I should have seen it, but I didn't . . .

She didn't say another word.

Rather, she closed her eyes and recounted a passage about a prophet who mentioned he would wait and watch from the tower, expecting to receive a reply from above after making his grievances known to heaven. Maybe she, too, would be reminded of a vision being yet for an appointed time. Maybe she'd be told to wait; it would surely come.

She went back to tossing and turning, but she stopped and groped for her cell phone nearby.

> **Trent, when can you, me, and Taylor meet? I think it's time that we talk.**

Next, she went to the bathroom. Upon returning, she sat on the bed, tucked her folded arms into her stomach, and began rocking slowly back and forth. She added closing her eyes and arching her neck moments later.

In a different day an era she might have broke out moaning and humming. But she was reflecting on what had transpired between Milner and her.

Their last phone conversation was at 11:40 p.m, which was nearly six hours ago. He hinted that their relationship might affect her long term should she make the wrong decision.

"How can you say that, Wharton?" she reacted. "That

doesn't even sound like you!"

"I'm saying it because I've been there before. I've gone through what you're now experiencing."

Selfishly, he hoped to continue his affair with her, but it was more exciting when he was a part of the unknown. Now he was a suspect. And there was a chance he might even be confronted at any point. Then it would be game, set, and match; he'd lose.

A more sober thought was also voiced. "Maybe I'm bracing myself for disappointment. You get used to certain things, and there's always a chance you'll never see it or have it again."

"Why didn't you say that at first instead of giving me something about you being concerned about influencing me the wrong way?" she said.

She voiced her concern aloud that Milner could easily move on to the next woman, winning her over with the same smooth dialogue and attentiveness as he'd shown her. He could lavish her with gifts even more expensive than what she received. He also had nothing to lose while she stood to lose a lot more.

"Wait a minute. I have not as much as given my number to another woman since you and I started dating," he said. "You have been the next biggest priority in my life after the restaurant!"

She was deadpan with her response. "Yeah, yeah . . . Tell me anything, Milner."

He was more forceful with his conversation. "Sonia, why would I spend money on you staying in a hotel room? I didn't have to do that."

"No you didn't. I had my own money!"

"I don't get it. Would you rather that I show up at your husband's job and apologize to him that I'd been doing his wife?"

"Mmmm, that might be nice for starters—"

He sensed the playfulness in her voice. "You don't really mean that, Sonia!"

"Hey, anything's possible. You just never know?"

Their conversation did not last much longer. Sonia claimed to have been mentally and emotionally drained. And Milner went along with it.

Yawning, she slid back under the sheets and covers, clasping her hands behind her head; she stared at the ceiling once again.

She was soon stunned by her cell phone's buzzing.

> We can talk. I don't know what it will accomplish.
> Where do you want to meet?

She nodded at Trent's reply.

> Anywhere you choose is fine. Just let me know
> what time.

> Meet us at the Columbiana Mall in the food court
> about 6:30 this evening.

> OK

Chapter 17

The moment almost seemed like old times. It was once conceivable that Sonia would meet up with Trent and Taylor at the Columbiana Mall where she'd spend time with the two most important males in her life. That picture would have been accurate back in, say, 2003 or before.

Look at them, she commented to herself.

She sent Taylor a text message informing him to look off to his right just beyond the merry-go-round. After spotting her, he nudged Trent to follow him.

Taylor had an athlete's strut similar to Trent. He was nearly as tall as his father. She should have been beaming with pride watching them instead of feeling ashamed. A broken spirit and a contrite heart should not be despised, she hoped.

She stood up and managed a smile once they stopped at the table. "I miss you two—"

Neither Trent nor Taylor responded. Instead, they merely sat down after Sonia sat back down. She immediately wondered whether Trent had coached Taylor on what to say and how to act around her, but she was determined to reconcile with them.

"I asked to talk with both of you because some things have happened that I'm not proud of, and I hope that we could possibly move forward as a family once again."

Trent leaned back in the chair and stretched his legs, making sure, too, that his feet didn't bump into hers. Meanwhile, Taylor sat more erect and folded his arms.

"I don't want to be the one talking the entire time," she said. "I hope that we'll all talk about this as a family."

"Personally, I really don't want to know why or who you were with," Trent said, leaning forward and resting his chin in the palm of his hand.

Sonia countered, "But you need to understand why things happened as they did."

Then she looked over at Taylor. "Baby, I'm sorry that you had to find out about this the way you did."

"Are you really that sorry?" he reacted. "How would you feel if your mother's picture is all over Twitter and everyone's talking about you at school?

"Today was my first day back and it was horrible. They were still teasing me and calling you a bop!"

Sonia attempted convincing Taylor that many of the kids who teased him might have parents who have done things far worse than what she did. And it's possible they saw teasing him as an opportunity to heap upon another child the pain they've been shouldering.

That didn't go over well with him.

"Mom, I can't speak for any of them." He then shook his head, emphasizing his next point; he also raised his voice. "All I know is someone I go to school with saw you getting inside another man's car, and he text me the picture just to prove that he wasn't lying."

Sonia looked over at Trent. She was inclined to bring up his past behavior simply to keep him from condemning her—it might also divert Taylor from being so critical.

"Your father and I have had many disagreements before, but none of them involved you until now," she said. "If I had to do it all over again, I never would have done anything that would cause you shame and hurt—"

"Then what would you have done?" Trent interrupted. "Because based on what I saw in that picture, it looked like you were really comfortable getting inside that car."

"Some things don't even deserve dignifying, and that's one of them, Trent."

"Oh, so it's going to be like that, huh?" he reacted. "You want to dismiss what I say? Well, let's see here . . .

"I've already had someone to confirm for me that you got inside a Mercedes. And if I really want to go further, I can find out where you were in Sumter and who you were with." He then tipped his head toward her.

There's no way that he's going to get away with that comment, she fumed.

First, she brought to Trent's attention the final straw was him forgetting about her birthday. Next, she listed several other examples which he seemed clueless about what it took to be attentive and considerate toward her.

"It's the simple things. Little things that really makes a difference with a woman," she added. "But you've refused to listen."

He sensed she was complaining again about her difficulty experiencing orgasms while having sex with him. "Look, I thought we've gone through that already."

Sonia ignored his comment and continued with her point.

"Trent, when was the last time we went out together just

you and me? It's not like we don't have the money because
we do. I stopped bringing it up because it would result in an
argument.

"And what about me telling you all those times if you know
I like certain things—fruit for example—why couldn't you
go and get it without me having to ask you? That's called being considerate. That's called doing the little things; they do
make a difference with a woman."

Trent rolled his eyes and snorted. To him, it was like a re-
cording stuck in a loop.

"Here we go again," he mumbled, shaking his head. "Now
she's trying to justify everything."

Annoyed, he also leaned forward and rested the side of his
face against his fist.

"Trent, I thought about it today and I realized that I've
known you nearly half of my life. I've spent most of that time
bringing to your attention things that are important to me
that you should have understood by now. It's a shame when
others see what you're not doing. And they're more than glad
to step in. That's what happened."

There was silence among them. Sonia darted her eyes both
left and right studying Trent's and Taylor's expression: Taylor looked down and away while Trent merely stared aimlessly at people walking through the mall's food court.

A couple of women did catch his attention, but he never
followed them with his eyes.

"Are you finished?" he asked after making eye contact with
her again; the sarcasm in his voice was unmistakable.

"You know what, Trent? Your words and actions don't
hurt me any more. I stopped crying over you long ago." She
brought her hands up beneath her chin, continuing, "We can
sling all kinds of mud at each other. But at the end of the day,
are we going to go forward as a family or not? My prayer is

that we would."

Trent leaned back, folded his arms, and stared at Sonia. She seemed to have maintained her appearance quite well despite being away from home nearly five days.

The tenor of her conversation was even conciliatory. Forgiving her was easy. Forgetting about her infidelity would take some time, but it was possible. But he had no peace about making that kind of decision.

That left him mulling whether he could live without Sonia. His pride said he could. But whenever he was confronted with similar moments of decision in the past, he often gave in to the notion that he could not live without her. And at least there was no guilt to bear having sex with her.

Changing thoughts, he glanced to his right at Taylor. They had a lengthy conversation the night before concerning Sonia. At the time, Taylor was still upset and he wanted his mother having no part in his life; it appeared to him that nothing had changed despite sitting across from her.

Then he thought about his own mother. Could he be so willing to move on despite the embarrassment?

"Sonia, I can't say that I'm willing to go forward," he said, somberly. "If it were just you and I, maybe I would; it wouldn't be easy.

"But like I told you last week after all this mess came to light, we have a son who's old enough to express his own opinion. He told me you've texted him while you were at work, but he asked you to leave him alone."

Sonia's lips parted as though she wanted to rebut, but Trent held up his hand indicating he wasn't finished. He first mentioned his past with her gave him no platform to judge anyone. Yet he also recognized a married woman of her character and personality simply doesn't enter into spur-of-the-moment affairs. It had to have been something she considered for a while.

"I remember you warning me about doing certain things before it was too late," he acknowledged. "You've basically said the same thing today. And you knew what you were doing when you decided to be with someone else—"

Sonia refused to hold back any further.

"So what do you want, Trent? I'm no longer seeing him; it's over!" she reacted, holding her hands outwardly. "I want my marriage. I want my family. I want a relationship with you and Taylor."

"But I don't want one with you!" yelled Taylor, who got up and stormed off.

That left Sonia and Trent staring at each other again. The tension between them quickly rose.

"I told you, Sonia. This is not entirely about me, although I'm the one who has the final say."

All this time Sonia managed to keep her emotions in check, but now she was crestfallen. It did not seem fair to her that she came to the mall showing contrition, but she still might leave without having her family intact.

"Trent, I used to get on you about not telling me that you loved me, and I'm just as guilty of not telling you the same thing; it's something that I've taken for granted." She slid her hand across the table hoping that he'd grasp it. He did not budge.

"For once, I just wanted to know what it was like to be the center of someone's attention even if it might have been a façade. But I want to be the center of your attention, Trent. I'm willing to be patient for as long as it takes—"

Why now? Trent thought while continuing to stare at her. He looked around hoping that he'd spot Taylor. He then sent him a text message asking where he was in the mall. He received a quick reply.

I'm with some friends. We're just walking around.

"Sonia, what if turned out that I did have sex with that woman from Brazil last summer?" he posed to her. "We wouldn't be having this conversation right now.

"You'd be collecting alimony and child support. You'd be staying in that house, and there's no telling what else you would have gotten; I would have deserved it!"

And with that, Trent stood up and walked off, leaving Sonia there to consider his words.

"Trent! Wait!" She rushed to catch up with him.

He turned around slowly, speaking sharply, "What?"

"Are you saying this is it?" she asked.

"Yes, so long as Taylor feels the way he does."

"Then I need to get my clothes since it's obvious you want to play tit for tat, and you don't want me there."

"I'll let you do that. But once you get what you need, I'm changing the locks."

Chapter 18

The sound of the drink mixer churning inside the book store always was annoying. But it wouldn't matter to Cortez if Ms. Wanda delivered on the good news she promised him.

"How long have you been waiting for me?" she said, standing a few inches to his left.

He looked up showing a mixed expression. He thought of taking her question as a joke, hinting at when was the last time they indulged in sweat-filled lust.

Instead, he shrugged his shoulders. "Maybe five minutes. Today's my off day from the car lot." He stretched his arms and yawned.

"It looks like they're working you hard in the car business," she observed, sitting down across from him.

"Actually, it's quite boring." He yawned again. "I was up most of the night trying to prepare for this lawsuit. I hope you've got something I can use."

Ms. Wanda leaned forward upon her forearms and elbows. "You should take back that comment."

"Why should I?"

"Because I can turn around and walk back out of here minding my own business."

"All right. Watcha have there?"

Shifting in the chair, Ms. Wanda started to grin. It wasn't often she did that.

"As of next week Wednesday, I'm no longer working at the St. Andrews branch," she said, while slightly raising her right hand and waving it. "Thank 'ya, lawd!"

"Okay, what does that have to do with me? I'm no longer working there, as well—"

She shook her head in derision. "I don't even know why I'm fooling around with you."

"You know why." He leaned back tugging at his slacks. "It's one reason why you're here sitting across from me."

"I'm a woman of my word," she mumbled, but catching herself.

He smirked. "Most of the time."

She persisted sharing with Cortez that she was hired as the loan officer at the main downtown branch. She even bragged of having connections in human resources up on the tenth floor that helped her get it.

"Well, aren't you going to congratulate me?" she insisted of him.

"Yeah, congratulations. Now why is it we're meeting here when you could have easily sent me a text message or called?"

She lowered her voice to say, "The friend who helped me get away from working under that sorry excuse for a manager, Trent Buckner, told me there was a lot of under-handed politics behind you being fired."

Wow, what a surprise, Cortez snorted.

"I could have told you that, Wanda—"

"But did you know the bank paid someone $750,000 in hush money? Did you know the person who was told to fire you is also gone? Did you know the reason why I was passed over was because Trent Buckner was told he had to hire someone outside of Palmetto Fidelity?"

Ms. Wanda sat back as if to suggest Cortez needed to consider what she related to him.

"I need more than what you just told me to have a chance with these people," he said. "I need a lot more."

"Cortez, you've got to start somewhere. What I told you was more than what you had when you woke up this morning."

"Ha! Wanda, I'm running out of time here. I need something that will blow their doors off the hinges. I'm talking about having something that will do some damage."

"Well, it's going to cost you, Cortez. Do you think in the real world you can get information like that for free? Come on now!"

Ms. Wanda explained to him that nobody at the bank had been willing to talk for fear of reprisal. And in the current economy, nobody's willing to lose their job just so that someone could say "thank you," get maybe a pat on the back—or behind depending on the relationship—and receive nothing else.

"Why are you so willing to help me?" Cortez retorted. "I haven't seen any results."

"Because it hasn't cost me anything as of yet." She shifted in her chair before sitting erect.

"You're now telling me I've gotten what I've paid for?"

She bobbed her head from side to side and hunched her shoulders. "Basically, what you've given me is something I could find out there on the streets. A piece of meat is what is—"

She tipped her head in his direction as if to dramatize her point with him. Without Ms. Wanda being motivated by her disdain for Trent, and with her telling him she didn't really need him for sex, there was no way he could keep her interested based on sheer hope that he'd win his lawsuit.

"Are you now telling me anything from this point forward involving you would be strictly business?" he asked.

"Quite possibly. But it has to be worth my while. I'm not going to risk my plans for retirement with someone who almost cost me my marriage."

Cortez reacted with bugged eyes to Ms. Wanda's response. He derided her as being not the sharpest blade in the kitchen drawer, pointing out that she was the knucklehead who volunteered to Trent about their affair.

Additionally, he claimed she was the bonehead who spoke briefly to the acquaintance who then told her husband that she was at happy hour with him.

He stood up from the table. "Wanda, find someone else to help you ride off into the sunset!"

"You're not going to leave me here wishing that you'd spank me, pull me by my hair, and tell me that I've been a bad little girl, are you?"

Ms. Wanda's voice was quiet but seductive. She cast an alluring stare at him once he looked down at her. She also ran her tongue across her lips and held it there.

"You know I just need to be handled a bit differently," she said. "And you understand how that should be done."

It was as if Cortez was frozen in time and movement. A woman's erotic talk was like words of affirmation to him, a professed weakness of his; they were a magnetic force.

Slowly, he inched back toward the chair across from Ms. Wanda and sat down. Vivid images of her glistening, sweaty skin and deep red bruises on her buttocks while she was bent over on all fours invaded his thinking.

"All right. We all have our wants and needs. It's a matter of reaching some kind of compromise," he said. "I've got an idea that might work for both of us even if the lawsuit doesn't pan out. But I still want you to find out whatever you can to help me."

Ms. Wanda leaned forward once again upon her elbows and forearms. "I'm listening—"

"Come over to my place and I'll fill you in on it."

* * *

Two hours later, Ms. Wanda and Cortez were lying next to each other in his bed And they held hands while they made pillow talk atop the bed sheets.

Casually, he mentioned to her that he'd been thinking of seeking payback from Palmetto Fidelity in the form of rigging up some fraudulent transactions.

Ms. Wanda immediately sat up. "You're not asking me to process them for you?"

"No, I wouldn't do that." He stroked her face then breasts, urging her to lie back down next to him.

"Okay, what's in it for me?"

"Something to help toward your retirement."

"How is that possible?"

Cortez said greed and carelessness were primary reasons why most people wind up in jail over fraudulent business loans. Although he acknowledged it was risky, he said the cases that reached the news often involved transactions linked to the Small Business Association.

The SBA, he explained, was the guarantor of a significant portion of those loans, so there was a greater amount of accountability and oversight.

"Therefore, federal government is always going to get its money back before anyone else," he said.

"Wait a minute," Ms. Wanda interrupted him, "bank fraud is a federal offense no matter how small it is. I don't know if I want to be linked to something like that."

She reminded him that she was a saved, church going woman who tithed regularly. And she was a believer in divine providence.

"That's great. I'm a saved, well, somewhat church going man who tithes when he's in a good mood. Lately I haven't been in a good mood," he retorted. "But haven't you heard of the wealth of the wicked being stored up for the righteous?"

"That same passage also said for us to rise and shine for our light has come, and His goodness was upon us. I don't recall it meant cheating the wicked out of their money."

"But the wicked cheats the righteous day in, day out."

He explained his plan would involve lines of credit extend ed by Palmetto Fidelity, and over time he would allow them to default using the bogus businesses and people who ap plied for them. He also assured Ms. Wanda there would be no risk with her participation. She would be merely a recipi ent of whatever he's able to secure from the fraudulent lines of credit—possibly twenty-five percent.

"We're not talking millions of dollars here. The stuff you read in the news like the one that happened last month in Virginia involving a group that defrauded the SBA for over $100 million. We're only talking about maybe a few hundred thousand, five hundred tops."

He joked with Ms. Wanda he once heard her say that she'd be happy accepting a $10,000 winning lottery ticket.

"I sure did say that." She got up and started dressing. It was nearly 7:30 in the evening. She already planned to say she visited her mother at the assisted living facility in the Harbison area after work should her husband asked what took her so long getting home.

"Your share of that over the course of two or three years would be about a hundred and twenty-five grand, if it works out the way I think it can."

"Five hundred thousand dollars is not a lot of money when you think about risking going to jail," she yelled from the bathroom.

After pulling on a pair of slacks, he joined her in the bathroom rubbing up against her. "You're right. But what I have in mind is merely to prove a point to those clowns.

"By the time they figure out what happened, it would be years down the road and they still won't be able to trace it back to yours truly."

He excused himself and raced over to his computer where he accessed some of his old record keeping from Palmetto Fidelity.

Pointing at his computer screen, he said less than two percent of all the loans he helped process ever went bad.

"I think I kind of know what I'm talking about here." He then smirked aloud, continuing, "If fraud by definition is willfully using inaccurate or falsifying information to obtain a loan, there's a lot of people out there who wouldn't have houses or cars. It's all about making the numbers work for them and for me.

"You'll find out for yourself what I'm talking about. Just wait and see."

Chapter 19

Sonia was on her way to the fax copier room when Vicki hailed her down from behind.

"Stop by here on your way back, okay?" Vicki asked, eliciting a shrugging-of-the-shoulders response from Sonia.

The printer assigned to her desk was out of toner, and it took in upwards of two weeks before a requisition was processed. So she figured she might as well get used to walking across the contract services workplace once again.

On her way back, she sat quietly in the chair opposite of Vicki's desk while she finished a phone call.

"Yes, that's right. Thank you." Vicki then let out a loud sigh and faced Sonia. "Have you read the latest e-mail update from Phyllis about this hiring freeze being extended?"

"I missed that one. Maybe it was intentional."

"Well, you ain't missing anything," Vicki reacted. "I can't believe there are people in this building who actually say they like working here!"

Sonia was careful to speak barely above a whisper. There had already been a spate of pettiness being reported to Phyllis lately, and she didn't want to contribute to it by voicing negative comments about contract services, and UCP for that matter.

"I thought you went on an interview not long ago at that place out in Ballentine—GSI?" she inquired.

Vicki sucked her teeth. Little did Sonia know she'd pushed open a flood gate for drama to spill over into their conversation.

"I thought I was gone from here," she said.

"What happened?" Sonia first scanned the workplace for Phyllis roaming the area before she leaned back in the chair.

"You were talking as if you were going on to bigger and better things."

Waving her hand dismissively, Vicki compared the job opportunity as a quality control administrator to her flash-in-the-pan fling with Gerald Conway, who arranged the interview.

Both were bogus. Both were a waste of her time. Both merely infuriated her further about her prospects of doing something life changing.

"I don't know which would have been worse, there or here," she said. "And that's scary."

"I know it's trivial to say some things happen for a reason. At least you didn't lose anything but a little time and gas." Sonia then gave her a sideways stare.

"I hope that's all you lost—"

"Don't you think that was enough?"

Vicki went into a tirade that Conway impressed her with his smooth personality and savvy. He was a man on a mission, and his stated goal was a five-year plan to leave his job once and for all and embark on managing a successful, cutting-edge side business.

When she showed up for the interview, she learned that Conway was nothing more than an entry-level manager; he was no farther up the corporate ladder than she was at UCP.

He was merely recruiting her to work in his department, but he would have no direct contact with her.

"I got to asking him more questions, and he finally told me this was his third divorce; he hated that he was likely to pay support for a fourth and fifth child," she said. "Once he told me that, I was through with him."

Sonia thought she had heard two different stories and needed clarification. "What about both of you meeting in Atlanta? Was he really there for business?"

"Sort of. He was there meeting his brother, who was willing to loan him some money so that he could pay his car note," Vicki answered, sighing. "I really know how to run into a real winner, don't I?"

She began mumbling and cursing. "Sonia, you just don't know how much I hate my life right now. You really don't." She leaned forward slightly and rubbed her forehead and temple.

I'd love to tell her that she's not alone, Sonia thought to herself. But she chose to offer something more encouraging.

"Vicki, it speaks of pressed down, but not driven to despair; persecuted, but not forsaken; knocked down but not destroyed."

Words of inspiration like that nearly provoked Vicki into rage. Too many people she'd known have wound up with shipwrecked lives trying to hold on to catchwords and phrases like those heard on Sunday mornings.

Meanwhile, there were other women she knew where she grew up on the other side of the state in Gaffney living the big life with cars, money, and big homes through mostly illegal means. They also had men clamoring after them to grace their lives by their mere presence.

"You know what? I hope sayings like that work for you because they've never worked for me," she said. "One thing that will work for me is that I refuse to be here in contract services by the first of June."

Sonia took a deep breath. "You really mean that, don't you?"

"As serious as a heart attack. I'm not going to wait for a hiring freeze to be lifted. And I'm not going to wait on some man to come by on a white horse and sweep me off my feet!"

"Well, it sounds like the one who tried not long ago was sitting in a rocking chair horse."

They both laughed at Sonia's wisecrack.

Sonia was the first to recognize Alvantrae standing in back of them with his left hand on his waist. He was now wearing his hair combed to back and placed in a large bun.

"Hey, Ms. Sonia."

Vicki, who had her back to him, also reacted to his voice.

"That must be Alvantrae—"

"It is."

"Whatcha got?" Vicki swung her office chair to her left, facing him.

Alvantrae called into question his most recent monthly evaluation. Contract services phone reps must meet a minimum overall percentage rating for the volume of inquires they log in monthly and achieve a low error percentage on screened calls toward meeting UCP's stated performance goals and qualify for cash incentives.

He was assessed a failing mark that disqualified him after he told a doctor that nuclear stress tests with specific procedure codes used for billing purposes did not require preauthorization.

He cited a page on UCP's intranet as his reference.

"I have a problem with that, Ms. Vicki, because they're messing with my money," he said. "I put up with too much every day I come here for them to be taking money away from me!"

"Wait a minute," she insisted, "did you refer to the resource directory for your information?"

Alvantrae shifted the weight from his left foot to his right before wagging his finger at Vicki. "If you would get off your tush and check things out for yourself, you'll see what I told that caller was absolutely correct."

She placed her hand on her thigh, retuning a *who-do-you-think-you-are* stare.

"And what side of the bed did you get out of?" He also mimicked her by placing his right hand on his waist.

"The same side as you."

"Well, if that's the case, you wouldn't be looking at me like that, and you'd bring it to those people's attention—that's at least $250 I could use toward my next shopping trip in Atlanta!"

Sonia, who looked to her right at Alvantrae and then to her left at Vicki, excused herself, leaving them to settle their discord.

Back at her desk, she decided upon a whim to check her personal e-mail address. There were none. It was as if she and Milner had ceased contact with each other right after she checked out of the hotel.

No phone calls. No text messages. Nothing.

Since moving in with her parents—she convinced her father to override her mother's objection—she was of the opinion she shouldn't be the one making the first move to reestablishing contact, if any, with Milner.

After all, wasn't she the one who stopped by The Groovy Soul the day Trent confronted her with being seen in Sumter?

But what if they were not spotted in Sumter? she also considered. More than likely they would be coordinating their next
tryst. She would have been looking forward to his e-mail and
possibly a text message by this time of day, or she would have
already called him during her break.

Going cold turkey from a habit she consistently fed for
nearly a year was not easy. It seemed as hollow as a deep, dark
cave and as lonely as solitary confinement.

On that thought, she glanced up at the ceiling and sighed.
She realized that maybe she'd become a prisoner of her own
lust or even worse, she'd been d-whipped; she still had only
herself to blame.

Chapter 20

Next time, Alcione promised herself she would fly from Miami into Charlotte and be picked up there rather than flying into Columbia Metropolitan via Atlanta. It cost less and the flights always seemed smoother from what she remembered, and there was more of a downtown skyline to view from the air. At least she had that possibility worth looking forward to whenever it would be time for her to return home to Brazil.

Her travel schedule between Brazil and the United States usually coincided with the weather still being relatively mild without any exposure to the extremes of the winter and summer seasons.

March was the most challenging month for her whenever she made her seasonal trip northward to the Carolinas while overseeing her family's Fogo de Janiero Brazilian steak house operations.

She'd leave Rio de Janiero where it was usually in the upper-eighties to mid-nineties. But then she'd arrive in Columbia where there was still a winter bite in the air. The average highs ranging in the fifties and sixties meant she'd have to buy a couple of warmer outfits just to get through the month.

This year, however, she arrived in the Carolinas a few weeks later. An afternoon high in the mid-seventies with a light breeze greeted her once she left the baggage claim area and stood outside waiting for her first cousin, Pauliño Robson de Oliveria, to pick her up.

A honking of the horn caught her attention. She waved at a platinum Audi A6 sedan that had stopped in front of her. A man in his mid-thirties with naturally bronzed skin scampered out of the sedan.

They hugged.

"*Bom ver você. Como foi seu voo?*" he said, while helping Alcione put her luggage inside the car and trunk.

"*Longo, como de costume,*" she replied. "*Eu trouxe-lhe algo de casa. Na minha mala.*"

Inside her car, Alcione handed Pauliño some soccer paraphernalia. Her home country and the entire continent of South America, for that matter, had been abuzz for several years now that it's being recognized as a major player in the international athletic arena—the FIFA World Cup soccer tournament's coming to Brazil in 2014; and in 2016, the Summer Olympics will also be hosted by Brazil.

"*Obrigado!*"

She reclined back and exhaled loudly. "*Eu gostaria de ter mais espaço para trazer mais. Talvez vou ter que sejam enviadas diretamente para você na próxima vez.*"

Enough of the Portuguese talk, she proclaimed. It was time to talk business, but in English.

Before leaving Brazil, Pauliño updated her about Fogo de Janiero's expansion project in Myrtle Beach was still on schedule. The restaurant's location was on Kings Highway about two miles north of the densely populated strand area, but still in proximity to all the hotels along the shore line. Its grand opening was set for the twenty-fourth of May, a Friday; it was also calculated to get a start on the peak season by creating some local buzz.

A second restaurant in Hilton Head also near its strand was awaiting final approval to start ground breaking. It was scheduled for a late Fall 2014 opening date. They hoped to take advantage of northerners who owned winter homes making their annual migration down south.

"I'm really concerned about keeping three restaurants opened in South Carolina," she said.

Pauliño still was not as fluent in English as Alcione. It was quite common for him to drift back and forth from Portuguese to English while conversing with her.

"It has not been a good last two years," he said. "We are barely breaking even."

Alcione arched her neck slowly as if to work out the stiffness after sixteen hours of flying and going through airport terminals. "This is becoming a big chance we're taking by opening restaurants in Myrtle Beach and Hilton Head, but everyone thinks we can have better success at locations close to the beaches like in Florida."

She looked in the back seat and grabbed her purse. Then she retrieved her cell phone where she previously transferred some other business files. After scrolling through them, she was reminded of why she felt uneasiness.

Along with Columbia, the Charlotte location also reflected similar trends of stagnation. There was no specific answer for it other than people simply didn't embrace Brazilian steak houses in those two markets. But no decision had been made to close either location so long as both restaurants were able to sustain themselves.

"Okay, let's talk about something else," she declared.

Pauliño merely glanced over to his right, smiled, and shook his head. Alcione was impulsive, all right. But she always been the more focused of the two.

"Did you bring a gift for your friend's wife?," he joked with her.

"Ha, ha! Why did you have to bring that up?"

He hunched his shoulders. "*Porque você realmente gostaria que ele deixe que ela fale com você do jeito que ela fez.*"

Alcione did not need any reminders about her making a special trip from South Florida to Columbia last summer to help save Trent's marriage. She took being cursed out and vilified by Sonia while she tried explaining to her that nothing improper occurred during their dinner date.

"Yes, I like him a lot while I was here last time." She returned a sneaky grin and glare at Pauliño. "Maybe he still likes me, eh?"

He wagged his index finger at her. "Be careful."

She nodded.

* * *

So far, so good. Taylor had not gotten into any more trouble at school, but it was tenuous at best. Trent noticed Taylor displayed more irritability and outbursts of anger since returning from his suspension.

It used to be when Taylor came home from school they might sit down and talk briefly. Now Trent had to allow Taylor a time of cooling off before he initiated any conversation with him. Even then, it was like navigating through a minefield because it seemed that anything spoken was a trigger word.

"How was school today?" Trent asked.

"Why do you want to know? They didn't call you at work today."

Trent raised his eyebrows and allowed himself a few seconds before reacting. "Yeah, that is a good sign."

Reluctantly, Taylor followed Trent into the kitchen where he had already prepared dinner. Neither sat at the table any more since Sonia moved out. They merely loaded their plates and went to their respective rooms in the house.

"Do you have any homework?"

Taylor sighed loudly and looked upward at the ceiling. "Yes, I have homework. The teachers still don't like me, and I still don't like them. What else you want to know?"

He stopped by the refrigerator, jerking open the door. Scanning it, he noticed none of his favorite assorted flavors of Calypso lemonade were in there.

"Dad, when are you going to the store? There's nothing in here!"

"I went to the store yesterday."

"But you didn't get anything that I liked or wanted!"

That confused Trent because he made sure to get his frozen waffles, pizza on bagels and hot wings; he also brought home beef flavored Ramen noodles, goldfish crackers, tortilla chips and salsa, and cracked pepper turkey meat.

Not to mention, he gave Taylor $45 spending money for lunch and after school—that should last him for the next three days.

"Did you mention anything about me getting you Calypso drinks?" Trent inquired.

Taylor stormed off to his room in a huff. "But you should have known that. I guess I'll just have water."

Kids these days could be so ungrateful, Trent huffed out of frustration. Parents providing a decent home to live in. Since everything's now electronic, providing them with some of life's conveniences despite the absurdity of how much it cost: iPads, smart phones, computers, and flat screen televisions. Making sure they had money to spend on some of the most frivolous of things—more than he could have ever fathomed having or spending—whenever they went to the mall.

And they still find reason to complain? That outburst was not going to go unaddressed.

Trent didn't bother to knock on Taylor's bedroom door. He pushed it open.

"Hey, I don't like your attitude lately!" He stood next to Taylor's bed with both hands on his waist.

"What did I do now?"

"Every time I try talking to you it's as if you want to go off on me. I'm the parent around here. You're the child. You need to remember that. You don't talk to me that way."

Taylor sat up, groping for his iPad. "Why don't you try talking to me like I'm a teenager and not a child."

"Maybe because you are still a child—"

"No, I'm not a child any more. I'm in high school, Dad, and why don't you treat me like I'm now in high school?"

Back when Trent's mother Melinda was a teenager, his grandmother Sadie Hightower would have considered Taylor's behavior as smelling his musk. That would have been reason enough to treat him accordingly by "slapping some sense" into him.

The same thing would have happened a generation later in the way Melinda handled Trent at fourteen years old.

Parents, however, no longer have that prerogative. It's as if any form of disciplining could result in them being arrested for abuse. And with the prevalence of the Internet, children have become equally adept at letting the world see what occurs inside their home via the social networks and YouTube.

"Taylor," Trent tried explaining to him, "I think you need to take a step back and realize just how good you have it. My mother used to tell me I was living the life of Riley and I didn't know it.

"I used to get mad when she'd say that, but now I understand what she meant standing here in front of you."

Trent's words hardly resonated with Taylor. In the next motion, he stuffed his ears with his earphones and turned up his iPad.

That was not a smart decision. Trent lunged forward and yanked the earphones away.

Taylor's eyes were bugged. "Hey, why did you do that?"

Along those lines, he now recognized his father's angry expression and bunched lips.

"I don't mind you voicing your opinion when it's necessary. But one thing I won't take from you is disrespecting me!" He put his finger millimeters from Taylor's face. "I'll knock you into next week, boy!"

"Okay, Dad. Okay. I get it."

Trent straightened up, placing his hands back on his waist. "What do you get?"

"I get that I shouldn't be talking to you that way. And I should be glad that you do the things for me that you have done."

After taking a deep breath, Trent went ahead with another item of concern.

"Let's see your grades."

Taylor began frowning. "Do you have to see them?"

"Yes."

Rolling his eyes, Taylor reached for his school bag that was at the far end of his bed. "You do realize that I missed some time from school, and they haven't given me a chance to make up everything that I missed?"

"Let's see them first."

Math was a seventy-four; History, seventy-eight; English, eighty-six; Science, eighty; Computers, a seventy-three. Trent had seen enough.

"What's going on here?"

Taylor sighed. "I told you. I missed a bunch of assignments while I was suspended."

"That shouldn't be. I brought home your work while you were out of school, so you're telling me that you didn't do anything?"

"I still have time to make it all up."

"When?"

"We're heading into May. School will be out in a few weeks."

Trent then lectured to him the importance of doing well every year in high school.

"Son, this time next year you'll be going to the eleventh grade. You'll have less time to get it right. How do you expect to be accepted into anyone's college with mediocre grades?"

"Dad, I'll make up my work. Can you just get off my back now?"

"I'll get off your back, all right—"

He then told Taylor he expected him to show his homework before 10 p.m. on school nights and before he went to school each morning. He also offered to help him with his homework or prepare for any test the remainder of the semester.

"You're not going to have any excuses. Now what I expect for you to do is to do your part. Is that clear?"

"Yes, sir."

Trent hoped his close relationship with Taylor might be the last line of defense preventing him from slipping in school. But this had been a difficult year, all things considered.

While sitting in his work office, Trent mulled whether he should blame himself since it all began with him being kicked out of the house—a little more than a month before school started.

He and Sonia always believed children from Taylor's generation needed both parents to help navigate through all the temptations and pressures that confronted them.

Dang! Who could this be calling?

"This is Trent. Who's this?"

"Hi Trent, do you know who this is?" The accent and broken English was easily recognizable from his cell phone.

I must not be living right, he mouthed before giving himself a forehead slap.

"Alcione—"

"Yes. I hope you're doing well."

He shook his head. "Where are you?"

"I'm back in Columbia. I got back yesterday. I hope you remember that you owe me?"

That's debatable, Trent thought. But how could he tell her that?

"Alcione, how are things with the restaurant? Are you still on schedule with opening in Myrtle Beach?"

"Pauliño said we're set to open on May twenty-fourth. If everything goes right, we should do very well," she said. "I would like for you to attend the grand opening with me."

"Can we discuss that later? My son and I were going over his homework."

"I've been waiting since last winter to talk about us."

"I thought I saw you in July of last year?"

"Yes, you did. But I forget when I'm back in the States our winters are your summers."

Thus, a quick geography lesson noting a distinction between the Southern Hemisphere and Northern Hemisphere.

He saw a second opportunity at getting out of this phone call.

"I'm sorry, Alcione. But I really do need to get back with my son and his homework. He's fallen behind in some classes, and the school year's almost over."

"You did tell me you had a son. How is he?"

He smirked. "He's been interesting lately. Typical teenager, I guess. Are they like that in Brazil?"

"I think kids are the same everywhere." She also chortled at the thought. "My brothers and sister always beg me to take their kids with me when it's time for me to return to the States."

Chapter 21

Sonia's idea of attending church was blending into a congregation without being noticed and then quietly departing without any interaction after the benediction.

An introvert at heart, she preferred not seeking out people when being asked by the pastor to greet someone she didn't come to church with at the start of the service. She wasn't comfortable wearing name tags, so serving as an usher was out of the question. And if it were left up to her, she'd sit in the far corner at the back of a sanctuary.

That was her comfort zone for more than a decade attending Bethesda Fellowship as a family with Trent and Taylor. Since moving out, she decided it would be best to start anew by attending another church.

She discovered Chairo Church, a converted K-Mart on Bush River Road across from the Dutch Square Mall, while at lunch one afternoon.

A church occupying that much square footage had to have

a large congregation, which it did. More than twelve hundred people filled the sanctuary during each of its three Sunday services. What she found different was it being a satellite campus—Columbia was one of a dozen throughout South Carolina; its headquarters was based out of Anderson, a half-hour southwest of Greenville. There was live worship, but the actual message was usually transmitted by satellite, so it was like attending a church in a movie theater.

But there was one other catch to the different setting.

"Good morning. How are you?" an assigned door greeter said to her, extending his hand to shake. "My name is Brian. And you are?"

If it weren't for being at church, she would have ignored him all together.

"I'm Sonia." She switched her purse from her right shoulder to the left and obliged shaking his hand.

"Pleased to have you here. Is this your first time at Chairo?"

"Actually, it's not. I've been here a couple of times."

"That's great. We hope you'll consider attending our new partner's meeting that we'll be offering next week. You'll hear more about it during service."

What was different about Brian other than his mannerisms was the way he dressed. Like many who attended Chairo Church, he was so casually dressed it was as if he'd been hanging out at the mall on a Saturday afternoon. He wore jeans, tennis shoes, and a Polo shirt. There were many who came to Chairo wearing sandals and short pants. Very few of the women wore dresses. None of them wore Sunday hats or made any other fashion statements that suggested they spent all of Saturday in someone's hair shop.

It was a form of culture shock or, better yet, church shock. Had someone like Brian showed up at Bethesda dressed as he was, it would have been assumed that he was a heathen and the call of salvation immediately awaited him. An usher might have offered him a last-row pew seat. Other members would have given him a cold shoulder until he showed conformity.

Chairo Church was what Sonia needed, and she already decided that she would continue going there even if she and Trent were to reconcile. The more than casual atmosphere took the focus off tradition, which she knew spoiled people, and placed it on the message, whose substance began helping her achieve wholeness in her life once again.

On this particular week, the guest speaker was Cliff Perkins, of Bellevue Worship Center in Seattle, Washington. He emphasized the importance that everyone's struggles can be overcome. The worst thing was to feel isolated, as if nobody could ever fathom the extent of the chaos in one's life.

"The best thing as believers is to realize you're not alone. You're no different than Sinner Joe. He knows he needs help. You have to remember you still need help," Perkins said. "That's why many of us fall from grace—it's when we fail to recognize we can't do anything without it.

"Remember, the last exhortation given in scripture was grace being with everyone."

There was a hearty applause from the audience both in the satellite feed from Anderson and live on the Columbia campus. It also perked up Sonia, who sat near the back.

After service, Sonia did something she would not have considered a month ago.

"Have a great week," Marlene, a greeter said to her in the lobby. She was in her mid-thirties, tall and slender. She wore her hair long and had on designer jeans and a long-sleeved blouse.

Sonia stopped and willfully shook hands with her. "Thank you. I hope your week is great as well."

Out in the church parking lot, Sonia thought of calling Trent just to see how he was doing with Taylor. It was mother's intuition, perhaps. She pulled up his entry and was poised to press the dial key, but then she balked.

She realized that it was only 12:45 in the afternoon and Trent would still be at Bethesda Fellowship. In fact, Pastor Middleton would just be stepping up to the microphone after the church offering. Depending on the flow of the service, too, the choir director, Joe Dawkins, might have led another song. Then Pastor Middleton would start into his message.

So, she considered sending him a text message—but why would she?

Now she needed boldness to accompany the grace she rediscovered. She started her car and took the surface streets back to her parents' home.

* * *

The Chandlers were gathered at the cherry oak finished dinner table in the dining room. Prentiss sat directly across from Tillman while Sonia sat to her right like when she did as a child. All that was missing in the family setting was Shonna sitting to Tillman's right.

Prentiss always made enough food to include Sonia eating with them, if she chose to do so. That proved to be about half of the time and always on Sunday. Sonia offered to give her parents money to help with buying food since she moved back home. But they never accepted it, insisting that she was not any burden on them.

"I remember growing up having a 'big' meal was when you served beef, a salad or cornbread—no, you usually made cornbread with spaghetti—and potatoes, and we had Kool-Aid to go with it."

"You remember those days?" Prentiss said; she then quietly

asked Tillman if he wanted more green beans to go with the baked chicken, rice and gravy, and corn on his plate.

"Who can forget?"

Sonia went on to recall some of the other combinations for dinner that Prentiss used to prepare for the family: ham hocks and cabbage; Rice-a-Roni, drumsticks, and mustard greens; hamburger meat and chili beans atop white rice; baked turkey thighs, green beans, and potatoes; salmon croquettes, white rice and canned corn kernels.

"I can't tell you how much I hated half of the stuff you used to make." She could not help but laugh at the memory.

Tillman chimed in on the subject. "You remember all the times your mother whipped you and Shonna for having those food fights?"

"Dad, that's not fair bringing that up—"

Sonia mimicked Prentiss in her maternal voice ranting about food was not to be played with in her household. And if anyone had a problem with it, they could leave 432 Bryant Avenue without a stitch of clothing she put on them.

"That's right, young lady," Prentiss answered. "I think you understand by now that food is not always as easy to come by, so you should be thankful for what's put in front of you."

"Mom, Shonna and I still don't like chili beans to this day. That should have been a sign not to make any."

Prentiss looked up, darting her eyes in Sonia's direction. "You were such a picky eater."

"Yeah, Mom. You used to tell me that I'd better keep all the food that I liked in my cabinets and refrigerator whenever you came to visit me once I was an adult, or you'd beat me if you didn't seen any."

Sonia sat erect in her chair, placing her left hand on her thigh, continuing with her thought.

"Yeah, when Trent and I moved into our home in Chapin, I

didn't let you come over until I went to the store, so I wouldn't hear you picking on me."

She went on to describe how she made sure that her cabinets had vanilla wafers, watermelon in the refrigerator, and fish in the freezer.

"Obviously, you listened."

"It's embarrassing telling your child some of these stories because all Taylor does is laugh and tease me."

Tillman scoffed at Sonia's reminder of life in the Chandler household from more than three decades ago.

"All I can say is that nobody told me how expensive it would be raising girls until after I had them," he said.

"Okay, Dad. Stop being a spoiler."

He looked over at Prentiss and gave her a knowing stare. "You and Shonna had to be everywhere and do everything. And guess who took you there?"

Sonia reached over and placed her hand atop his. "Thank you so much for what you did."

* * *

It wasn't so bad being home, Sonia thought. Her mother wasn't as overbearing as she feared. She was allowed to come and go as she pleased, and she was given a key to the house. Prentiss also didn't antagonize her with reminders about the fallout from her affair with Milner.

Out of respect, Sonia usually adhered to a self-imposed nine o'clock curfew, meaning she tried to take care of everything right after she came home from work during the week. It also meant she didn't go out socializing because she didn't want to contribute to any rumors that might get back to Trent or even worse, Taylor.

Beyond reading books, Sonia spent her time listening to

music on YouTube. She was quick to understand why Taylor had so much music on his iPad when he didn't spend any money buying CDs or mp3s.

Through YouTube, she discovered she could build up her collection of mp3s by ripping the music from the videos she downloaded. Then she could transfer the mp3 file to her cell phone or flash drive. There were nights she'd be up as late as one o'clock in the morning.

It's never a good thing going to UCP short on sleep, she'd remind herself; the problem was still going to sleep because her mind was still engaged with her music. Sunday nights were the worst because it marked the start to another work week. Being such a light sleeper, it did not take much to awaken her. She attributed that to being attuned to Taylor while he slept as an infant.

So it was not uncharacteristic that she jerked her head up trying to track where the buzzing sound went off in her room. But she didn't hear it again; she settled back under her sheets and covers.

Moments later, she heard the buzzing again. She recognized it coming from her cell phone. It seemed odd that somebody would be sending her text messages at that hour. She got up and checked her phone, which she had charging. The first thought that came to mind was Trent or Taylor had finally relented with his anger and made a passionate appeal that she'd return home. But there were no messages on her regular cell phone.

She heard the buzzing again. It came from her purse. She'd forgotten that she still carried her Tracfone.

> Sonia, I miss you. I've been miserable not hearing from you.

Why would Wharton be sending me messages at this time of the morning? I haven't heard from him in more than three weeks.
She then opened the second message.

I hope you're doing well. I wish you good luck and a good life if you choose not to respond.

He's got to be kidding me! Wharton Milner probably has five other women lined up after me. Now that's an example of hidden things of dishonesty that I've got to renounce!
She deleted his messages, but another one came before she turned it off.

We made a good couple, didn't we?

Yeah, right. Got me in the mess that I'm in...
Sonia tried going back to sleep. But thoughts of Milner got the best of her. She sat up in bed. Then she leaned over the side and retrieved her purse.
Toying with the Tracfone in her hand, she mulled replying; and of all things, she felt more boldness thinking about him than she did with Trent after church.
She closed her eyes and imagined being with Milner at Lake Murray on a warm evening. The magnetism that attracted her to him still was strong, she conceded.
Yeah, we did make a good couple.

Chapter 22

The TV was watching Milner more so than he watched it. He was consumed with browsing Web sites for restaurant equipment.

He opened The Groovy Soul with used ovens, refrigerators, and freezers. At the current rate of success, he sensed he would need to upgrade with brand new equipment much sooner than later.

Total cost: In upwards of thirty grand to do it right with all the necessary trimmings.

Nothing's cheap, that's for sure!

By 2:30 a.m., Milner was dozing off at the computer. He got up and went to the bathroom the last time he caught himself nodding off. Upon his return, he noticed there was a text message in his inbox.

> **Wharton, you've not said a word to me. It's obvious you've decided to go in a different direction.**

Milner was hardly surprised that Sonia got around to re-plying. A smirk appeared on his face. The right kind of male attention can be so doggone addictive, he bragged to himself.

> I could easily say the same thing about you. But how are you?

He decided to take his cell phone into his bedroom where he awaited another reply.

Five minutes had passed. No response. He began feeling drowsy again. He placed his cell phone, which was plugged to its charger, next to him while he curled under the bed sheets.

Another five minutes passed before he recognized the phone buzzing nearby.

> I am trying to get my life back together again. May-be you should be doing the same thing.

He yawned and stretched. Although his body was tired, he was still mentally alert, but how much longer?

> Can we talk? I'd rather hear your voice than keep sending you text messages.

> It's after 2 a.m. I don't even know why I'm still awake doing this?

He closed his eyes again. This time, the feeling was sooth-ing and relaxing. Maybe contacting her later in the day would be best for both of them. But as logical as that seemed, Milner refused to give into give into fatigue. He counted to twenty with his eyes still closed thinking it might help him sum-mon the mental energy to complete his text message. Then he opened them; the words didn't easily come to him.

He tried it again. But he conceded she was winning the waiting game, if there was one being played.

Sonia, I'm going to call you. I hope it's OK. I'll try again tomorrow if you don't answer.

Before scrolling to her number, Milner turned onto his back; he also positioned a pillow under his neck.

"I was trying to go to sleep but you keep texting me," Sonia answered.

"Where are you?"

"At my parents' house."

"You went there the same day after you checked out of the hotel?"

"Uh-huh . . ."

He heard Sonia sigh heavily into the phone. A conversation like this reminded him of being in high school when he and a girl would talk on the phone until she or both of them fell asleep only to be awaken by the busy signal.

"It's nice hearing your voice even if it's after two in the morning."

"Wow, that's really a profound statement." She spoke in a low tone, making sure that she didn't wake up her parents with her conversation.

"All right, all right. I admit that I'm fishing for something to talk about."

"Why don't you just tell me what's really on your mind?"

Milner thought about the romantic activity that had been the highlight of their affair before all hell broke loose. It was something he missed. And from his perspective, he hoped the window of sexual opportunity was still open to him.

"What's on my mind is that I should have called you much

sooner. But I wasn't sure when the right time was."

"Wharton, there was never really a right time for me having an affair, but I made time for it because it was something I wanted." She sighed after commenting.

"I understand what you're saying, Sonia. But you're also asking that I make a wild assumption that things were back to what they used to be. There's no way I can do that."

He went on to remind her that she was the one who came to him with the bad news. And for that reason, she should have informed him when it was okay for them to resume contact.

"That's not exactly the way things happened," she corrected him. "We hadn't spoken since the night before I checked out that hotel. And from I recall, you were acting like you were ready to move on to another woman.

"It felt like you threw a few dollars at the situation just to say you didn't immediately run away—you still had nothing to lose!"

Maybe not materially. Maybe not in a marital sense. But it became increasingly apparent to Milner there was no way he could continue glossing things over with Sonia. He was in a fight not only to preserve his reputation, but any continued contact with her.

She now had his full attention.

"Sonia, please accept my apology for missing it with you," he said. "I shouldn't have done anything to imply I was shying away from you.

"I spoke of doing things mind, body, and soul with you. At a time like that, I should have taken as much a risk as you had already risked with me. I should have told you to call me as soon as you found another place to stay. Or, I should have offered additional help, if that's what you needed.

"That's when a woman knows she has a man who has her back, rightly or wrongly."

Milner spoke as if those were thoughts and emotions that he had repressed over the past several weeks. He then arched his neck and gazed upward at the ceiling.

There was silence on Sonia's end.

"Are you still there?" he queried.

"I'm still here. What am I supposed to say now?" She also hunched her shoulders.

"I don't know. That's really up to you. But let me ask you this: Are you any closer to getting back with your husband?"

She inhaled through her nostrils. "Nope."

"Do you still hope that you will?"

"It would be nice."

He spoke more forcefully. "I asked do you still hope that you'll get back with your husband?"

"Yes, but—"

"But what?"

She considered explaining the dynamics involving Taylor, but she changed her mind. "It's complicated."

"Situations like these are always complicated, to some degree. But all I want to know is are you all right? Whether you are or not, I want you to know that I'm here for you."

He then asked her what time it was. He sensed maybe, just maybe, a long, smooth stroke to his ego might be in the making.

"It's going on three o'clock." She paused and chortled. "I should have gone to sleep long ago."

"To be honest," he said, "I didn't plan on going to sleep until I heard from you tonight."

"Really?"

"Yeah, that's right."

"Five weeks is a long time to decide on going to sleep, don't you think?"

"That is a long time to stay awake," he quipped with her.

"But you know what? I'd stay awake a little longer if you were to come here right now—"

"Wharton, I'm under these covers, in my bed at my parents' house, and it's 3 a.m. The last place I need to be is at your place."

"Actually, it should have been the first place." His voice had turned seductive and mesmerizing. "How soon will it take for you to get here?"

Sonia was torn. The past five weeks were spent building herself up spiritually. Now it was being put to test, and she found herself wilting and giving into sensual thoughts of their past encounters.

Surely, she thought, she was a much stronger woman than the way she was feeling.

Mindlessly, she grazed her breast, which sent impulses throughout her body that she had not acknowledged since she last seen him. Next, she stroked her inner thigh and inched upward. She felt her heart beat faster and her body temperature rise.

I can't deny it. This is like a drug.

It seemed so ironic to her that one of the naughty thoughts she entertained while lying awake next to Trent was a ren-dezvous in the wee hours of the morning with Milner: She'd sneak out of the house around 2 a.m., drive to his place; they'd give each other something to think about for the rest of that day, and she would return home before the crack of dawn.

"Sonia, you're still awake?"

She yawned into the phone. "I'm still awake. It's going to be really rough for me today at work. I just know it."

"I don't care if you don't have on any makeup. I don't care if your hair is in rollers. I'm also sleepy, but it would be worth the wait—and while—to see you."

"Come on, don't you think that's going a bit too far?" She

chortled afterward.

"Sonia, please come on over. This is as good a time as any to talk this through."

It all seemed too crazy to believe. But what had been sane lately, anyway? It was very much possible she'd consider the same thing had Trent called her.

"You really must want to see me?"

"I do."

The mattress beneath her squeaked to each movement she made. The queen-sized bed itself had to be at least twenty-five years old. It hadn't been slept on for any duration since she graduated from college. Prentiss was a sentimental person and never saw fit to get rid of her bed or Shonna's.

A still, small voice from within reminded her about not being drawn back into perdition. But all she could think about was giving herself some attention. Her body and soul was yearning for the same thing.

"I really shouldn't be doing this," she said. "But haven't we all said something like that before?"

"Do you remember how to get here?"

"I know how to get to Garners Ferry Road. I'm not sure if I'd be able to recognize when I was in Eastover, let alone where to make that turn at nighttime."

Milner said he would drive out to the Choo-Choo Station convenience store, which was about two miles from Antioch Zion Church Road. Then he would lead her back to his place.

He mused, "At least if I fall asleep, I'm sure you'd wake me up."

"Are you sure about that? I might decide to turn around and come back here."

* * *

"This doesn't make any sense!" Sonia told herself periodically while driving.

It was far from her ideal rendezvous scenario. Her lone piece of rationalization was that she wasn't sneaking out to see him. This was completely out of her volition—well, sort of.

If her parents asked her where she went at 3:30 in the morning, she figured she would tell them she simply couldn't sleep and went out driving around. Then she stopped off at a Waffle House and got something to eat.

She called Milner once she reached the I-20 and I-77 interchange. There was no answer.

Less than ten minutes later, she reached the Garners Ferry Road exit. She called Milner again. This time he answered.

"Where were you when I called a few minutes ago?"

"I was getting dressed."

"Okay. I'm now on Garners Ferry Road and I just passed the car dealership. How far am I from you?"

"At this time of the morning, it shouldn't take you long. Maybe fifteen, twenty minutes. You forget you're coming out to the suburbs—"

"No, I'm just returning to the scene of the crime."

Sonia tried convincing herself that maybe she could see Milner one more time and get it out of her system. Then she might have the strength next time to resist seeing him. It was like having a chocolate bar a final time before fully committing to a diet. Even worse, it was like the struggling addict who figured on another high before getting help.

It all made sense for a few moments. But she returned to berating herself. "I really shouldn't be doing this. All I have to do is find somewhere to turn around. Then I wouldn't need to apologize for anything!"

But she kept driving farther along Garners Ferry Road. She

passed by the shopping center with Lowe's and Walmart on adjacent properties on her left. The next landmark was a business complex occupied by Richland County government on her right—WNPW's business office and station was about a quarter-mile away from there.

Five minutes later she passed by a high school on her left and the shopping center with Food Lion and an Shell gas station across the road on her right. Milner also described her last check-off point would be passing by the air and army national guard facilities another five minutes away. Then she would be officially in "the suburbs."

"Are you still awake?" she greeted Milner.

"I'm right here waiting on you." He was reclined back in the driver's seat. "Where are you now?"

"I don't know. I'm not really paying attention. I'm just driving."

Whether she told him the truth or not, he sensed his instincts about her were proving him correct. A woman couldn't stay away from something that's been good to her, although it actually went both ways; it still was a long, smooth stroke to his ego.

"Just be on the lookout for Choo-Choo Station, which will be on your right. My lights will be on. I'll be in the Mercedes."

Milner noticed in his driver's side mirror a car slowing down and its right-turn signal blinking. He sat up and looked over his shoulder. An Infiniti M35 had stopped beside him.

"You made it out here to the suburbs!"

"I can still turn around and go back to my parents' place, you know."

"But you're almost to my place. We'll be there before you know."

He put his car into DRIVE and eased onto Garners Ferry Road. She never turned around, but followed him all the way into his front yard.

When Sonia emerged from her car, she'd already given him fair warning that she would not be mistaken for being glamorous. She wore a red and white sorority cap, a dark blue sweat suit combination, and her hair was combed to the back. She also wore sandals.

Likewise, he was not dressed for a big gala, either. He wore baggy cotton sweats, a suede leather jacket, and tennis shoes.

"Can I at least get a hug?" he asked her.

She looked around. "Not out here. I just want to get inside where it's warmer!"

"The door's already open. Go right ahead."

"I hope you have the heater on, too; I can't believe how much cooler it is out this way!"

"It's just that much hotter during the summer time."

* * *

The heater was set at an accommodating seventy-five degrees. That was definitely more to Sonia's liking as she stopped in front of Milner's living room sofa, yawned and stretched before him.

It was also an inviting view from behind, which Milner exploited by wrapping his arms around her and kissing her on the neck. A sense of calm came over him now that he was tangible to her. He caressed her breasts. He noticed them reacting to his touch.

"I can tell that you're really glad to see me," she said, reaching behind.

"At least you know that I'm sincere about it."

He did nothing to hide the protrusion in his sweats. Rather, he turned her around and drew her toward his body; he then squeezed her buttocks. The fullness and firmness of her cheeks were worth bragging to others.

She wrapped her arms around his trunk and stroked his back with both hands. They stood there in that embrace for several moments generating their own heat.

"Wharton, I'm still not sure why I came all the way here to see you," she said upon separating from him. "There's really no logical reason."

"Would you have made the same trip had your husband called you?"

"That's my husband!"

"Fair enough."

At first, Sonia's spouse was merely the punch line to jokes Milner once told to himself. Now he held Trent in contempt. The man did not deserve to have a woman as captivating as her, and he was the one who had what it took to make her feel her worth in a relationship.

Had it not been four in the morning he would have been content with leading her to sit down with him on the sofa. But the bedroom was a more logical place especially since they already had some history in there.

She put up some resistance following his lead. "Why are we going in there?"

"You've been here before," he answered. "So why do we have to be formal?"

The night light was the only form of light in his room. She noticed once she was inside his top cover was crumpled. It also appeared to be where he spent his time talking to her from his cell phone. The room was otherwise kept orderly. It was something she could appreciate, considering that Taylor and Trent would not earn anyone's recognition in that area.

They stopped about halfway inside, a few feet from the bed. He turned toward her and reached for both her hands. She looked up at him wondering what was next.

"Sonia, I've really missed you. I'm glad you're here with me."

He kissed her softly on her lips, hoping that she might indulge with more vigor and conviction.

"It has been a while, hasn't it, Wharton?"

He made an awkward move leading her over to the bed where they sat down simultaneously.

"If you hadn't thought about divorcing your husband, I would like if you did. I'll even help pay for it."

Humph.

She paid $750 toward divorcing Trent only to change her mind after his bold gamble that saved his hide. So divorce had not been anything that she considered since then—and nothing she ever divulged to Milner.

"Can I ask you a question, Wharton?"

He nodded.

"When you got your divorce, who filed for it? Was it you or your ex?"

After yawning, Milner answered, "She didn't really want a divorce, but she was willing to go along with it if I paid for it. So I did."

"Why did you two divorce?"

He pondered the question while looking away from her. Valorie Dingle Milner was from Ettrick, Virginia; a city on the outskirts of Petersburg, which was famously the hometown of pro basketball legend Moses Malone.

"Do you really want to know?"

"Yes, I do."

"I walked in on her screwing another soldier. A freakin' corporal, at that."

Sonia sighed while she mulled his answer. "Wharton, I'm sure there was a reason why she was with that corporal. It sounds like she was getting back at you."

Milner admitted that he asked Valorie to marry him because he was scared of going to hell for committing rampant fornication, a product of the holiness-or-hell teaching that he adhered to during his early adult years.

Barely a month into the marriage, he realized that he made a bad decision. His way of dealing with it was ignoring his wife's pleas that he spent more time with her and treat her as his equal in their marriage. He hung out with other soldiers, and he eventually gravitated to having adulterous relationships of his own.

"The best thing that happened was our divorce became final a couple of months before our tenth anniversary. She missed being entitled to half of my military benefits." He shrugged his shoulders.

She shifted her weight on the mattress. "You know what? You really sound like you were selfish. Like you pressured her into getting a divorce to keep what you had coming."

"Hey, she didn't add one thing to that relationship," he snapped back at her. "She acted as if she sat on a gold mine. And it wasn't worth much, if you ask me!"

He shifted his eyes and stared aimlessly at pieces of furniture in the bedroom. Sonia remained stoic and studious of his behavior.

"Wharton, was the only reason why you called me over was because you wanted a piece?"

He stared at her for several moments. It was an uncomfortable feeling that she had discovered his intentions. "Is there anything wrong with that?"

"Only because you hadn't spoken to me, and you think we can simply pick up where we left off?"

Milner thought fast. "Sonia, I hadn't told you this. But I also had to go out of town for about ten days. I had some things on my plate, too."

The easiest and most believable alibi he rigged up was explaining to her that he went ahead with helping MacArthur out of jail, but it took longer than he expected.

"The thirty grand that was needed to get him out of trouble was the money I wanted to use toward equipment upgrades with the restaurant," he said. "I sure hope this is the last time anyone in my family will be calling me about him because I'm through with him!"

He stopped talking and watched her.

"Wharton, you have a way of layering things together, and I'm not sure if any woman can deal with that. I know that I'm having problems with it." She then hunched her shoulders. "Why couldn't you tell me all this while I was on the phone with you a while ago?"

"I told you that I felt it was better to speak with you in person rather than texting and explaining things over the phone."

"And you think that would have gotten me in the mood to give you a piece?"

She broke out laughing at the thought. "Even my husband knows better than that!"

"Are you calling me a liar?"

She shook her head.

"I'm only saying it's difficult keeping up with your intentions, Wharton. I'm not a chess opponent. I'm the woman you said you wanted to please mind, body, and soul. And all you're doing right now is turning me off mind, body, and soul—"

He reached for her hand while making eye-to-eye contact with her. "I'm not out to play games with you. I'm too old for that.

"I knew what the risks were the first time you caught my attention. But I thought the reward was more than worth the risk."

She stood up immediately, placing her hands on her waist. "I'm also not a pair of dice that you throw around on a game board, either!"

"Sonia, I know it was not the best time to be calling you. But I had to start somewhere."

He stood up and walked toward her, to which she began taking steps out of the bedroom. She stopped by the living room sofa and gathered her purse and sweat jacket.

"Sonia, I never heard you say that you wanted a divorce," he said, catching up with her. "I never heard you say you wanted to reconcile with your husband. I haven't even heard you say that you missed me at all.

"Do you really know what you want?"

"Right now, I don't." She sighed loudly and raised her eyebrows.

He nodded. "I see."

"I'm leaving, Wharton. I don't need my parents worrying about where I'm at this time of the morning."

* * *

It was after 5 a.m. once Sonia turned onto Garners Ferry Road heading back into Columbia. She reached into her purse and retrieved her Tracfone right after she drove past the air and army national guard facilities.

Just like she'd done a few hours earlier, she toyed with it in her hand. She considered calling Milner and apologizing to him. At that moment she recalled Pastor Perkins defining falling from grace as an individual failing to recognize he or she can't do anything without it.

Maybe it was grace that kept her in that moment of temptation despite her indecisiveness and lack of recognition. But with great certainty, she let down her window and tossed her Tracfone into the median of the road.

The phone sounded as if it disintegrated upon impact. But

she didn't bother looking back into her mirrors to notice where it occurred.

Chapter 23

It appeared as if Tondy Pratt, Paula Freese, and Maytreka were talk show panelists by the way they sat in their teller chairs and swayed while offering opinions about the popular cable TV reality series *Real Housewives of Atlanta.*

Tondy sought a high-five from Maytreka after mentioning former football player Kordell Stewart was a jerk, and men like him didn't deserve sincere and loving women like Porsha Williams.

"He was a control freak and tried to be a dictator with Porsha," Tondy said. "You wouldn't catch me with someone like him."

Since Ms. Wanda's departure, Tondy had the second-most seniority among bank tellers after Maytreka, who came to the St. Andrews branch in 2008; a year before Trent took over as manager.

Tondy, a week shy of her twenty-ninth birthday, had two boys before she was twenty-one. She's a single mother. Her boyfriend Omar Fitchew's a pharmacist at a Walgreens in West Columbia.

"But you know what? I really thought they would last. I can't believe that he would do that to her. She finds out on Twitter that he's divorcing her."

Maytreka grunted, but was hesitant about returning Tondy that high-five. She'd been a fan of the show since its debut and was the one who started the discussion.

"If you really check it out, it seems none of them stay married or together after they've been on that show," she said. "I think half of 'em are divorced."

"I never liked Kordell, too. But I think Porsha needs to work on herself before she goes on with another man," Paula chimed into the conversation. "But at least she should be getting some alimony.

"That's always a good thing."

Paula, a divorcée and mother of a ten-year-old daughter, swung to her right and looked at Tondy, who took a moment to inspect her face in her makeup mirror. She shared with Tondy the only drawback about receiving alimony is whenever she's had to claim it as income.

"I wish her good luck," she added. "She's a beautiful woman, and many men would love to allow her to be free and happy to pursue her dreams."

"What dreams?" Maytreka reacted.

She was of the opinion that Porsha was an airhead and simply was out of her element being involved with Kordell. She had nothing to offer in their relationship.

"How can you say that?" Tondy argued.

Paula agreed. "Yeah, how can you?"

"She wasn't all that bad while he was chasing after her. And if he was thinking with his other head, which was probably smarter than the one with all those scars on his face, she definitely had plenty to offer," Tondy went on to say. "I say she was the one who was deceived by him."

Maytreka, who had a reputation for charming male cus-tomers, laughed at both Tondy and Paula.

"That girl was as dumb as a box of rocks," she said. "And did you see the way she dressed in the episode before this last one?

"Can you say 'ratchet? I bet Kordell saw that she was all about da' money, and he had enough. Shoot, cut his losses be-fore she turns up pregnant. She isn't wife material. I bet his ex-wife probably told him that, too!"

Those were like fighting words, in Tondy's opinion. The conversation among the three became so spirited that it caught Trent's attention, considering his office was on the other side of the building from them.

Curious, he emerged from his office and approached his staff.

"What seems to be going on here?" he inquired, placing his hands on his waist.

Paula was quick to fill him in the details. "Kordell didn't even have the class to discuss with Porsha that he wanted to divorce her. He's off in another part of the house and she finds out on Twitter that he's outta there." She hunched her shoul-ders, adding, "With all the rumors there's been about his sex-uality, anyway, I guess it's not at all surprising he would be a punk about it."

Twitter. Divorce. Internet. How fitting, Trent thought to himself. But he was slow to react.

"Mr. Buckner, do you watch *Real Housewives of Atlanta*?" Ton-dy queried him.

Trent held his hands outwardly and shook his head. "I can't say that I do. I'm familiar with Kordell Stewart because he played football in college and in the pros, but that's all."

"What rock have you been living under?" Maytreka reacted. "I'm not into shows like that."

"Humph, even my boo watches *Real Housewives of Atlanta*, Mr. Buckner," Tondy said.

She then cut a menacing glare at Maytreka. "I bet you have a different man with you each time you watch *Real Housewives of Atlanta*—"

Maytreka placed a hand on her waist and rolled her neck at her. "You know you ain't right for saying that!"

"I bet Mrs. Buckner watches *Real Housewives of Atlanta*, and she tells you about it all the time. Ain't that right?" Tondy asked Trent, smiling at him.

This was a conversation Trent realized he should have avoided. He was aware that Sonia watched reality shows, but she was the last person he felt like making any references to.

Although he'd been estranged from Sonia, he had yet to consider filing for divorce. He still viewed it as a final option, but it was fast making its way up his list.

"Ladies, I think I'm going to leave that discussion alone. I know it's slow right now, but I ask that you tone it down."

He turned around and strode back to his office.

Paula whispered behind his back. "I bet he's watched all the episodes."

All three erupted in laughter.

The regular mailman Wayne Madison came by the St. Andrews branch later than usual. He waved at Trent, handed him a stack of envelopes, and hurried back to his delivery van.

Sifting through the stack, Trent noticed there was an enveloped addressed to him; it also came from an attorney's office, which placed him on guard. His neck tensed at the notion that Sonia had possibly filed for divorce once again.

He was careful to open the letter that was addressed from

the Duckett Law Firm on Assembly Street in downtown Columbia. And after reading the first paragraph, he sighed in relief. This was a letter requesting that he give a deposition in
Cortez's wrongful termination lawsuit. He was to appear in
three weeks.

I'm not surprised at all, he mumbled to himself.

Then he contacted Palmetto Fidelity's corporate office
where he was instructed to speak with Amber Cohen, the
bank's in-house legal counsel.

"To this day, I still don't know all the particulars why Cortez was let go by the bank," he said. "It was always shaped as
a matter that was way above my head, so I stayed out of it."

Amber replied, "You're not the only one who has received
these letters, Trent. And we really don't expect much to come
out of it, anyway. So we've been telling everyone to give them
what they want."

She leaned back in her chair, adding, "Just answer the questions truthfully."

Trent shrugged his shoulders. "I wouldn't do anything less."

* * *

The Buckners lived in a cul-de-sac where there were more
older, established home owners than young families with
children. Trent had a good rapport with most of the neighbors, and he knew most on a first- and last-name basis.

It always amused him whenever he saw Mr. Dennis Rembert, a widower who lived next door to his right, because he
was eighty-five years old and bona fide curmudgeon.

Mr. Rembert walked his dog, which Trent estimated was
around fifteen years old, at least four times a week. Between
the two of them, he often joked to himself, there had to be at
least two hundred years and they looked every bit of it.

Neither had spoken to each other since 2010. That was after Mr. Rembert accused Trent of stealing his garden tools.
In that relatively short span, Trent noticed Mr. Rembert had
lost weight and he'd become more feeble. The dog walked as
slow and wobbly as Mr. Rembert, and it barked at everything.

That's served as a reminder of his last conversation with
Mr. Rembert.

"I may be old, but I'm not crazy," Mr. Rembert said. "I
loaned you my tools, but you never returned them."

"Mr. Rembert, I don't have them. And how could I have
your tools if I've never been inside your house, let alone your
garage?"

Since then, Trent instructed Taylor never go near Mr. Rembert's property for any reason. He cited there had been several
incidents in the media about cantankerous old coots like him
shooting kids. All the confrontations were unprovoked. And
it was later learned in each case the elderly person had some
form of senility.

Life without Sonia was increasingly bearable. Trent was
still getting used to not encountering the smell of her perfume after he went into the bathroom behind her, the feeling
of her not sleeping in bed next to him, and him not having sex
even if it was sporadic at best.

He was, though, more than okay with knowing Sonia was
no longer nagging, ranting, and sentencing him to the Dog
House Inn over something stupid; or she wasn't needling him
about them having God time together, and then using it to
find fault in him.

The biggest transition was the laundry and ironing for himself and Taylor. While he was banished from the house last
summer, he merely took his clothes to the cleaners. But it did
not take long for him getting used to the routine of Sonia doing those things once she took him back.

In fact, it was something she insisted on because she considered it a labor of love for the family's benefit. Now Trent had to get up earlier or start the night before ironing clothes. He also had to take time out putting clothes in the washer and being mindful of taking them out of the dryer.

On this particular afternoon, Trent arrived home earlier than usual. He figured that he would get a head start on the laundry. That meant after perusing the mail he would stop first by Taylor's room and sift through his clothes that he usually left all over the floor or hanging on the closet doors.

Trent was no more than five strides away from reaching Taylor's room when he heard a headboard bumping consistently against the wall.

"Hey, Taylor! What's going on in there?" He followed by knocking on the door.

There was no immediate response, but there was loud whispering.

"Taylor, I do have a key to this room. I'll go and get it—"

"Can you come back in a couple of minutes?" Taylor yelled.

"What? You don't ask me to come back in a couple of minutes. Open this door. Now!"

"Crap!"

Loud thuds for footsteps approached door. Then Taylor fumbled with opening it, which infuriated Trent. Once he saw a hint of light from the room, Trent pushed the door and barged inside.

"Did you have to do that? I was already here!" Taylor complained.

That was the least of his problems.

There were pathways to the bed and bathroom amidst the clothes all over the floor. The room smelled of a girl's loud perfume. Standing nervously to the right of Trent was Dawn, peeping from behind Taylor's closet door. Taylor, himself, was shirtless and his pants were unbuttoned. His bed sheets were crumpled.

Trent's eyes bulged. "I know I'm not seeing what I'm seeing in here!"

He stepped over a pile of shoes and lunged at Taylor, grabbing him by the shoulders. Next, he shoved him out of the bedroom, stopping in the hallway.

"I told you NO GIRLS! Didn't I?" He pushed Taylor hard into his chest.

Visibly stunned by Trent's sudden rage, Taylor protested, "Dad, not now. Can she at least leave first?"

"Are you finally dressed, young lady?" Trent asked from the hallway.

"Yes, sir," she said; her voice was faint.

"You need to call whoever brought you here and go home!"

"Yes, sir."

Seconds later, a fifteen-year-old girl hurried past them wearing skinny jeans, a pullover sweater, and carrying her school bag. Her hair was partially disheveled.

Trent put his finger directly in Taylor's face. He spoke loud enough that only Taylor heard him. "Your ass is grassed!"

Taylor rolled his eyes, provoking Trent to smack him aside his head just as he started down the hallway.

"You didn't have to do that!" Taylor reacted, with his hand covering most of his left ear.

"That ain't all I feel like doing when I get back!"

Trent approached Dawn in the living room. "How long will it be before your ride gets here?"

"My sister's coming from the mall, sir. She said she just left there."

Don't worry about closing the door when you leave."

He stormed back down the hallway seeking out Taylor. Once he reached the bedroom, he started yelling again at him;

his arms flailed during each sentence.

"You're lucky it's the other way around because I'd still be on you right now!" Trent said. "If I do what I really want to do right now, they'll be taking me away in handcuffs!"

Trent then demanded that Taylor look at him and not fidget for his iPad.

"In fact, gimme that thing. You won't need this anytime soon!" He lunged over to his right and snatched it up from Taylor's bed.

"Dad, come on. You didn't have to do that!" he protested. "Where do I go? What do you really allow me to do? It's not like I go see any of my other friends—"

"Oh, but you made sure you had something to do today! You can't have it all, and you won't!"

This was far from an inner struggle. Trent could not fathom at Taylor's age bringing a girl over to his mother's home without her knowledge. For that matter, he didn't bring girls to her home even after he graduated from high school and while he attended college in Ruston, Louisiana.

The first—and only—woman to visit his mother's home was the one he married—Sonia.

"What you don't understand is that too much is going on out there," he tried explaining to Taylor. "You bring a girl to this house, and let's say nothing happens. But she goes back home and says something did happen.

"Guess what can happen?"

Taylor looked around without any intention of answering. He then hunched his shoulders. It was Trent's impulse to smack him aside his head again for his apparent lethargy.

"I might have to get you out of jail because it would be her word against yours. You'd be seen as guilty, and you're behind the eight-ball trying to prove your innocence. That's what can happen!"

Taylor appeared more concerned that Trent's tirade might be insulting to Dawn, whom he suspected was still waiting for her sister in his living room.

But Trent didn't care.

"Man, I've put too much into you to be making bone-headed decisions like this." He pondered quickly about how Taylor's school year had already unfolded. "I'm going to have to create some accountability for you after school."

He went on to tell Taylor that he would have him riding a cab from school over to the bank for the remainder of the school year.

It was non-negotiable.

"Even when your mother was here, there was always a chance that you might do something like this," Trent said. "I can't afford to allow you to find trouble for that little bit of time, which is obviously too much!"

This had taken a life of its own, Taylor fumed. He did not think it was a big deal inviting Dawn over. He tried explaining to Trent that she came over to help him with his English class since he still was catching up on missed assignments while he was suspended. And they actually did some work.

"Okay, Dawn and I decided to take a break and things happened. But we had already promised to each other that we were only going to go so far."

Trent's face frowned first then it contorted. "Do you expect for me to believe that?"

"Pretty much—"

"Boy, I'm about two seconds away from puttin' something on you!"

Trent went back into the living room and checked on Dawn. The area was quiet.

"Taylor, what's her name?"

"Dawn."

"Dawn, are you still here?"

There was no answer. Trent then checked the front door. It was not locked. But it bothered him that there was no way of knowing what the girl might say or do once she was back among her people.

For the moment, his focus was disciplining Taylor for breaching his trust.

"You want to be treated like a man, and what you did was something that deserves a man's punishment."

Trent glared at Taylor, who was visibly uncomfortable with the confrontation. He brought to Taylor's attention about his recent woes, starting with his grades.

"Dad, I missed time from school!" Taylor argued. "You've been on me every day about getting my work done. I'm doing it!"

"Look what it took, though."

Then Trent reminded him about being so irritable and quick to having outbursts. It's been as if he's wanted to fight and argue about everything.

"Now you're sneaking girls into this house. What's next? Parties? Drinking? Maybe hanging with the wrong crowd and getting into more trouble?"

"You can't talk about anyone," Taylor retorted. "Mom didn't want you back because of what you did!"

"You only know half of the story. The other half is why I'm back here!"

Chapter 24

Trent walked away from Taylor before things escalated into something worse.

"I'm not finished with this!" he yelled.

Taylor spoke cautiously—at least that's what he thought was doing. "Can I at least have my iPad back?"

He watched Trent freeze in mid-step and slowly turn around; his father's chest heaved and fell and his lips were bunched.

Trent finally spoke. "Hell no!"

He waved Taylor off, grumbling and cursing to himself, and sought refuge in his work office. After plopping in his chair, he closed his eyes and took long, slow breaths in an attempt at calming himself down from his fury.

After contemplating his recent behavior, it appeared to him that Taylor had reverted to mischief and lethargy as a means of coping with the tumult at home.

Blaming Sonia was more than a convenient excuse. But it

was also important to him that he got a handle on Taylor before it was too late.

His phone went off. He glanced on his desk. The number was one from his contact list. Initially, he scoffed at the notion to answer. He allowed it to go into voice mail. Then he called back.

"What was it you wanted?" he asked.

Sonia answered, "Trent, did you at least listen to the message I left you?"

"I didn't." He sighed into the phone.

Under different circumstances, marital and paternal instincts might have taken over and he would have rattled off describing how their son gotten into mischief. He figured Sonia would have a conniption. She would want to know who the girl was, where she lived, and who her parents were; those were questions he'd already considered asking, although he had yet to act upon them. It would have also been characteristic of her to demand that Taylor be included in any God time they had.

Even worse, he would be faced with defending himself from Sonia's accusation that his lack of spiritual leadership was responsible for the crisis.

"Trent, if you would have listened to the message, I told you that I've spent all this time away from you and Taylor working on getting my life back in order," she said.

Trent looked around his work office. Nothing she said registered with him.

"I'm a bit surprised that you would be calling," he said. "All these years you've been telling me about one day it might be too late for me. Have you considered it might be too late for you?"

She inhaled long and deep through her nostrils. She covered her brow with her hand and stared down at the carpet in her bedroom.

"It's not like I can block you and my son out like that." She also snapped her finger.

"I called because I want my husband and my son back in my life. I hope we can talk about it again."

Trent sighed.

"What's wrong?"

He didn't answer.

"I know you, Trent. Something's wrong."

A part of her hoped that he would simply tell her to come back home. She would be more than glad to pick up her clothes another time.

"Maybe it's a good thing that you called—"

She perked up and sat upright in her bed. "Can we talk about it?"

"What are you doing the rest of this evening?"

"What time is it?"

"It's about 6:45 [p.m.]"

"Nothing. I'm usually in once I'm back from work."

Trent rolled his eyes at her response, but he was in no position to judge.

"Can you meet me and Taylor at 7:30?"

"Where?"

"Have you eaten?"

"Yeah, but that doesn't matter. Where do you want to meet?"

He suggested they meet at the Chick-fil-A on Dutch Fork Road in Irmo, a location that she was more than familiar with after Taylor's basketball practices.

After he hung up with Sonia, Trent waited until 7:25 before he walked down the hallway and knocked on Taylor's bedroom door.

"Taylor!"

There was no delay with his response. He was also fully dressed when he opened the door.

"Yes, sir?"

"Put on your shoes and come with me. We've got a couple of errands to make."

"Okay."

* * *

Sonia left her parents' home almost immediately after hanging up on Trent's callback. She turned into the Chick-fil-A parking lot around 7:20.

It amused her to be waiting at the ultimate of soccer mom locations, considering how much she detested being a sports mom. She counted at least eight minivans that had passed through the drive-in, and another dozen or so crossover style vehicles like a Nissan Murano, Buick Enclave, Toyota Venza, or Ford Edge that had stopped in the parking lot.

Humph.

She was more than content in her M35 without any car magnets decorating her rear quarter panels or school team sport logos with her child's name in her rear window.

Once 7:30 passed, Sonia started fidgeting being that she was a stickler for punctuality. She hoped that Trent would be a man of his word and not play games with her.

Another five minutes passed. But she breathed a sigh in relief once she noticed an Acura sedan model that looked like Trent's making a right-hand turn from Dutch Fork Road. She peeked into her rear-view mirror and checked her makeup.

Try keeping an open mind, she told herself.

She was heartened to see Taylor had come with Trent. But she noticed a scowl on her son's face once he got out the car.

Meanwhile, Trent scanned the parking lot, made a pointing

gesture at Taylor, and they headed inside the establishment.

"You two wouldn't wait for me?" Sonia said behind them while they were in line.

Trent recognized her voice and turned around. "We figured you'd already be inside since we were late."

This was not the time to be nitpicking with him. He had a semi-valid point. She then shifted her attention toward Taylor.

"What was that frown on your face I saw out in the parking lot?"

Taylor looked over at Trent. She noticed his chest heave. Instinctively, she glanced over at Trent.

"What's going on with him?"

"That's why I asked to meet with you."

"Okay—"

"What are you having?" he inquired. "It's on me."

She replied, "I'll have a large ice tea, sweetened."

Trent then instructed Taylor to find them a table. Minutes later, he walked over to the far left corner of the dining area, carrying a tray with two large lemonades, Sonia's tea along with two large orders of waffle fries, four regular sandwiches, and several packs of ketchup and barbecue sauce.

The Buckners now had more family moments together—two—since she moved out than they had all year. Sitting across from Trent, she asked, "Can we at least pray before we start eating and talking?"

It was more than tempting for Trent to deride Sonia for requesting a moment of prayer. The righteous one who so famously called out the sin and shortcomings of others was herself sitting among sinners.

Yet there was something nostalgic about her request. She was right. They'd been in each other's lives too long to block each other out just like that.

"I'll lead," he said.

Sonia's eyes widened. She hoped it was an encouraging sign.

"*Thank You for this time together. We look to You as our author and finisher of our faith. We look to You for Your grace to abound this moment. We thank You for the provision you've provided for us this day . . . Amen.*"

Trent could really be a leader when he really wanted, Sonia thought to herself. But her curiosity could no longer go without being satiated.

"I called you wanting to talk about us, Trent. But I sense there's something else."

Taylor squirmed in the seat next to Trent, who noticed from the corner of his eye.

"Yeah," he answered, gesturing with his head to the right of him. "Taylor decides he's going to invite a girl over without my permission. I caught them in his bedroom. I don't know if they were right in the act; Taylor came to his door without a shirt and his pants were unbuttoned."

Sonia focused her eyes directly at Taylor while adjusting her posture. She spoke slowly and quite maternally.

"You had a girl in your bedroom?"

She continued staring at Taylor, who had stopped eating; he merely looked down at his food. "I know your father has already gotten on you about this. If it weren't for us being here, it would be my turn."

Regardless of their differences about how their marriage should be, Trent and Sonia always agreed on what was right and best for their son.

She looked over at Trent.

"Taylor's been acting out his anger by doing some bone-headed things," he said, pausing to take a long sip from his lemonade. "I've already set some things in place to avoid another episode for at least the rest of the school year."

"I hate to say this, but all this started with you," she replied. "I was afraid what happened last year would eventually affect Taylor."

Trent eyes widened. Any rage that he had ignored or suppressed in the name of solidarity and conciliation came back with vengeance.

"There you go again," he said, sitting back against the cushion. "I went against my better judgment doing this!"

Taylor saw an opening for escape. He was quick to interrupt his parents.

"Mom, Dad, both of you are to blame!" They looked at him with surprise.

"You can't judge me at all, Mom. You should be the last person to tell me I was wrong for having Dawn over," he said. "And you, Dad, I already told you that Mom talked about you all the time while you were gone last summer."

"Taylor, I have my faults. Your mother has hers. But you're under my roof," Trent countered. "That means you abide by my rules and regulations.

"You're a teenager. You don't work. You're barely getting your act together at school. And the last thing you need to be doing is something that could land you in more trouble than you could ever imagine."

Out of mischief, Sonia was gleeful that Trent had lit into Taylor so fast. She would not have expected anything less.

"Your father is right," she added.

"Mom, nothing happened. Dad walked in before anything did. And we both said that we would stop before we got too far."

Sonia placed her hands on her waist. "You think you have that much self-control?

"Hah! Famous last words."

Trent quieted the exchange and suggested that she accompany him when he took Taylor over to Dawn's residence, informing her family what transpired.

"When did you plan on doing that?" she asked.

"Right after we leave from here."

"I think that's a good idea. With the way people are these days, she could tell her mother anything."

Trent then asked Taylor, "How long have you two been talking to each other?"

"A couple of weeks now."

"Who's idea it was that she come over to the house?"

"It was both our idea. I asked her if she could help me with a paper that I have due in English. But we both wanted to see each other."

Sonia interrupted him again. "Taylor, I'm sure if your father knew that you were inviting someone over it wouldn't be as big of an issue. I'm willing to bet money that he would have been there to keep an eye on both of you."

"That's the whole point," Trent added, "You invited a girl over without my permission. How many times have I told you no girls?"

* * *

The Buckners drove in separate vehicles over to an apartment complex just off Lake Murray Boulevard, about ten minutes away from the Chick-fil-A where they met.

Based on outward appearance, the apartments reminded Trent of where he once lived in Louisiana: Children bicycles and tricycles outside the apartments. Older, lesser maintained vehicles were outside many of the buildings. A few young males bounded along in a pack holding up their sagging pants with one hand. This was the kind of setting that made him more than appreciative for the athletic scholarship opportunity he was given to attend college, which opened an entirely different world to him.

"How many times have you been over here?" Trent asked Taylor.

"A couple of times."

Trent merely stared at Taylor. "Have you ever met her parents?"

"She lives with her mother. Her name is Shawnetta."

Trent rolled his eyes.

"Now how far do I go off in this place?" he asked.

Taylor pointed ahead to his left. "Usually, there's a burgundy colored Chevy Malibu in front of their apartment." He then updated Trent that he was coming up on it.

"Did you tell her that we were coming over?"

"Yes, she knows."

"I hope her mother's there."

"She is." Taylor shrugged his shoulders.

Sonia followed closely behind Trent, and she was quick to meet up with him and Taylor as soon as they got out of his car. She made it known to Trent that she did not like going there, and this was not her element.

"You know you weren't a child of privilege," Trent said.

"That has nothing to do with where we are right now." She looked over at Taylor. "My instincts say you could have done a lot better."

"Mom, she's not a bad girl. You shouldn't be so quick to judge."

"Taylor, all you had to do was let me know you wanted to invite a girl over," Trent chimed in to say. "We might not be going through this now."

Taylor sucked his teeth while Trent nodded at him to go ahead and knock on the girl's door. There was no music blaring from inside.

Moments later, a comparatively short woman wearing a black wrap cap, purple short-sleeve blouse and black shorts answered the door.

"Who are these people with you?" she asked Taylor.

Then she cocked her head back in a dismissive manner. The appearance of Trent still wearing his white long-sleeved business shirt and dark slacks and Sonia in her ivory and black business pant suit gave her the impression that his parents were highfalutin.

"I'm Taylor's father," he volunteered.

"And I'm his mother," Sonia added.

"The reason why I'm here is because your daughter was over at my house visiting Taylor, and he did not ask for my permission," he said.

Shawnetta placed her hand on her waist. "And what does that have to do with me?"

"When I walked in on Taylor, both of them were partially dressed. They say they hadn't gone all the way, but I asked that your daughter leave, which she did without any problems."

"Well, I don't know what happened. But if I were you, I'd keep your son away from my daughter." Shawnetta looked back in the apartment. She yelled for Dawn to come into the living room.

There was no response or Dawn appearing. "Dawn, I'm not going to call you again!"

"Mama, I don't have anything to say to him!" she yelled from her room.

Shawnetta looked back at Trent and Sonia. "And I suggest that you leave from in front of my home. From what I hear, you two have your own issues!"

"Come on, Taylor," Trent reacted.

Sonia, who didn't waste another moment standing in front of the apartment, hurried back inside her car. Taylor walked rather reluctantly back to Trent's car. She followed them closely out of the complex.

"I had a feeling something like that might happen," Sonia called him to say; she still followed him once they were on Lake Murray Boulevard.

"I'm not surprised, either."

Sonia asked to speak with Taylor. "I'm not pleased with what I've heard about you. You can do much better than that."

She felt somewhat handicapped by what she could say further because of her estrangement to Trent.

"You don't need to be messing with girls like that. Those are the ones who can ruin your life. Before you know it, she's telling you she's pregnant. She's the type who would have you paying child support, and you're not even eighteen years old."

"I get it, Mom. I get it. Now will you leave me alone?"

He handed the cell phone back to Trent.

"I don't think this would have happened if both of us were together," she told Trent.

"So, you think that's reason enough for me to let you come back?"

"Trent, I don't want to be separated from you—"

"You know what? Not once since all this has happened you've apologized to me. Not once! And you expect me to just say, hey, come on home?"

He shook his head. "I don't think you really mean what you've been saying."

"Trent, none of this would have happened had you taken me serious all those years," she retorted; they had already been driving their separate ways since passing the railroad tracks at St. Andrews Road.

"All you had to do was be more thoughtful. All you had to do was treat me with sensitivity. But it was far from you. Let's not talk about all your past behavior—"

For a brief while, Trent wondered whether he'd been holding Sonia to a double standard. He changed his mind and the animosity was back—again.

He felt inclined to curse at Sonia. And he would have done just that had he been alone.

"You're stuck in the past. That's part of your problem," he said, sneering. "You need to spend better quality God time. Obviously, that wasn't revealed to you!"

He then hung up.

Chapter 25

L ance and Shonna had known for nearly a month that his mother, Barbara, would be coming to Columbia to visit him.

As fate would have it, his oldest sister Lauren had also indicated that she'd be visiting him. But Lance still had not mentioned anything to his mother or sister about Shonna being his girlfriend.

"Aren't you bucking for any trouble with them?" Shonna asked.

He looked at her with a wry grin. "I'm already in trouble with them because I hadn't gone to see them since I moved here."

"They didn't want you to settle here in South Carolina?"

"I wouldn't say they were against it. We have a close-knit family, but I've always been the one who wanted to go different places."

Shonna still seemed genuinely interested in meeting some

of Lance's family. Whether his mother and sister liked her or not, she figured it was one less barrier removed in her relationship with him.

She even went as far as offering her GMC Acadia SUV so he could pick his mother up at the airport. She was scheduled to arrive at Columbia Metropolitan at 7:50 p.m.

"I can handle it in my car," he said.

"But what if I want to meet her at the airport, too?"

Lance was stunned. "You actually want to come and meet my mother?"

"Yeah, why not?" she answered. "Or did you plan on having me appearing from behind door number three or pop out of a box, yelling, 'Surprise!'?"

The offer seemed nice, but Lance was quick to think it would not send the right message using her vehicle: It would appear as if he was dependent upon her for everything, and as if he were her boy toy whom she supported.

His job as a systems analyst paid nearly twice as much as what she earned running the radio station. Admittedly, he was too cheap to consider buying another vehicle, although his primary bills consisted of rent, car insurance, student loans, lights, cell phone, and cable.

"I'm telling you, I've got this one," he said. "You're welcomed to come along. My car isn't too small that it can't handle you, my mother and her luggage. She's only going to be here for four days. "

"Okay, I'll go along with it. But the offer still stands."

Shonna then questioned him about living arrangements for his family.

"Do you plan on putting her up in a hotel room, or you have that one handled as well?" she asked.

"Where else did you think my mother was going to stay?" he replied. "She's staying with me."

"What about your sister when she arrives?"

"She'll stay at my place, too. You forget that I have two bed-rooms—I guess that's possible to miss since you've always slept with me."

"Lance, two women don't get along well under the same roof. Trust me on that."

"I have three sisters," he reminded her. "I know exactly what you're saying. But I think these two won't have any problems."

Lance explained to Shonna his mother and Lauren were similar in personality much in the way she once described Sonia and her mother. But it went even further with them. They bore strong resemblances all the way down to the way their feet and toes were shaped.

"I find that hard to believe," Shonna remarked.

"It's true. My mother has told me the story a couple of times that when my grandmother on my father's side visited us she noticed Lauren as a young child had feet and toes just like my mother. It sort of freaked her out."

"Well, I guess that's as similar as one can get."

"Just wait until you see them together. You'll look at me and say that I was right," Lance said.

He further related to her his mother once showed him a black and white picture. He made the mistake of thinking it was Lauren.

"I told my mother that I didn't recall Lauren taking any black and white pictures at school. My mother laughed and told me that was a picture of her when she was in the fifth grade. Then I looked in our family album for one of Lauren in the fifth grade. They're like twins."

Shonna could not resist bringing up the obvious with Lance. "If you say your mother and sister are that much alike, what will they think of us?"

Sighing loudly, Lance was slow to respond. "What do you think?"

"If she's anything like my mother, it's going to be pretty interesting."

* * *

Lance and Shonna agreed on parking his Hyundai Sonata in the three-story garage adjacent to the airport terminal. Then they would meet his mother in the baggage claim area. Since they arrived early, they killed time by taking a walk along the outer concourse.

"This is the first time my mother has ever flown anywhere to visit me," he mentioned. "I'm beginning to feel a little nervous."

"You, nervous? I find that hard to believe."

"I am. I haven't seen her since I left D.C. to come here. I'm sure she's going to be nitpicking about everything in my place."

"Lance, all mothers do things like that. They wouldn't be mothers if they didn't."

He went as far as to say his mother had a tendency to be overbearing especially since he's the only male in the family.

"I thought you had a brother?" Shonna turned to ask him. His face contorted. "I've never told you I had a brother. My father died when I was sixteen, so I'm it among the males in my mother's house."

They stopped walking.

"You never mentioned your father died—"

"I never saw any reason to tell you," he replied. "But, yeah, he's been dead since I was sixteen."

They resumed walking, heading over toward the car rental parking lot. It afforded them a view of the airplane hangars and runways. The seven o'clock hour was one of the airport's peak periods for arrivals and departures.

Lance first mentioned that his father, Curtis, worked for the U.S. Department of Agriculture as an inspector. He attended college in Alabama, earning a degree in veterinarian medicine.

"How did he die? How old was he?" Shonna asked as they began heading back toward the airport's terminal.

"He was forty-five when he was killed fighting off two punks who tried robbing him at a gas station."

According to witnesses' accounts, two young men approached Lance's father while he was pumping gas in his Lexus sedan. It appeared as if one of them asked Curtis Miles for money, which he flatly refused and told them to go find themselves a job. The taller of the two accosted his father by grabbing him by the collar. But Mr. Miles broke the man's grasp and they engaged in a fist fight, which he was the immediate aggressor. The other robber, who was much shorter, took off running. It was assumed that he had stranded his partner.

Mr. Miles had beaten the man down to the ground; he begged Mr. Miles to leave him alone and he ran away in the opposite direction. Just as Mr. Miles reached for his car door, gunshots were fired and he fell forward against his car. The other robber had come back seeking revenge. He died from his wounds a day later.

When they were asked by police their motive for shooting Mr. Miles, the one who shot him said it was because "he disrespected us by telling us to go find jobs."

Lance said it took him several years—until his final year in college—to have any closure from his father's death. "That's how long it took for both of them to be locked up for good. A damn shame, if you ask me.

"You float a bad check, people want to press charges on you

and have you arrested the next week, if you don't make good on the check. You kill someone, and it's possible you can avoid being sentenced for years."

He shook his head at the thought. Shonna placed her hand on his back.

"Your father sounds like he was nobody to play with," she said. "I bet he was well respected."

He nodded. Then he reached over and grasped her hand. She smiled back at him and gave him a peck on the cheek.

From a distance, Lance noticed Barbara Miles riding the escalator down to the baggage claim area. In his own way, he was still getting the nerve to stand up; he clutched onto Shonna's hand slightly longer. Then he leaned over closer and whispered in her ear. "See the woman wearing the brown jacket and matching slacks?"

"The tall lady, right?"

"Uh-huh."

"She looks like she's looking for someone, Lance. Is she your mother?"

"Yeah, that's her," he answered. "Guess we better get up."

Lance and Shonna held hands while they walked in her direction. She immediately recognized him—not hard at six feet, four inches. And Shonna, who was five-six, complemented him nicely in appearance.

"My baby!" Barbara said, holding out her arms for him; he finally let go of Shonna's hand and walked alone before stopping to hug her.

"Hey, it's been a while," he said. Then he kissed Barbara on the cheek. "How was the flight?"

"Not bad at all. We didn't have to wait forever on the runway in Atlanta. I was actually surprised." She then looked over his right shoulder. "Who's your lady friend?"

He released his hug, smiling. "She's Shonna, my girlfriend." He then looked back at her. She stood with her hands folded waiting patiently for her moment.

Barbara waved in Shonna's direction. "Hi!"

"Hi, Mrs. Miles," Shonna replied, walking toward them. "I'm Shonna Chandler."

She held out her hand, which Barbara was cordial to accept shaking. "I'm so glad to meet you. I've probably been more excited than Lance."

"Is that right?"

"Yes, ma'am."

"I'm Barbara. Everyone calls me Babs."

The announcement came over the system luggage for Barbara's Delta flight could be picked up at carousel three, which was on the far end of the claim area. Lance hurried over toward the smattering of people.

"Which one or which ones will be your luggage, Mom?"

Barbara waited several minutes before she recognized her travel set. "It's those two and that large one over there. Flying sure ain't the same as it used to be."

While Lance retrieved her luggage, Barbara acted upon her curiosity. "How long have you two known each other?"

"A year, but we didn't really start dating until, like, almost nine months ago." Shonna replied.

"Is that right?"

At least to Shonna, she was off to a far better beginning than when they visited her parents. She figured she had the kind of personality that could get along with most people given that radio's mostly about connecting with an audience or advertisers.

She also figured that she would try to find a common ground with her other than it being Lance.

"Early in my career, I worked in Washington, D.C."

"Is that right?" Barbara excused herself to bark orders at Lance.

"Hey, let me pull that travel case and you take the large suitcase."

"Mom, I got this."

She shook her head. "You have always been so stubborn just like your father."

"Lance, stubborn?" Shonna instigated.

He merely turned and looked back at her and Shonna, who was on the brink of giggling at him. This was the kind of interaction she had hoped would occur last month at her parents' home.

Barbara quickly turned to her left. "Shonna, that's your name, right?"

"Yes, ma'am."

"I have to ask once, maybe twice. Then I'll remember it forever."

She first mentioned to Shonna as they walked across the driveway toward the parking garage that as a child Lance tried emulating Johnny Gill, a fellow Washington, D.C. native; the Miles family also lived in the same neighborhood as Gill, which also produced Stacy Lattisaw.

"Lance, you never told me you used to sing?" Shonna blurted out to him.

"She's already telling you about me wanting to be the next Johnny Gill?" he reacted. "Oh, brother! Here we go . . ."

Whereas Gill's musical beginnings could be traced to the church—first performing in a group his father formed with Gill's brothers and later singing in a group his mother formed after they divorced—Barbara said she couldn't get Lance sing in front of crowds.

His biggest obstacle was himself, she said; he never took it serious enough to discover the extent of his talent.

"Mom, can you—"

"Listen here, I'm telling this story!" she chided him.

She was still eager to tease about him singing Gill's early hits "My, My, My" and "There You Go" in the bathroom before he went to school in the mornings.

Given the baritone voice that Lance actually grew into, she said, that was not a bad idea wanting to copy Gill's style. But she always thought her son would have been better suited trying to emulate someone whose style was even smoother like Ronald Isley's, if that was what he really wanted to pursue.

She looked over at Shonna. "You gotta admit my baby looks better than both of them, doesn't he?"

Shonna didn't expect to be put on the spot so soon by his mother. Clearing her throat, she commented, "I'm biased like you, Mrs. Miles—"

"Barbara or Babs," she interrupted.

"Barbara," she said, "Lance runs loops and circles around both of them." She was careful not to elaborate any further.

Then she spoke to Lance. "Aren't we parked on the second level?"

"Yeah. Why don't y'all wait here on the first level, and I'll go bring the car down."

"We don't have to stop here. I can still get around," Barbara said; she then shot a look in Shonna's direction. "Ain't that right, Shonna?"

She felt obligated to reply, "Yes ma'am."

Chapter 26

Lance was poised to follow the road signs out of the airport that led him northward to Platt Springs Road. His apartment was no more than ten minutes away. But then it dawned upon him that he had passengers.

Saving face, he asked, "Shonna, [do] you know of a good place where we can find something to eat not far from here?"

"It means you'll have to turn around and go back toward Airport Boulevard."

Barbara was more than eager to chime into that discussion. She complained about flying on planes don't include anything to eat worth mentioning.

"We're talkin' about a gulp of a drink poured onto three ice cubes and a couple of salty, roasted peanuts to gag on," she hissed. "Of course, if you really want food it's gonna cost you."

She also sucked her teeth. "You'll be lucky if you can get past airport security with anything you bring. If not that, you pay more for the convenience of eating at the airport.

"Humph!"

Shonna assured Barbara the place she had in mind would be worth her while. She reminded Lance about The Groovy Soul.

"I've eaten there a couple of times, Barbara. The food was really good." She looked over at Lance. "Do you remember how to get there?"

He hunched his shoulders. "Wasn't that the place you called yourself introducing me to Sonia?"

"Yes, it's the same place."

She instructed him to remain on Airport Boulevard and make a left at the intersection where there was a K-Mart. That was Knox Abbott Road. He was to drive another mile and a half or so until he saw the multi-story bank building on his left. The restaurant was in that shopping center.

Lance hurried over to the passenger side opening the door first for his mother. After Shonna got out, he was unsure whether he should walk with her or his mother inside The Groovy Soul. But all it took was one look at his mother. He figured Shonna would have done the same thing had it been Prentiss visiting.

"When I came here last time, Shonna's station had something out here in the parking lot," he mentioned to Barbara, then looking back at Shonna.

She actually lagged behind a couple of steps appearing somewhat miffed by him walking along side his mother than with her.

An overbearing mother was something she felt she could handle. But a test of her patience was the notion that Lance was possibly a mama's boy at heart. Those were the kind of men she was careful to avoid since there was nothing good she'd ever heard or read about them making great boyfriends or even more. Okay, so what if he won her approval. Could that lead to something that she'd regret?

Swallowing her pride, Shonna managed a weak smile. "Lance, you've now been to several of our remote broadcasts. You can probably explain to Barbara how they work better than I could."

"Mom, don't believe her. All I know is that people come by and talk to the on-air talent, and they give away lots of items. If it weren't for me meeting Shonna, I wouldn't have known that much."

Once inside the restaurant, they were immediately greeted by a man who wore a collarless ivory long-sleeved shirt and brown slacks. He looked to his left at Shonna and then to his right at Barbara, grinning.

"Have I not seen you before?" he asked. "I know two of you look familiar—"

Shonna was quick to respond, "Mr. Milner, you have a very good memory."

"Oh, yes. That's right. You're the station manager!" he reacted, wagging his finger rather coolly. "I've been thinking about your station coming here again. When will be a good time to contact you?"

She searched her purse and handed Milner another business card. She advised him to contact her early during regular business hours.

"I'm at this restaurant all day. Things come up all the time," he said. "But I'll definitely do that."

He then turned his attention to Lance's mother. There was a gleam in his eye as he spoke to her.

"Good evening, thank you for visiting us. Do you have a special seating preference?"

"Anywhere you select will be fine, thank you." Barbara looked him up and down with much admiration. She was more than tempted to say that she'd eat alone just to savor the sight of him all to herself.

"Okay, follow me."

He led them over to a booth not far from the buffet bar—it would allow him an unobstructed view of Shonna and Barbara.

He scanned the restaurant again. It was about half-full despite it being nearly 8:30 in the evening. "Would you prefer this table or another?"

"This will be fine," Lance answered.

A portion of Shonna's ego was soothed as Lance took the initiative of sitting next to her. He also suggested to both she and Barbara that they visit the buffet bar first.

Since Shonna had previously dined at The Groovy Soul, she shared with Barbara how she became familiar with the establishment.

"What Lance didn't tell you was one of my advertising reps came here for lunch, and he simply raved about this place. He suggested to Mr. Milner that he consider us hosting one of our shows from here."

She looked around and noticed there had been some changes in The Groovy Soul's aesthetics. She continued, "I've even brought my sister here to eat, and I know she liked it as well."

Barbara listened halfheartedly while she scanned the dining area to find out where Milner had gone.

"Sounds like this is the place to be," she said, filling her plate from the salad bar. "We have a couple of places like this up in D.C."

Once they returned to the booth, Lance took his turn visiting the buffet bar. Barbara figured this was as good of an opportunity as any to convey what she'd already suppressed since being introduced to Shonna.

"You're right, the food is really good. That brother who runs this place definitely knows what he's doing," she started off saying; she glanced over at Lance, who was still browsing the selection.

Shonna nodded. "I've wanted to come back here for a while. Hopefully, we can work something out with Mr. Milner for another remote show."

Their eyes finally met in a mother-to-girlfriend showdown. Shonna was more than familiar with the type of stare that Barbara made at her: the eyes moved subtly up and down looking her over.

"How old are you, Shonna?"

"Forty-four."

Barbara blinked her eyes a couple of times while Shonna sat motionless.

"I'm barely ten years older than you. I'll be fifty-six later this year. Don't you think you're too old being with my son?"

"May I still call you Barbara?" Shonna asked, shifting her weight on the cushion.

She nodded.

"Barbara, I know you may not agree with me dating Lance, and I think I can understand why. But I didn't go into this relationship with my eyes closed. They're wide open."

"Is that right?"

Shonna spoke matter-of-factly to her. "Yes, that is correct."

Barbara glanced over toward the buffet bar again. She noticed Lance was returning.

"I'll say this real quick. You may still feel young and sexy. It may even feel real good to you right now," she said. "But at some point, you're going to feel like an old woman around my son; Ms. Clairol's not going to be able to hide that. He might even realize he doesn't like being around an older woman. Then what you're going to do?"

Shonna, who did not respond, also noticed Lance from the corner of her eye. She moved her purse, ensuring that he had room to sit comfortably next to her.

There was no dialogue among the three over the next several moments. It was not long before Milner, whose timing's often uncanny with his customers, stopped by their booth checking for refills.

He positioned himself to make eye contact only with Barbara, whose features reminded him of Olivia Brown of *Miami Vice* fame. She appeared as if she would pass her phone number on to him by telepathy if he was capable of receiving it.

"Would you like more sweet tea?"

"Please, thank you."

He also checked with Shonna on her tea and Lance with a refill of Coke before leaving. He'd taken a couple of strides toward the drink fountain before he thought of returning.

"Excuse me, but I know I've seen you here before," he asked Barbara. "I never forget my customers."

She chortled. "Well, I think you've mistaken me for another customer of yours. This is my first time coming here."

"Well, that makes it even special. How did you find out about us?"

Barbara glanced at Shonna, prompting him to look across at her.

"I should have known," he said. "But didn't you come here before with another attractive lady?"

"You don't allow anything to get past you, Mr. Milner. The other lady you're speaking of is my sister."

He shook his head emphatically. "Now this picture's becoming much clearer!"

Then he finally struck a conversation with Lance. "If my memory serves me correct, you've come here before with her?" He nodded over at Shonna.

"Yeah, once." He returned to his plate of broiled fish and steamed vegetables.

Right after Milner left, Lance looked up and started a conversation with his mother.

"Mom, I think I'd be watching out for that guy. He's trying to lay it on really thick with you."

"Can't you tell?" she said, chortling. "There's nothing wrong with a man having good taste."

"But he shouldn't try hitting on anyone's mother while her son's around. I've got something for him the next time he comes over here with that silly talk of his." He looked over his shoulder in the direction of the cashier's counter where Milner hung out.

Barbara reacted with raised eyebrows. "I can always come back here alone."

"All right, Mom. You're here visiting me!"

All three resumed eating once again. But Lance suddenly spoke up. "I should have done this before I went over to the buffet bar. Excuse me." He took off for the bathroom. He had been holding it all evening.

Barbara waited until Lance was beyond an earshot's distance before she resumed with Shonna. She leaned back against the cushion, shifting her weight.

"What does your mother think about you dating a twenty-eight-year-old man?"

Shonna placed her fork down. "Nothing. She won't even talk to me."

She felt as if she was being engulfed in searing flames of intense scrutiny, working its way from her feet to the tip of her head.

"Do you understand why?"

Shonna took a sip from her tea. "I'm sure she thinks I have no business with Lance."

"That's the first thing most people are going to think when they see you and Lance together—I know I was wondering what in the world you were doing with him when I saw you two back at the airport."

Barbara then lectured to Shonna that she had no intention on telling her what to do with her life, and that she'd never stand in the way of her children's choice in a relationship—within most realms of reasoning.

Pausing, she scanned the restaurant again for Lance and then for Milner. Then she returned her attention back to Shonna.

"If you can deal with all the circumstances that are against you, I wish you well, because you're going to need every bit of it." She sighed after making her comment.

"Thank you," Shonna answered. "My mantra has been taking it one day at a time."

Clasping her hands first, Barbara placed her chin atop them and proceeded staring at Shonna.

"Well, let me ask you this while I'm at it: Do you like my son?"

Shonna, who leaned forward slightly, did not flinch or take her eyes off Barbara.

"Yes, I do."

Barbara nodded again. "I see."

* * *

Twenty minutes had passed since Shonna left Lance's apartment returning to northeast Columbia.

Lance had already helped his mother store her luggage in his other bedroom. And he even made a special trip down to his car bringing his mother's purse back inside—at her request since she'd forgotten it.

The things a good son will do, he mumbled to himself.

Barbara joined Lance in the living room after changing out

of her pant suit into a sleep gown. They had not had a mother-son moment in more than a year. He had no doubt who would dominate the conversation.

"It appears to me you and Shonna got along well," he said. "I was hoping that would be the case."

"She says you two have been dating for almost a year." Barbara folded her arms and leaned against the sofa's back cushion. She also spoke rather dryly to him. "I didn't know you like 'em older."

She told Lance she tried dismissing him dating Shonna as a stage that many young men go through, but even she realized that was far from the truth. Being a widow for more than a decade, she then posed the question to him: How would he handle his own mother dating a man approximately the same age as he?

To this point, Lance had never heard any criticism about them dating. For that matter, he had few acquaintances in South Carolina, so it didn't matter. And he'd only shared bits and pieces of about Shonna with Derek Casey, a college classmate.

"I don't know what I'd do," he finally answered.

"I'll tell you what you'd probably do. You'd tell me to go find someone who was much closer to my age."

Lance partially hid his face from Barbara. He recalled to himself she seemed far more open to him dating Nayla Ramsey, whom he followed to South Carolina only to be stranded after she ran off with a childhood sweetheart of hers.

"Mom, I didn't go out looking for an older woman. In fact, I didn't really know she was in her forties when I met her. I thought maybe she was thirty-five at the youngest; thirty-seven or thirty-eight, tops," he said. "It sort of just happened."

"A lot of things just 'happen' and they turn out to be good. I don't think this is one of them."

Barbara began rocking back and forth in contemplation. She said the only the only concern she failed to voice with Shonna was in the event she became pregnant. At forty-four, the chances for complications during pregnancy would be greater as her child-bearing years waned.

Beyond that, raising a child would require energy that Shonna may find difficultly having.

"Mom, we're dating. You're talking as if we're getting married. That has never come up."

"Lance, it's obvious you see this only one way. But that's expected at your age. It's all good right now to you; she even thinks that way."

Barbara stopped rocking back and forth. She yawned and stretched. Then she scratched her head before sighing loudly.

"Let me ask you this. Do you like her?"

"Yeah, uh-huh. I like her."

"Lance, do you really like this woman?"

He hunched his shoulders. "Yeah. I like her."

Barbara resumed rocking back and forth, but giving him a side-eyed glare.

"I can't tell you who to date, Lance. But if you'd ask me, I think you could do much better," she said. "This woman will be fifty years old in a few years—about the same time women begin going through lots of changes."

He shrugged his shoulders.

"That's my point, Lance. You need to think about that. So does she."

She then told Lance that she planned on returning to Washington, D.C. a day earlier, and she had already text messaged Lauren advising her that she should cancel her trip to Columbia.

"All because you don't like who I'm dating?" Lance reacted; he got up and headed toward the kitchen. "You just think there's no woman out there good enough for me. She could be same age as me and a different race, and you'd probably still act the same!"

"Lance, as long as you're happy that's really what's important; it's not about me. But sometimes a mother can see things around the corner before her child. The last thing we want to see is our children running into those pitfalls.

"We would rather not see you experience the pain that comes with them."

She got up and followed him into the kitchen, taking a seat at the table; he didn't bother to join her. She conceded she hated hearing the adage when she was younger, but as she'd gotten older she found it to be quite true: "Experience is the best teacher. There's no other way around it."

Chapter 27

L ance and Shonna were in agreement that they were the ones penning the chapters of their lives. It didn't matter what others said about them.

The skepticism and cold shoulders by family members hadn't discouraged them. If anything, they felt it cemented their relationship.

"Do you really love this old hag you've been sleeping with?" Shonna joked with him before entering into a long, sensual tongue kiss.

After separating and wiping the sides of their mouths, Lance answered, "I sure do. So, do you really love the boy toy they say you've been sleeping with?"

"With all my heart!"

Void of drama, pomp and circumstance, Lance simply asked Shonna if she would marry him while she was lying atop of him in bed.

"Are you sure that's what you want? Are you sure I'm what

you want?" she queried, while looking herself over.

He returned a wide grin. "With all my heart."

"Then, yes, I do."

"Really?"

"Yes. I've never been so happy with a man as I have with you."

They were naked and without shame entering into another realm of commitment. After celebrating their decision beneath the sheets, Shonna decided she would share her news with an unlikely person.

She nuzzled up to Lance while she made the call to Sonia late that Sunday evening.

"Surprise, it's me!" The giddiness in her voice was unmistakable.

"This is a surprise," Sonia replied. "And how did I deserve this privilege?"

"I'm calling because you were the first person who came to mind."

Sonia brushed her hair back from her forehead. "I'm not sure how I should react—"

"Is this a good time to speak with you?" Shonna asked. "I figured since it was Sunday night that you might be in your usual time of deep meditation."

A remark like that might have triggered Sonia hurling a flurry of insults back at Shonna. This time, though, Sonia merely went along with it and told her anytime had been a good time lately.

She explained that she still had not reconciled with Trent, and she'd been staying at their parents' home for the past several weeks.

"Have you spoken to Taylor?"

"He doesn't want to talk. He's been upset about the whole thing."

Lance was in a playful mood, prompting Shonna to shoo his hand away from between her thighs. There was no time for foreplay or afterplay during this call.

"Remind me of what happened," Shonna asked.

Rather than giving her another blow-by-blow account, Sonia summarized that Taylor was the one who first discovered that she was involved with another man. And neither he nor Trent wanted her back in their home despite her having made two attempts at asking them to reconsider.

Sonia sighed into the phone. "I don't know what else to do. Lord knows I've repented and asked Him to forgive me."

"I'm sorry to hear that. I mean, I never thought you would have gone outside your marriage, anyway," Shonna said. "But I didn't call to be judging you."

"Thanks. It has been tough. It really has."

Sonia went on to share that she never knew there was so much she needed to work on with herself. "I always thought since people came to me with their problems that I had it together." She chortled at the thought. "That's been far from the truth."

"I'm sure everyone goes into a marriage hoping that things will work out beyond their wildest of dreams. I'm sure that's what Lance and I are hoping right now."

Sonia made a double-take. Then she interrupted Shonna in mid-sentence wanting clarification about what she heard. "Did you say you and Lance are thinking of getting married?"

Stunned was the softest of words to describe the way she felt. It was as if her legs had given out from under her.

Meanwhile, Shonna grinned after she'd sneaked a peck on Lance's lips.

"That's what you heard. We hadn't set a date, but I'm going to become Shonna Chandler-Miles."

"Wait a minute. Let me check something real quick," Sonia

said. She held her cell phone out in front her and read the date.

No, it was not the first of April; they were already into the month of May.

"Wow, both of you really clicked, didn't you? I guess congratulations should be the next thing I say."

She then asked Shonna if she had shared the news with their parents.

"No, you're the first I've shared it with."

"Has Lance told anyone?"

"Only a college classmate of his."

"Not his family?"

Shonna shook her head. She was careful to describe Lance's mother as a likeable woman, but she didn't care too much about them dating.

After smirking, Shonna added, "She visited us a few weeks ago, and she left earlier than expected."

"I wonder why—"

Lance squirmed around in bed next to Shonna after she shared that bit of news with Sonia. It was a topic both agreed not to discuss since her parents also shared the same sentiment.

After all these years, nonetheless, Shonna mused aloud that she felt proud to say she'd finally found love; there was no recipe for it.

"They say it might come once, maybe twice in a person's life," she said. "And it rarely comes a third or fourth time. There's no way of preparing for it. You just live and hope that it will come."

Sonia reminded Shonna about the day she shared the news with her after she accepted Trent's marriage proposal.

"It was so cute. He took me to dinner. After dinner, he drove me past the bank where we first met. We stopped by

Shekinah's since it was not far from that bank. And while we were there, he asked me to marry him.

"So, when did Lance ask you?" She held up her hand and stared at her wedding and engagement rings.

"Right here in my bedroom."

Sonia frowned into the phone. "I wouldn't say that's the most romantic of places."

"But it was. I promise you."

She followed with a long giggle. Then she turned to her side and wiggled her hips, inviting Lance to spoon up against her. She also reached back and brought his hand across so that he would cup her breasts.

After another five minutes of additional small talk, Shonna felt compelled to ask Sonia about the status of her relationship with the "male friend" that she would only describe to her the last time they spoke on the subject.

"You mean Wharton?"

"As in Wharton Milner?"

"Humph!"

Shonna, who jerked away from Lance and sat up in bed, was stuck between cursing Sonia out or hanging up. "That man has to be at least ten years older than you!"

"Eleven, almost twelve years." Sonia barely spoke above a whisper. "You don't have to tell me. I know I'm a hypocrite no matter what angle you view me from."

"You got that right!" Sonia said. "And would you believe we went by his restaurant when Lance's mother was here?"

Sonia said she had not seen Milner in more than a month. "You suddenly realize that all things that glitter aren't gold." She thought of his nice home and car and all his attentiveness.

"You know you really hurt me with the things you said about Lance and me," Shonna said. "And to think you fell for his weak lines, thinking he's still Mack Daddy? You should have seen how he tried hitting on Lance's mother.

"Humph, I bet he once wore a jerri curl back in the day . . . Girl, what was wrong with you?"

"Obviously, a lot of things. I'm sorry to say I did sleep with him. I'm sorry to have hurt you. Will you forgive me?" There was contriteness in her voice.

Seven times seventy came to mind with Shonna; that was just for starters, according to her teaching. Some things in life simply weren't fair, she hissed.

More so, it was important that Shonna knew someone other than her long-time friend Dana was an ally of hers entering this marriage.

She calmed herself to ask, "I need your help with something."

The moment was humbling to Sonia knowing that her sister accepting her apology.

"I know by the sound of your voice this doesn't sound like something pleasant. But what is it you need?"

"Prentiss Chandler will listen to you. I need you to talk with her about Lance and I getting married."

There was a long stretch of silence. Sonia peered over her shoulder in the direction of her parents' bedroom, giving thought to what she could possibly tell her mother.

"I'll do it, but I need to think about it. Can I get back with you?"

Chapter 28

Trent saw going to this deposition as an annoyance. Since it was not considered Palmetto Fidelity business, he received no reimbursement for mileage and parking.

To him, Cortez, whom he once called Bishop Moneymaker, was nothing more than a deposed womanizer who had a talent for making money. He had not spoken to Cortez since the day he was fired.

Humph.

Thirty years would be not be soon enough.

The deposition was held on the seventeenth floor of the Palmetto Fidelity building, one of the tallest in Columbia's sparse skyline. Upon exiting the elevator, he was hardly intimidated by Dutton & Winston Law Firm's glistening mahogany wood doors and cherry wood finished furniture, which to him was like entering into a movie scene.

"Good morning, you're here to see?" the receptionist asked.

"I'm supposed to give a deposition," Trent answered. "Mine is at eleven o'clock."

"Please have a seat. We will call for you once they're ready to have you."

Trent, who did not bother to prepare for the deposition, picked the Cambridge black leather lounge chair to sit in and wait his turn; he figured there was nothing really special to say. Just do what Amber Cohen told him: Answer the questions as truthfully as he possibly could.

When it was his turn to go back into the meeting room, Trent unknowingly walked past Neal Scanlan, the former generalist in human resources. Neither spoke to each other.

An attorney in an Armani suit wearing Hugo Boss loafers, and his hair slicked back greeted him as he entered. Trent was no slouch in the way he dressed, but shopping for suits at The Men's Warehouse and shoes at Sears was about as far as his budget allowed him.

"Trent, my name is Doyle Tharp. Please have a seat over there. We'll get started with this shortly."

Within minutes, a stenographer and videographer entered the room along with a second attorney, who wore a pin stripped power suit and Ferragamo loafers. Trent was quick to presume the other attorney was Cortez's; he was the one who'd be asking the questions.

"I'm Tim Duckett," he said. "Thank you for your cooperation in this case."

After being asked to state his name, Duckett reminded him that his deposition would be used in an arbitration hearing between Cortez and the bank.

Trent nodded and sat back in the swivel conference chair that made his office chair seem like a laminate desk from high school.

"How long have you been employed by Palmetto Fidelity?"

"Since 1999."

"How do you know Cortez Anderson?"

"I was his manager at our St. Andrews branch location."

"How long were you his manager?"

"From 2009 until last summer."

Trent was quick to assess these were the perfunctory questions. The tone of questioning shortly changed. They were still probing but increasingly specific.

"As his supervisor, did at any time you ever discipline Cortez Anderson?"

He shook his head. "Never."

"Did at any time another employee complain of him doing anything that was found offensive?"

"No."

"How familiar are you with the course of events that transpired last May twenty-five?"

Trent frowned slightly. The date had no apparent relevance to him.

"May twenty-fifth was the day that Deloria Lovett confronted Cortez on his job." Duckett leaned forward and checked off a couple of notes that he made. "Are you aware now of the date?"

"Yes."

Trent explained he was the one who instructed the security guard to contact the Lexington County sheriffs about an altercation inside the bank, and one of the principals involved had a gun. He also mentioned he instructed his staff to quietly adjourn to the employee's break room.

"At the time, were you aware of anything that Cortez did that day might have violated Palmetto Fidelity's policy, uh, I mean Code of Ethics?"

"No. My concern was for the safety of the employees under my supervision."

"So, you're telling me that it appeared to be a random occurrence?"

Trent nodded again. "Cortez was a loan officer who had clientele visiting him on a daily basis. There was nothing to suggest anything was abnormal—that was until the deceased customer threatened to shoot him with the gun she was carrying."

"I see."

Duckett leaned back in his chair and looked to his right at Tharp, who was taking notes of his own. Trent continued staring directly at Duckett.

"Have you ever feared reprisal for any decision you've made in the time you've been employed at Palmetto Fidelity?"

"No."

"Have you ever felt discriminated by your employer?"

"No."

"Have you ever been asked to do anything unethical by your employer?"

"No."

"Have you ever been told to instruct the employees you supervise to do anything you knew was unethical?"

"No."

Trent took a deep breath and looked around. This was unfolding like he thought it would—an absolute waste of his time.

Meanwhile, Duckett remained focused on his list of questions. He flipped through another page of notes. Then he looked up at Trent.

"Are you familiar with Palmetto Fidelity's Code of Ethics?"

Trent paused before answering. He recalled it being among several documents new employees were whizzed through when they're hired by the bank.

"We're given updates to the Code of Ethics on an annual

basis." He then shrugged his shoulders. "At least for me, I remind myself to use common sense in that if I have any doubts about anything that I'm doing, it might be something I shouldn't be doing. That is something I've also stressed to employees who work under me at the St. Andrews branch."

Duckett sensed an opportunity. His eyebrows were raised and he leaned forward once again.

"Approximately how many employees have you had to terminate for violating these codes of ethics?"

"Do you mean by me directly referring to it?"

Duckett hunched his shoulders as if to entice more from Trent. "Let's just say . . . Do you recall how many people you've had to terminate being a branch manager? And you say you've been a branch manager since, what, 2009?"

"That's correct." Trent then leaned back in his chair and stretched his legs. "To answer your question, I've terminated three employees, but they were all for different reasons: One was for being late too many times. Another was because an employee had too many shortages, a common reason for termination; the last employee was absent too many times."

"I see."

He was quick to come back with another question. "Did you ever sense Cortez pushed the limits ethically in keeping up with the demands of him doing business on behalf of the bank?"

"I can't say that I did. I mean, we get regular reports about the performance of loans. I can say overall that our branch has done quite well with a low default percentage."

"And what is considered a low default percentage?"

"Anything better than five percent."

"One last question, who's decision it was to terminate Cortez Anderson?"

Trent took extra time to form the right response. "I have

never been knowledgeable of whose decision it was letting go Cortez. All I know is that he spoke with our generalist on a couple of occasions. And the last time we spoke, he pretty much conceded that he was gone when he was asked to speak with the generalist a second time."

"Were you aware of any customer complaints against Cortez Anderson?"

Trent shrugged his shoulders. "No, I wasn't." He chose not elaborate on an unfounded complaint made by a customer who blamed Cortez for documents being mailed to the wrong address.

Duckett appeared to have asked all his questions. His face was flush from going at it continuously for more than forty-five minutes. The deposition that Trent gave was consistent with the eight other current and former Palmetto Fidelity employees that he'd already interviewed.

Nevertheless, he thanked Trent for his time and advised him not to divulge anything from the meeting to anyone.

The deposition was the last thing Trent wanted to recall, he thought to himself. He was more so concerned about Taylor's well being since he was in the final days of the school year.

Chapter 29

A week had passed since Shonna shared the news with Sonia, and she had yet to approach her mother. She'd already apologized to Shonna for not having given her any updates.

"You just don't know how much I've prayed about this," she told Shonna the night before.

Part of her dilemma was getting past herself. She still battled feelings of inadequacy since being estranged from Trent and Taylor.

"Well, Lance and I are going to look at engagement rings tomorrow," Shonna said. "I can't believe I'll actually put something on that finger!"

"Sis, you'll never be the same."

Humph.

Their mother might not be the same, either. But here went nothing. Prentiss had a routine of preparing toast and topping it with margarine and having hot tea with five teaspoons of sugar added to it. Then she'd commence to reading the newspaper—as if anyone did these days, Sonia mused. Even she recognized newspapers were merely a remnant of what they once were compared to less than two decades ago.

"Mom, everyone reads their news information online. They even read it from their cell phones or iPads. You need to get with the times!"

"You do what you're going to do. I'll do what I do." Prentiss blew into her cup and took a careful sip. Talking about being set in her ways, she had yet to warm up to text messages.

Sonia joined her mother at the kitchen table. Immediately, she thought back to when Trent earned major points with her. That came during a fourth of July weekend when he volunteered to cook dinner for her parents. She had never seen her mother eat anyone's cooking other than hers, but she ate Trent's—and even had seconds.

Trent scored a daily double that same day when Tillman led him out to his garage and showed him under the hood of his 1982 Ford F-150, which he still owned.

"Easy to work on. Everything's right there in front of you," he told Trent. "One of the best trucks they ever made."

Trent was no mechanical genius. But he knew how to watch, listen, and ask the right questions. It also helped that he got Tillman to talk more about himself.

If Lance might get past the handshake, which Sonia believed was possible, he might also earn Tillman's acceptance, and Shonna would be beside herself.

"Mama, do you recall what it was like being in love with Dad?"

Prentiss returned a long stare at her. "Are you trying to say that I'm too old to remember anything like that?"

"No, I'm not." Sonia leaned forward resting her chin atop her hand. "It was on my mind."

"Well, to answer your question, yes I do. Most women remember things like that. First kiss. First date." She ended the list on that thought.

"Why would you ask me that question?"

"I was thinking it seemed like yesterday that Trent and I came over and told you, grandma, and Dad about us being engaged." Sonia looked down and began fidgeting with her wedding and engagement rings. She then chortled at the thought.

"To this day, I still don't think you liked that Trent impressed you with his cooking."

"He just had a good day."

Sonia gave her a side-eyed stare while Prentiss returned to reading the newspaper.

"We pay $25 a month for this?" she hissed. "There was a time when reading a newspaper really meant something."

Sonia shook her head. "See, you can read most of the same stuff online for free."

"You don't say?"

"I'll show you, if you want me to show you."

"I might have to take you up on that, child."

Now if she could ascribe to another thing. Sonia shifted her weight in the chair.

"Mom, I asked you about what it was like being in love because Shonna's in love with Lance."

"Humph, that doesn't surprise me. She looked like she was in heat and her nose was wide open." Prentiss then bit into her toast.

"I don't know about all that, but what I do know is that she's also engaged to Lance."

Prentiss stopped chewing. About that time, Tillman came bounding into the kitchen."

"Chandler, you missed what I just heard!"

He looked back at both of them.

"Dad, good morning."

"Morning, lil' girl."

"Chandler, Sonia says your daughter's marrying that boy!"

"What daughter?"

"You only have two!"

"Shonna?"

Sonia nodded. "I'm told they're going to look for an engagement ring for her today."

Tillman looked first at Sonia then over at Prentiss. Then he ran his hand through his thinning mane of graying hair. "I didn't get a good look at him, but your mother says he's way too young for her."

"That ain't all I've said!"

He joined them at the table. "What do you know about him, Sonia?"

"I used to be his boss. I actually hired him."

"You what?" Prentiss reacted.

Sonia looked directly at Prentiss. "It's true. Shonna thought she would be surprising me when she introduced him. She was the one who was surprised when she learned that we already knew each other."

Prentiss tossed her teaspoon in her cup. She leaned back in her chair. "He still has no business asking her, but nothing surprises me. He should find someone closer to his age.

"Does he have any children? It seems like most of these young fellas already have children."

"None as far as I know and what Shonna knows."

Sonia figured she might as well play up Lance's strengths to her parents.

"Lance is a focused young man He's not a bad person to deal with. I can see why Shonna's in love with him."

"Humph, I won't say anything about that." Prentiss

squirmed in her chair while looking over at Tillman.

"I'm telling you, Mom. Women love him." She recalled to herself the callers who had asked about him after he left. Then there was Charlotte, of all people.

"Well, if she goes through with it, like I told both of you when you were teenagers, I'm not takin' care of nobody's kids. If you can have 'em, you can take care of 'em."

Tillman leaned forward upon his forearms at the table. He appeared to have heard enough of the cackling between wife and daughter.

"Prentiss, why don't you cool it with that talk. I may not agree with what she's doing, but she is forty-four years old. Don't you think she's lived long enough to know what she's doing?"

"You would say something like that, Tillman. Every time we go to the store you can't walk in a straight line for looking at another woman. You think that I don't be paying any attention—"

He jerked his head to his left. "Woman, what does that have to do with the tea in China?" He shook his head. "If someone doesn't agree with you, then you're ready to find fault in them."

He sat up in his chair. "Say what you want, Prentiss. Shonna is grown enough to make her own decisions. She's going to do what she wants, anyway; we don't have to agree with it."

She waved him off. "I don't want to hear it! It says we're supposed to ask for wisdom, which will be given liberally to us."

"All right. So you're sitting there with all that wisdom. Now what?" Tillman retorted, hunching his shoulders. He then left the kitchen and headed outside in the backyard inspecting the shrubbery that needed trimming.

Prentiss went off into another rant about her telling Shonna that she wouldn't speak to her until she knew what Lance's mother had to say about them dating.

"You'll then need to talk to her," Sonia interrupted her. "I remember her saying his mother came to visit them a few weeks ago."

"You don't say?"

"That's what she told me."

Prentiss announced that she had enough discussing anything about Shonna and Lance. So she aimed her scrutiny arrow at Sonia.

"When was the last time you've seen Taylor?"

"Last month. And he hasn't said much to me."

"Don't you think you've gone too long not seeing your own child?" she asked. "I don't get it."

Sonia glanced down at the table. "I agree." She did not want to divulge anything about him discovering her being seen with Milner.

"I know Taylor's really upset about the way things have been lately. That's really tough on a fourteen-year-old child. He's not yet ready to handle any interaction with his mother."

This was prime material for Prentiss. She relished in the notion of sharing the gospel to all who would listen—whether they wanted to or not.

Meanwhile, Sonia partially hid her face from her mother's view, bracing herself for the onslaught of righteousness. It took all of her not to roll her eyes derisively. That would be disrespectful to one of the persons who allowed her to live there at no charge.

"It speaks of blotting out one's transgressions and being purged with hyssop—"

"Yeah, I know, and a broken and contrite heart are not easily despised," Sonia interrupted her. "But you know what?"

"I understand now what it means to be told I'm not condemned and to sin no more. That's what I'm trying to live up to."

"Humph, I hope for your sake that's true."

Sonia did not bother commenting. Over the past several weeks, she'd come to understand she'd been as critical and cynical to others as her mother was toward her. It was a scary thing to acknowledge, and it was hardly attractive. But was she too far along—at age forty—to change?

Chapter 30

It was a work of mastery the way Tanya managed to weave answering the phones, placing her caller on hold, and describing another wacky episode from her personal life. She had seven years' experience perfecting her craft.

"Did I tell you what happened with Natroye and me over the weekend, Ms. Sonia?"

Sonia shook her head wondering how in the world she got suckered into another of these conversations. "What happened, Tanya?"

Three minutes passed before Tanya cycled through another call and continued with the details: Bad sex was the reason that Natroye Bivins and her parted ways after dating for three months.

Another phone rep, Kai Long, whose desk was in back of Tanya, craned her neck to hear how this interaction might unfold.

"I know we're at work, so I'll try and keep it clean."

"Please do," Kai instigated.

"The first couple of times, I thought maybe it was a matter of him being nervous. I mean, it takes a real man to properly handle all of this," Tanya said, looking herself over; she often complained that her breasts were too large and her backside wasn't big enough but she wouldn't trade either of them for the world.

"After each time, he told me that his problem might be the result of him getting out of a bad relationship with his ex-girlfriend. I went along with it and tried not making a big deal out of it. Things happen, you know? I figured we could talk and get to know each other even better."

She went on to describe things were just as bad on their third attempt. Natroye still struggled with achieving and maintaining an erection. It was extremely disappointing to her because she was really in the mood that night.

Natroye told her that he had no problems with his blood pressure or circulation, he was not on any medication, and he was reasonably fit; he also drank alcohol at extremely moderate levels and his job had mandatory random drug testing, so the latter was out of the question.

"How can you not make a big deal out of a man having a problem with, you know, getting up for you?" Kai said. "I thought all men want sex."

Tanya agreed with her on the latter. "You would think, huh?" She then looked over in Sonia's direction.

"Ms. Sonia, wasn't I right for telling him that maybe we should go our separate ways after giving him four chances?"

"Let me pose a question to you like this: What if you two were married? Would you leave him over that same issue?"

"I guess that's why I'm not married, because I want it all and I feel like I deserve to have it all," Tanya answered. "I'm sorry if that's being selfish."

The final straw was broken over the weekend, Tanya added, after they agreed on going to a pool party at a mutual friend's home in Irmo.

"You should have seen him in those cut-offs. Lawd, he made hell seem like the North Pole." She fanned herself at the memory. Her eyes also widened with incredulity as she described the way Natroye piqued her curiosity the moment he guided her hand inside his cut-offs while they were near the deep end of the pool.

"I was like [Betty White's character] Rose from *The Golden Girls* asking for the check, please! But when we got back to his place, it was like an ice cube in hell; it had no chance."

Kai butted into the conversation again. "You're a better woman than me. I don't think I would have given him as many chances to prove himself." She then returned to answering the call that dropped into her queue.

Tanya was quick to point out the difference between her and Kai was about fourteen years. She was thirty-seven with a fifteen year-old son; Kai was barely twenty-three years old and starting out in life.

Meanwhile, Sonia recounted to herself the frustrations she's had with Trent when it came to experiencing orgasms. But which was worse? A husband who failed at reaching his wife emotionally or a husband who could not sustain an erection? She mused that it was probably a coin flip.

"Did you ever think that he might not be attracted to you?" Sonia asked. "I mean, it does happen—"

Tanya frowned at the question.

"If he was never attracted to me, he should have told me rather than waste my time!" She lowered her voice to share her mantra being if there's no erection then there's no way of tapping into a woman's emotions, and her attraction for the man would quickly disappear.

It had been a while since Sonia felt comfortable offering sound wisdom to anyone, but the nature of their conversation and the moment seemed right to make that foray.

"I think it's difficult sometimes for a man or woman admitting to anything when it might offend the other person," she said. "But the problem is you're still hurting that person when you don't tell them anything."

"Well, he didn't hurt me if it were about him not being attracted to me, because it was his loss!" Tanya shimmied her shoulders and wiggled in her seat. "If I don't get what I'm looking for at that moment, I feel I've wasted my time. As for the man, well, tough on him!"

Another call dropped into Tanya's queue. Sonia took that as an escape opportunity from her cubicle before another phone rep approached her with another set of problems. She walked across the workplace to Karen Partridge's desk, checking on whether the department's requisition order for toner was fulfilled and had arrived.

With cartridges in hand, Sonia was on her way back to her cubicle when she passed by Phyllis, who was in an unusually talkative mood. She went as far as inviting Sonia into her office.

"I've wanted to chat with you for a while," Phyllis said, gesturing for Sonia to sit in the chair across from her desk.

The prevailing contract services staff sentiment about Phyllis was one of derision: Their boss was opportunistic, heartless, and lacking personality. But Sonia seemed to enjoy a rather favorable working relationship with her.

She last sat in Phyllis' office nearly nine months ago to discuss Lance's punishment for his role in the confrontation he had with Charlotte. She was surprised at the fairness of her decision, which took into consideration her lobbying on Lance's behalf.

"Are we looking at Saturday overtime?" Sonia asked. "I thought we've been doing well managing our backlog of inquiries."

Phyllis rubbed her forehead. "I didn't ask you to come in here for that. I would have sent you an e-mail." She then sat straight in her office chair, shifting back and forth in it.

Okay, no Saturday overtime.

"Has someone made a complaint with any of my phone reps?"

"Not this time." Phyllis followed with a weak chortle.

"I give up."

Phyllis leaned forward upon her elbows, which rested on her desk.

"Isn't your son named Taylor?" she asked.

"Yes, that's his name. He's in the ninth grade."

"I thought so. The reason why I asked you to come in here is because your son and my nephew are classmates."

What a coincidence, Sonia thought. *This is nothing more than small talk.*

Phyllis went into a discourse about her family being from the North Augusta area, a South Carolina city close to the Georgia border, and her having relatives who lived in Columbia. Some family members had moved to other places nearby North Augusta like Aiken, Barnwell, and Edgefield, while others were living in the Atlanta metropolitan area.

"I was at my oldest sister's home this past weekend—are you familiar with those large homes on Wescott right down the street from their school?"

"No I'm not. I've never driven back there." Sonia then hunched her shoulders, hoping that Phyllis would get to the point with her.

"Well, anyway, we were talking and she mentioned that Da'Mitri was suspended earlier this semester for getting into a fight with a boy named Taylor."

"You don't say?"

"Uh-huh. She told me that your son beat him up because he saw you in Sumter with another man."

Phyllis' expression changed from conversational to concerned—it dawned upon Sonia that was the day she arranged to leave early and visit Milner. Immediately, she began thinking that was leave time that she accrued. It didn't matter what she did with it since it was approved through the proper channels of communication.

". . . He said he'd seen you and your husband before, so he knew the man you were with was not your husband—"

Rather than feeling ashamed, Sonia was perturbed that Phyllis would take time out of their workday to divulge about her nephew who was beaten up by her son.

"And what you're getting at?" Sonia sat back in the chair and folded her arms.

Phyllis leaned forward again upon her elbows. "I was shocked that it involved you both directly and indirectly."

"Your nephew was wrong for posting things like that on his social network. And he didn't have to go around school harassing my son."

"I agree with you. And I'm sure you talked to your son that he shouldn't resort to fighting to solve everything at school."

She glanced down at her desk before looking up at Sonia. "I'm not even sure why I'm telling you all of this. But I've been there and done it as well—"

Sonia, who was unsure how to react, asked Phyllis for clarity.

"I've cheated on my husband, too. Maybe what I did wasn't put on blast." She shook her head in wonderment. "But it's been just as bad."

Phyllis volunteered to Sonia some of her exploits involved

both single and married men. The most outrageous tryst was meeting a married man one night in the parking lot of a church in a rural South Carolina town, and they had sex in his motor coach on church property. And on several occasions, she met another married man at his home where they had sex in the same bed he and his wife slept. She also went as far as having sex in public places, which she cared not to mention, in broad daylight and at night with various men outside her marriage.

There was no sudden rush of compassion or sympathy that Sonia felt toward Phyllis. Surely, she didn't find Phyllis any more courageous for making such an admission.

She made a quick scan of her office and spotted the portrait of Phyllis and her husband displayed prominently on a shelf over her left shoulder.

She smirked. Hard, in fact.

"You know what?" Sonia reacted. "That's really none of your god blasted business what I was doing. As long as it wasn't *your husband*, you shouldn't really concern yourself about me!"

Phyllis sighed. "I expected an answer like that from you."

There was a burning urge to bolt out of Phyllis' office, but the tenor of their conversation did not allow for it. A more tactful, graceful exit was needed.

With contempt in her voice, Sonia asked Phyllis about her motives for cheating. She then clutched onto the printer cartridges.

"My husband is a weak man. He has no backbone. He can't make a decision on his own, and he acts so needy. It makes you think there are three children in the house instead of two."

She snorted at the thought. "When he doesn't get his way, he tries to act like a dictator, which is laughable. My kids hate him, and I hate him. He's the type of person I'm ashamed of admitting that I'm married to him."

"Has he ever found out about you?"

She shook her head with a look of resignation much like the tone she used describing her husband. Her hazel colored eyes seemed to focus aimlessly beyond Sonia.

"It's been pure hell," she said. "Now he follows all of my moves."

Over the years, Phyllis said he's paid for a private investigator to provide him periodic reports of her whereabouts; he's monitored her cell phone calls; he's tracked her use on the computers at home; and he's even placed a tracking device on her car that he could monitor from his cell phone.

"He's even spied on me in the bathroom. He showed me the video of me having a moment to myself before I'd taken a shower."

"Why haven't you divorced him?"

Phyllis sighed loudly. "He knows I can't afford fighting him, and he'd take everything from me, including our kids. I'd never get to see them again."

A seemingly shameless and unremorseful cheating wife and a questionable husband hated by his family still had no resonance with Sonia. All that registered with her was having spent nearly fifteen minutes in Phyllis' office, and it now felt as if she'd been in there an hour and fifteen minutes.

At this point, Tanya's ranting and histrionics now seemed melodic and welcomed. Humph, she'd even gladly handle a call from Hassiba if it meant leaving Phyllis' office.

"I appreciate you bringing to my attention about there being consequences for our decisions; I better get back to my team," Sonia said.

She took a couple of steps toward the door but Phyllis implored her to wait a moment.

"I shared all that with you to remind you that nothing you do is really done in secret," Phyllis said. "If I can find out about you screwing around on your husband, you can imagine who else knows what you've been doing—"

Sonia shrugged her shoulders. She didn't really care who knew if she'd been with Milner.

For that reason, she resumed walking toward the door. But Phyllis insisted on stopping Sonia once more. Looking back, Sonia noticed that she was now sitting back in her chair with her arms folded.

"I can't tell you how you should live your life, but one thing I can tell you is to make sure that your son never puts another hand on my nephew," she said, tipping her head toward Sonia. "So consider what I'm saying as fair warning."

"Too flippin' bad," Sonia hissed back at her. "You tell your nephew to leave my son alone. And that's my fair warning to you!"

She grumbled at the notion Phyllis would bring up something that happened roughly two months ago. That was a case of pathetically poor timing and sour grapes being vicariously expressed by the victim's aunt. She was not even worth an invitation to kiss her butt. That would have been too much respect given to her.

Chapter 31

The invitation came by e-mail and postcard. Fogo de Janiero's grand opening in Myrtle Beach was Friday the twenty-fourth at 7 p.m. A reply was needed by the end of the day.

Trent had procrastinated long enough. It was 3:30 in the afternoon. He figured he'd use some of his clout with Alcione by calling her personally to confirm that he was attending the event. While he was at it, he might be able to gauge whether she was still serious about him making good on the favor that he owed her.

"I would be very disappointed if you were not coming," she told him.

He recognized the enticing tone in her voice, but he didn't consider it any stroke to his ego. If anything, he reasoned it may not be a bad idea getting out of Columbia for the evening. His life had been a repetitive cycle of work, home, Taylor's activities, work, Taylor's activities, and then back home.

"I'm actually looking forward to being there," he said.

Alcione said the restaurant's actual opening for business would be on Saturday. But the management had planned on making a big splash with its grand opening event.

More than nine hundred invitations were sent out, and they received about three hundred and eighty-five replies as of Trent's call to her; they considered their forty-five percent response rate more than encouraging. Some of the expected guests include local and state politicians, the U.S. congressional representative for Myrtle Beach and surrounding areas, the local four-year university president along with faculty and several board of trustee members, the local media, and prominent local business people.

Recently, their South Florida location received a prestigious four-star review from a nationally recognized critic based in Miami, lauding the food as unique, inventive, generously served, and unquestionably authentic Brazilian cuisine. The management had already incorporated it in their Internet, social media, radio and cable television promotions. For her part, Alcione secured a commitment from international star Aña Carvalho Malhieros, a high school classmate of hers as the guest performer; they also planned on sending clips from her live set to Univision for added promotions. And with the weather expected to be in the mid-eighties, it was ideal conditions for a successful effort.

"You should know I don't like to talk a lot about business. What are you doing tonight?" she asked.

Trent initially balked at answering. He didn't have Sonia as an excuse.

"I don't have anything planned."

"Mmmm . . . You are not worried about getting in trouble with your wife?"

Alcione had long since decided that she would handle Sonia much differently if she encountered her again.

"My wife and I are separated."

"I am not sorry to hear that," she said. "Your wife did not seem to be a reasonable woman."

Trent grimaced. He recognized there appeared to be no true way out of this favor that he owed her.

"We're just separated. I have not decided if I want to file for a divorce."

"Do you still love her?"

"I can't say that I do. But it's not as if I hate her. We've had our problems, and maybe this is the best way of handling them."

For a moment, Trent's words never registered with Alcioine. Her mind had wandered back to last year when they first met at the St. Andrews branch. It stunned her that she had such an instant attraction for him. She regretted having met Cortez so soon, but his sensational affair with Deloria Lovett created a convenient reason for her to dump him. Trent's smooth, simple delivery and unmistakable athletic appearance was a bonus. His large hands were strong and reassuring.

Fogo de Janiero was poised to commit to a more advantageous proposal offered by a larger bank last summer. But Alcione took it upon herself by inviting Trent for dinner, claiming that her family's business wanted to go with Palmetto Fidelity as its financier of their expansion projects.

Although Trent was under the impression it was a done business deal after their dinner date, Alcione spent the rest of the night begging and pleading with her parents to override plans and dictate to upper management and investors their new plans, which now involved Palmetto Fidelity.

Alcione took as big of a gamble as Trent. Now, she was determined to get more of a return on her investment.

"I see so much potential in you, Trent. All you need is the right situation."

Trent's brow furrowed and he darted his eyes left and right. "My marriage aside, I'd like to think I'm already in a pretty good situation."

"I believe it could be better."

"How?"

"By knowing the right people."

She had a point. He's had his sights set on upward advancement in the corporate world—there was nothing wrong with that career path.

"I agree that we all need the right people in our lives and careers," he said. "I also think that we need to constantly reassess who means us well and who doesn't."

That was American gibberish she was willing to ignore. She still felt there was an upside to drawing Trent into her lair.

"Have you thought that maybe it was meant that you and I meet each other?" she asked.

Trent felt something grab him in the gut. "I never thought of it that way."

"Why don't you give that some thought. I would love to continue this conversation."

Before hanging up, Alcione also told Trent in no uncertain terms that he was more than welcome to come visit her home in Lexington County. All he had to do was call ahead and let her know that he was on his way.

Chapter 32

Cortez could not resist laughing at the memory while turning into his driveway. A pale-faced reporter with makeup caked on her face confronting him about rumors that went viral over the Internet. And a large-framed man who could have benefitted by losing forty pounds huffing and puffing to keep up with her.

It was people like them that cost him his job at Palmetto Fidelity, but now he was making more money at Midlands Ford than he did at the bank. Some were in awe at the way he was able to get car deals financed when it seemed they were hopeless. And the women loved him.

It was risky venture charming some of the female buyers who were already lured to the dealership by the salesmen. He didn't care at all. Most of them were predatory habitual liars, cheats and losers who prostituted themselves on asphalt. They deserved their twisted fate.

He let out a loud yawn at his mailbox. Then he looked back

at his home. He realized the long hours had prevented him from taking care of some things. The roof gutters needed cleaning and debris removed from up there. The grass had finally turned green thanks to several inches of spring rain during the month. He would need to get in contact with Nathan Royster, who did his yard work.

Inside his home, a three-bedroom and two-bathroom dwelling with vaulted ceilings, the sofa had been transformed into a drop-off point for clothes, ties, socks, his briefcase, and junk mail. The walnut finished dining room table became his work desk for his mortgage brokerage side venture. With the economy showing sustained signs of improvement, he might be on the ground floor of a financial sector making a rebound.

Bishop Moneymaker was making a nice comeback, and it had a nice sound to it.

An envelope from Stabler & Hewitt Associates was in his tidy stack of mail. They were the arbitrators in his case against Palmetto Fidelity. He took a deep breath while he dug his finger under the flap and ripped it.

It wasn't about the $500,000 he sought in damages for being wrongfully terminated. He sued in protest to being a piece used by the bank to placate an angry bank customer who was paid three quarters of a million in hush money.

"*Dear Mr. Anderson,*" he began reading to himself, "*in pursuant to your employment agreement with Palmetto Fidelity, this case was brought before an arbitrator for an impartial resolution ...*

"*In consideration of the facts presented, we side with Palmetto Fidelity since the legal test necessary to prove wrongful termination was not satisfied ....*"

Cortez's eyes bulged. He felt as if something stabbed him in the gut. A case that was methodically presented with logically supported facts failed to meet a freakin' legal test?

What a joke!

He brought his hand up to his chin and stared blankly at the bare off-white dining room wall for several moments. He couldn't even put together a string of expletives that was fitting for the decision.

Phooey!

It was more like eff'em!

He tossed the letter aside. Then after tapping on his computer keyboard, he looked over his left shoulder recalling where he'd tossed his cell phone. It was on the khaki upholstered sofa with warm tones in a pile of clothing.

He reminded himself while he scrolled through his contacts even the great apostle's arguments fell upon deaf ears when defending the gospel before prominent rulers. What he encountered was merely an opinion.

Can you talk? I really need to talk to someone.

Ms. Wanda was in another part of her home when she recognized the text message on her phone.

What's wrong? Give me a few minutes.

Without any regard for her husband who was asleep, Ms. Wanda left her house and took off driving her maroon Mazda CX-7 around in her neighborhood. The urgency of Cortez's text was why she did it.

"Are you all right?" she inquired. "It's not like you to contact me this time of the night. You know the rules—"

"Yeah, I know 'em. That's why I first asked you if you could talk."

"This better be good now that you've gotten me out of my house, or I'm hanging up and going back."

"Why do you have to be so witchy with me? You lose a little

weight and rediscover being freaky again, and you think that you're all that and a bag of chips. Humph!"

"Keep on, Cortez. I don't have to put up with your jive."

Cortez smirked at their dialogue. At least she still acted as if she still had a need for him, although he now regarded her as merely a senior member of his replenished harem.

"I wanted to talk to you because I got the arbitrator's decision."

Ms. Wanda turned into an apartment complex that was four blocks from her neighborhood so she would not be distracted while driving.

"What did they have to say?"

"What do you think?"

"Uh, why don't you tell me?"

"They sided with the bank. They said I my complaint didn't meet the legal definition for wrongful termination."

The letter spelled out that his rights were not violated. There was no retaliation or reprisals made by Palmetto Fidelity. He was not coerced into doing anything that was unethical, and he was not fired for it. There was no discrimination. And there was no breach of any agreement between him and the bank.

After considering what was said, Ms. Wanda turned the engine off and reclined back in her dark charcoal cloth seat. She figured she might as well be comfortable once she shared what was really on her mind.

"I know we didn't talk about it much after Trent and Scanlan came in for their depositions. Did you really expect you had a chance to win, if that was what you had to prove?"

Cortez was dismissive of that reality. "My attorney told me going in that lawsuits are always fifty-fifty. I understood that, and I felt it was worth taking that chance."

Ms. Wanda had mixed emotions. She was glad a decision

was made. Maybe Cortez would find something else to do with his time. Along those lines, she was mildly disappointed that she would not get a cut of any settlement money. Now she wondered whether he would actually go through with defrauding the bank and give her a portion of the money to help fund her retirement. He'd already promised her so much while making pillow talk that it all sounded the same.

"I actually prayed for you," she said. "But I only prayed that His will would be done. I can't say that I ever felt any peace or confirmation about any of this."

Cortez despised what he dubbed as bandwagon prayer warriors; they were never sincere. "You could have kept that to yourself."

"Did you ever think that you had any righteous cause behind what you were doing? You were trying to blame them for the mess that you created."

He got up and began pacing from the dining room into the kitchen and back.

"Wanda, I really don't care what you have to say. People sue people all the time. This is a litigious world we live in. You sling something against the wall, and you hope that it sticks."

"I guess that's the difference between you and me," she said. "First of all, I wouldn't have jeopardized my job by having all those women come see me."

She had to go there, didn't she?

It bothered him that she was hardly any help while he prepared for his arbitration case. All that he got from her was warmed-over information that he'd already figured out for himself along with some kinky thrills whose memories were already distorted by time.

"See, that's where I have a problem with people like you," he said. "As long as I made the bank money, and there was nothing over the Internet about it, everything was fine."

Ms. Wanda disagreed with him. "You don't realize how many people had a problem with what you were doing."

"And I suppose you were one of them?"

She sucked her teeth after starting her vehicle. Then she began backing out of the space where she parked.

"Oh, I see. In other words, you were jealous—"

"Why would I be jealous over a whore-chasing heathen like you?"

Cortez was moved to laughter. He took a few extra moments to collect his thoughts.

"You've got some nerve, hypocrite!" he retorted. "You know what? I'm tired of arguing with you all the time. It's been real, Wanda."

She mimicked his laughter in retaliation.

"Hey, it's no skin off my back. Freely come, freely go. That's what I live by—"

The feeling was mutual—somewhat. Cortez countered, "It doesn't matter. You're still a hypocrite; I'm out!" He was quick to hang up on her.

Chapter 33

All this wedding talk had Shonna thinking differently. It was no longer about herself only. She had a fiancé to consider. Lance was her present and future.

Admittedly, Shonna also needed help. Sonia was her best and closest asset.

"I really didn't pay any attention to the things you did when you and Trent got married," she said. "Marriage was the farthest thing from my mind."

Sonia chortled "I know. You also didn't appear all that comfortable standing up there as my matron of honor." She reminded Shonna about her constantly scanned the church for an exit door that day.

"Hey, I had to go to the bathroom. And I'm sticking by that story, thank you!"

Sonia could tell Shonna was still giddy about being engaged. Most thoughts expressed included some reference to Lance. Everything was a cute or sweet experience, including their search for her engagement ring and their wedding rings.

They went to three locations in the Columbia area. The first store was Lawson's in the Village at Sandhills. They had a ring that she liked, but . . .

"Lance and I saw this ring for nine hundred, right? I mean, I've waited all these years to put one on my hand, but I've never thought [that] I needed to break the bank just to say I had one," she said. "So, we asked the man about the diamond that supposed to go in it. He told us that we had to pay for it separately. Then he showed us a couple of stones that cost about two grand each."

Shonna said she couldn't leave Lawson's fast enough. Both laughed at each other once they were in the parking lot.

"Hey, I've never owned a ring of any kind," he told her. She replied, "So I guess I know about as much as you?"

The next store they visited was Boulware Diamonds in the Harbison area. They had a good reputation for its selection at reasonable prices. The problem, however, was nobody in the store wanted to help them.

"We stood there at the counter for, like, fifteen minutes. Three couples came in after us and the people who worked there went out of their way to help them."

"And you said this happened over in Harbison? That sounds like something maybe our parents would have gone through. This is 2013," Sonia reacted. "How did Lance handle it?"

"He was furious. Eventually, he approached someone and he gave him some choice words before he stormed out of the store," Shonna said. "They looked really stupid once they realized they lost a buying customer, but it was too late. I guess they didn't think a young fella like him had money *and* credit.

"Humph, they must have thought he came in wanting to buy used jewelry or hock some for money. Oh, well . . . I don't recall them having any advertisements with any of the sister stations. But if they ever approach us wanting to buy some air time, guess what's going to happen?"

So, they went over to the Columbiana Mall. Both were on edge after Boulware Diamonds. They walked into three stores, taking cursory glances in each of them, and kept walking to the next. It was the fourth store they entered—Zindler's— nearby the food court where they felt comfortable with the store's selection and most importantly, the salespeople.

"It was really cute what happened in there," Shonna recalled. "One thing I've always liked about Lance is his decisiveness. But even this one took the cake."

Shonna described them having approached a counter and Lance suggested a ring set to her. "I told him I wasn't really feeling any of them. He shrugged his shoulders and we kept looking."

This went on for another forty-five minutes until Lance became impatient with her. "He's a typical guy. You know they hate shopping with us women after a while."

"You don't have to tell me, sis. I can tell you a few stories about Trent."

"Well, we went back to the first counter and I spotted this gorgeous one-carat cluster that had both the engagement and wedding rings. I pointed it out to Lance; he rolled his eyes and looked at me like I'd spilled food on myself."

"Why?"

"You know Lance has that sexy, deep voice. He mumbled to me that he'd shown me that same ring about an hour ago when we first came into the store."

"Didn't you tell him that it was all a part of the shopping experience?" Sonia asked.

"Well, not really. I told him that it just took me a while to make up my mind."

Shonna went on to casually mention that Milner contacted

the station about coordinating a remote broadcast at The Groovy Soul. He wanted it to coincide with the restaurant's second anniversary.

"I was only listening in on the conversation. I had nothing to say either way," she said. "Hey, when was the last time you last talked to him?"

Sonia recalled him broaching that subject to her several months ago, so she was not surprised that he finally gotten around to calling WNPW. But any mentioning of him was uncomfortable at best.

The last time she saw Milner was the same week she ditched her Tracfone. On what was a cool, breezy Thursday night, she felt lonely, bummed out, and she was having second thoughts. She had convinced herself that maybe she was better suited with someone like him. So, she drove by The Groovy Soul with intentions of making an impassioned appeal to him.

When she turned into the parking lot, however, she saw Milner from a distance escorting a woman, whom she figured to be in her mid- to late thirties, out to her car. Once there, they stopped, hugged and kissed each other.

Sonia was speechless. Instead of confronting him or even driving past them, she turned around and went back to her parents' home. The mere sight of him doing that was enough of a wake-up call to forget about him once and for all.

"It's been a while," she said, sighing. "Can we talk about something else?"

"Sure."

Shonna then mentioned that she'd already come up with ideas about who and what she wanted in her wedding. Starting with Sonia, she wanted her to be her matron of honor. She wanted Tillman to give her away. And she wanted Taylor serving as an usher.

"Do you think you can get Taylor to be in it?" she asked. "And to think I haven't seen my only nephew in over a year. I can't believe it's been that long. We live in the same city."

Inhaling deeply through her nostrils, Sonia told her that she would have to contact Trent. Each of her previous attempts were contentious.

"What's the latest with you two, anyway?" Shonna inquired.

"There's nothing to say. I can't really blame him. I'm sure I'd be the same way with him. In fact, I had filed for divorce last summer."

"You never told me you did that?"

Sonia mentioned it happened shortly before they stopped speaking to each other—another uncomfortable item for discussion.

"The only thing that saved Trent's hide was him getting that foreign hussy whose family owns restaurants in this country to fly here to Columbia and speak with me."

"Wow. That's deep."

Sonia closed her eyes. She still envisioned Alcione, in her matching beige Garbardine pant suit, sitting at the table across from her in Fogo de Janiero. Her heart rate increased rapidly. Her temple pulsated. And she felt rage welling up within her recalling Alcione's heavy accent.

Although she'd forgiven Alcione—and Trent, for that matter—the memory was too fresh to forget anything from that meeting.

She hissed. "Can we talk about something else?"

"What's with you?" Shonna reacted. "You're about as bad as that football player's agent who kept repeating 'next question' every time he was asked one."

Shonna was determined to pry something out of Sonia just to say that she did it during this conversation.

"Well, can you answer this: Do you miss Trent?"

There was silence between them.

Initially, Sonia dropped her head and brought the heel of her hand up to her forehead. She then looked out of the driver's side and passenger windows of her car. There was nothing that piqued her attention in the Food Lion parking lot not far from her parents' home.

"I do. I think about it sometimes," she finally answered. "I also think it's not fair that I'm in this mess. I made one poor decision."

Sonia hissed again. "Can we talk about something else?"

"Here we go again!"

They both laughed.

* * *

This was a call that Sonia cringed to make, but what other choice she had? Until things changed legally, she felt as his wife she had every right to call Trent, and more so as Taylor's mother.

It all seemed odd that she would be calling Trent on a Saturday morning, considering this was the time of day once set aside for interacting with Milner. She would go to the nearest Dunkin Donuts just to call him.

The phone rang only twice. Sonia took a deep breath.

"This is Trent—"

"Hi, Trent." She hoped that he wouldn't hang up on her.

"Sonia?"

"Yes, it's me."

"How have you been doing? I talked with Shonna yesterday, and she asked about you."

"That's nice."

Trent seemed to welcome hearing from her. His relationship with Shonna was always cordial. They actually played well as domino partners whenever the Buckners hosted gatherings at their home in Chapin. Their success made Sonia jealous because it should have flourished for her when Trent was her partner; it never did. So they agreed it was best they didn't play as partners.

"Listen, Trent, the reason why I'm calling you is about Shonna, anyway; she's getting married."

"Really? Now that's news."

"I know. And she's marrying Lance. You remember him?"

"Who can forget? Isn't she much older than him?"

Did he just have to bring that up? Time and circumstance had already forced Sonia to change her attitude toward Shonna and Lance.

"Yes, she is by sixteen years. But they're happy; they're very much in love with each other. There's no other way I can explain it."

He shrugged his shoulders. "Well, tell Shonna congratulations the next time you speak with her."

The apprehension between them was heavy as fog settling onto the city at night. Neither saw it fit to relent from the positions they'd held over the past two months.

Sonia felt that Trent should let his guard down and be conciliatory; he felt she should pull her head out of the sand and recognize she needed to apologize and ask him for forgiveness.

They attempted to speak simultaneously.

"No, you go ahead," they both said.

Sonia managed a weak chortle before proceeding. "Shonna also wants Taylor to be in her wedding."

Raising his eyebrows, Trent leaned back in the leather surfaced office chair that he recently bought, replacing the old one he previously kept for a decade.

"Why don't you ask him if he wants to do it?"

He paused then yelled out Taylor's name.

"Sir?"

"Come here!"

Trent mentioned to Sonia while waiting that Taylor seemed to be getting his act together once again. His grades had improved significantly since she last saw him, and he's not been as prone to outbursts of anger—he took credit for providing a steady, guiding hand and structure.

Sonia swallowed hard and remained silent. "I'm glad to hear that. Lord knows I'm really glad. It's a mother's prayer being answered."

Taylor appeared in the work office with Trent. "You called me?"

"Yeah. Your mother wants to speak with you." Trent handed him his cell phone.

Taylor hunched his shoulders and darted his eyes in one direction. Then he greeted Sonia.

"Hey, baby!"

"Mom, I'm not a baby."

Sonia still was overjoyed to hear him. Now if she could only be there. She also hoped that her son's heart toward her would soften. Maybe Trent would go as far as putting his foot down and declare that she was returning home whether he liked it or not.

"I know you're not one. But you're still my baby. You'll always be. No matter how old you are or how tall you get." She wiped a tear away.

"Why you want to speak with me?"

Sonia took a quick breath, composing herself. "Your aunt Shonna is getting married, and she wants you in her wedding. Would you be interested?"

"Sure, why not?"

"Okay. Good. She wants you to be an usher. You'll be escorting the ladies down the aisle to their seats. I'll get back with you once the date's been set. "

"Does that mean I have to wear one of those silly tuxes?"

"Yes, you have to wear one of those silly tuxes."

"Okay, I guess I can deal with it for one day."

"Thanks."

"Here's Dad—"

Sonia looked upward and smiled. Then she nodded her head. Trent was right. He did sound as if he was more stable emotionally. But she sensed things were still far too delicate to declare any definitive victories. It was more like taking a step forward—progress in its smallest of measurements.

"Do you remember when Taylor was our ring bearer?" she asked Trent.

"That was just a few years ago." He recalled it took bribing Taylor with an entire set of Transformers toys before he agreed.

"I'm about to get off the phone, Trent. I just want to know if you've thought about filing for divorce?"

Trent stared aimlessly off to his left. His wood finished bookcase had four shelves. The top two were full with Taylor's trophies from participating in team sports along with various track and field medals that Trent himself earned during his career as a sprinter. The bottom two levels had a mixture of pictures and books.

"I can't say that I have," he answered. "But you'll know once I decide."

What was she to say?

For all she knew, he could be lying; his petition for divorce could be in Monday's mail.

"Taylor needs both his parents," she said, adding a sigh to dramatize her point. "I think we need to work out some kind of visiting schedule."

"You do need to see him," Trent replied. "Text me what you propose as a visiting schedule next week."

At least this call was civil. Neither of them raised their voices or cursed at each other.

"Trent, take care of yourself. I'll give you more details about Sonia's wedding as she gives them to me."

"Sure. Bye."

She allowed him to hang up on her, but she sensed there was some hesitation on his part. Maybe only prayer could change things—it was all that she had.

Chapter 34

Trent was unsure how he would be received by Alcione since he never took up on coming by her house. All he had to do was show up and make it happen, setting in motion something that could be life changing.

When he tried calling her during the week, it was like playing phone tag. He'd leave her a message. She'd leave him a message. But they kept trying all the way until Thursday morning.

"I couldn't get away like I wanted," he explained to her. "And then when I could get away, I couldn't catch up with you."

"Don't worry about it, Trent," she assured him. "I am looking forward to seeing you tomorrow."

Alcione told him it probably worked out for the best because she'd been in Myrtle Beach since Tuesday morning to oversee final preparations for the grand opening. That included meeting her parents, co-founders of Fogo de Janiero, as well as her school classmate Aña Carvalho Malhieros and her band at the airport.

"They came in on separate flights," she said. "It has been very crazy this week. But tomorrow will be the easy part; I also get to see you."

"Well, seeing you will probably be the best part of my day, for sure."

Trent said he anticipated arriving in Myrtle Beach around six in the evening.

"Can you come earlier?" she asked.

"Why would I need to come earlier?"

She was coy with her response. "Are you not a man of your word?"

"Meaning?"

"You owe me."

"Oh. Yeah. I do owe you," he said. "What time were you thinking?"

"How about three o'clock?" she answered. "I get to see you before the grand opening and you can put your things away in the hotel room."

"Hotel room?"

"You're staying with me for the night. That is part of our agreement."

Even so, he'd already anticipated bringing a change of clothes; the carnality in him was curious of what it would be like with her.

Had this occurred maybe seven years ago, he would have already reserved a room. Then he would have come up with a scheme about attending a company training program in the afternoon, and that he'd be spending the night instead of driving back that same day. If there were any issues with Sonia, he would have dealt with them once he returned to Columbia.

"I know you Brazilians know how to throw a good party," he said. "I guess I'm about to find out first hand what it's like."

Alcione licked her lips, smiled, and began twirling locks of her long, thick curly hair through her fingers. "That is true. We do."

* * *

Alcione huffed in annoyance. Another call had come in on her cell phone. It had been like that since she woke up at seven in the morning.

"*Olá!*"

"*Este é Alcione—*"

While most things had gone smoothly leading up to the evening's grand opening event, Alcione had not had much time to herself until now while she waited for Trent's arrival at the Embassy Suites Resort in the Kingston Plantation.

She felt she had every reason to think that they would get along well. He shouldn't have to concern himself about looking over his shoulder since there was no wife in the picture. All he had to do was represent himself well both publicly and privately. There were many options that awaited him.

"I don't speak Portuguese," Trent blared into her ear. "You're going to have to teach it to me!"

Her eyes lit up. The anticipation increased with each heart beat.

"Where are you?"

"According to my GPS, I'm less than a couple of minutes away."

"I am waiting in the hotel lobby. I can't wait to see you, Trent."

"I'm about to turn into the complex now. Look for me getting out of a metallic blue Acura sedan in the parking lot."

Whatever Trent drove was the least of her concern. What mattered most was him showing up since it had been a relatively stagnant year in her social life. Telling her parents, Nelson and Tassia Amaral de Oliveria, that she had an American friend who would be her date at the grand opening rekindled her confidence—and possibly more.

Before leaving Brazil, her main go-to guy João Aznar got engaged to an up-and-coming model Maria Bertrami rather than maintaining a semi-annual relationship with her.

Another option, Gilberto Rioz Conti, a spoiled playboy who wanted things on his own terms, also went his separate ways. He did not like that Alcione played the same game as him by openly exploring her own male options as he did with women.

It also didn't help that her parents were prodding her to get married since she was now thirty-five. They even went as far as playing the role of matchmaker. They arranged for her to meet Marcos Dias do Nasciemento, who was the son of telecommunications magnate Carlos Antonio do Nascimento; a business partner based in Rio de Janiero.

That didn't work, either. Marcos was too passive and clingy, and he lacked ambition. Those were not traits she preferred in her men. She then told her parents that she would do things on her own terms.

She gave herself once-over a final time while waiting in the hotel's restaurant. The navy lace overlay dress by Eliza J was not what she planned on wearing to the grand opening, but it should serve well as a reminder to Trent what he passed up on last summer.

Then she looked up. Trent was walking in her direction. He wore charcoal slacks and a white Polo shirt with a Palmetto Fidelity logo over the pocket, and it was succulent to the eye. His V-shape upper body, muscular shoulders, and thick thighs that filled his slacks triggered a sensual feeling between her thighs.

"You're here!" she said, standing up and holding her arms out for him.

She moaned into his ear as she felt their bodies press together. "We're going to have a good time today. I know we will."

"It's nice to see you again," he whispered to her; he also inhaled a deep sample of her fragrance.

"Is that Sun Moon Stars?"

She gave him a broad grin as she separated. "Beyoncé Heat." Then she cast an alluring stare at him, adding a growl.

"Come, let's go up to our room."

If this is evil, I don't want to be delivered, Trent thought while they rode the elevator up to the eighteenth floor. He glanced over at her repeatedly. Tall. Well put together. Refined. Affluent. Not to mention, he was already well aware of her having freak tendencies. Adding the Brazilian element to the equation made him feel as if life had presented him an enviable twist of fate. Not every man could brag of meeting a woman like Alcione.

Maybe she was right after all. We were meant to be together.

* * *

Alcione handed Trent the card key after exiting the elevator.

"We're in No. 1812. It's to the right."

He looked to his left at her. "I'll need to get my bag at some point."

"Don't worry about that right now."

Trent walked carefully toward the end of the corridor, turning right as indicated. The room was the first door also on their right.

After the door clicked open, Alcione was the first to enter. She went over by the suite balcony window and drew the curtains back. She peered out at the ocean and then down at the beach. The dunes and tan sand and the hotels that lined the shore reminded her of home, although Myrtle Beach itself would have compared to lesser known beaches.

Trent walked quietly across the suite and stood behind her. Their attraction for each other was just as strong as it was a year ago. She turned around and clasped her arms on his shoulders. Then she leaned forward and pressed her soft lips to his.

Both closed their eyes, filling their minds with lustful imaginations; the hotel suite itself was filed with their kisses and moans.

"I am in so much need, Trent," she said, upon them separating briefly.

Trent was incredulous. He saw himself as a neglected husband before his estrangement, and having deprived himself since then. His instincts took over, allowing his hands to roam down her spine and settling on her backside. He gave her buttocks a firm squeeze—they felt so full.

Mmmph!

And to think all this had been at his beckoning. Shame on him for not checking it out last time.

Alcione, looking up slightly at Trent, placed her hand behind his head, and pulled him closer so that she pushed her tongue inside his mouth. He sucked it soft then hard while she gave him all he could accept. Then he reciprocated with her. She was more than eager taking his inside her mouth, starting softly then sucking it so hard that she could have triggered his gag reflex.

They paused again for air. Both had a look of relief. Any

doubts about this connection being worth their while was answered.

"I never thought I would want another woman. That was until I met you," he said. "You are the total package."

Alcione was not familiar with the term, but she sensed it was all good.

"I don't care that you are still married," she said. "*O que é suposto ser destina-se a*—what is meant to be is meant to be; I believe that."

They hugged and kissed again.

Meanwhile, Trent considered his options: Sit down and talk or simply go with the flow. But if he talked, it might be perceived as being conditioned by his married life with Sonia; she'd imposed that so many times whenever he tried initiating any bedroom activity with her. If he went along with removing her clothes, which was his true inclination, he'd be gambling on not getting to know the person for whom he had this strong attraction.

He opted for the latter.

In his next motion, he slid down her thong piece and acquainted himself with the arousal between her thighs. He wasn't the only one who gasped.

She did not swat his hand or jerk her body away. She enhanced the moment by gyrating her hips to his touch. She even widened her stance to accommodate him inserting his middle finger.

Suddenly, she tensed and shuddered.

"What's wrong?" he asked.

"It feels so good."

"Mmmm."

He teased her by tasting his finger before kissing her. Then he inserted his finger again, withdrew it, and offered her a sample; they both sucked from the same finger.

"I want you inside me, Trent. Right here."

Alcione's accent was mesmerizing and intoxicating. And at the rate things were going, he might as well add addicting. He didn't care that he was at the cusp of venturing beyond the point of no return, and that his conscience would forever be etched by this moment.

Without any urging, he dropped to his knees and proceeded pushing his tongue between her outer folds. After shutting her eyes tight, she nudged him with lateral movements, ensuring that he was properly positioned in front of her. She was quick to gyrate her hips to his tongue flicks and then work them back and forth to his prodding.

"Oh, deus... Sim, sim!"

"Eu não sei se posso segurá-lo por mais tempo..."

Trent did not need any translator to understand Alcione's reaction. His timing with her was uncanny. Their movements were also complementary and effortless. Lust, sex, and passion was universally understood, breaking down any language or cultural barriers; the culmination of an attraction between man and woman was being satiated, regardless of its morality.

* * *

Alcione was happy. Trent was off to a torrid start making good on the favor that he owed her, and there was a nice turnout of invited guests at the grand opening; they estimated the crowd to be in upwards of two hundred and fifty. That meant she didn't have to resort to Plan "B" with the latter, which would have been opening the event to the public as a sneak peak. As for Trent, she didn't have a back-up; it was all or nothing.

One of her proudest moments of the day came shortly before the grand opening program was to begin. She introduced Trent to her parents. They were a stately couple considered as socialites in Brazil.

Her way of dodging any suspicion of being involved with a married man was stressing that Trent was the person who was instrumental in securing the financing for Fogo de Janiero's expansion in South Carolina.

Serving as translator, Alcione told her father that Trent had traits that reminded her of him. He looked at her then at Trent and smiled.

"Thank you very much," he said with heavy broken English.

Alcione looked back toward Trent, explaining, "My parents do not speak English well."

"Tell him it is a pleasure meeting him. I am very humbled by the comparison."

Alcione showed much exuberance when she introduced Trent to her mother. And while she interacted with her daughter, she looked continuously back and forth at Trent.

Maybe mother's intuition had already come into play. It was as if she tried looking into his soul as she made eye contact with him.

"I am pleased to meet you," she said, also with heavy broken English.

Trent shook her hand, but he struggled with not giving himself away as someone who had already spent an hour in her daughter's hotel room releasing several months of pent-up sexual energy.

"Tell her I appreciate her confidence in our bank to serve them. I have heard so many good things about them."

* * *

Alcione was stunning in appearance wearing an ivory Calvin Klein evening dress. Her hair was combed to the back and it flowed freely down her spine, and her Lillian drop pearl earrings outlined with fourteen-karat gold blended well with her toned olive complexion. She was very much in her element mixing among the crowd, introducing herself to strangers and then thanking them for coming to the restaurant's grand opening.

For his part, Trent held his own whenever he was seen paired with Alcione. He wore a single-breasted Ralph Lauren taupe colored shark skin suit and black Kenneth Cole loafers. He seemed most comfortable interacting among other business people. It also helped that nobody seemed to be remotely curious about what his relation was to Alcione, which was fine with him.

"I told you that we were meant to be together," she said about halfway through the event. "My parents like you."

Trent was stunned. That shouldn't be. "When did you first tell them about me?"

"Last year."

"Last year?"

"Yes." She did not divulge to him how much it took to convince her parents to change their plans and go with Palmetto Fidelity. "I told them about meeting someone very handsome here in the States, and I had good feelings about him."

Trent gave her a side-eyed reaction. "Stop jiving me."

"I'm sorry. I am not familiar with that term—"

"Stop kidding me!"

"Why would I do that, Trent?" she reacted. "My parents only know that you are the banker who made this beautiful night possible. That is why my father was so glad to meet you."

"I don't know about your mother."

She chortled. "Mama likes you, too. She whispered to me that she knows you and I have already been romantic."

"That's mothers for you. I knew she had already picked up on something about me."

"It's okay. They want me to be happy, and I am." She grabbed Trent's hand and led her over to the food section. "I know you have not eaten much since we've been here."

She paused and gave him a mischievous stare. He was not slow to pick up on what she meant. In fact, his stomach growled at the mentioning of food.

Like it was in Columbia, there was an abundance of food served. Alcione said the staff began preparing all the meats three days ago so that everything would also be on schedule for Saturday's opening.

"That was important. Getting off to a good start with the customers is everything."

She then picked up a couple of plates and filled them with cuts of top sirloin and pork loin along with grilled vegetables.

"I never told you that I actually started as a waitress in our restaurant in Rio de Janiero?"

He shook his head. "This is the first time I've heard about it. So that's why you're so comfortable around this setting?" He wondered briefly whether he would have learned any of this about her had they taken the time and talked back in the hotel room.

"My father wanted me to learn as much as I could about the business," she said. "Then I worked in the kitchen preparing the food on the menu."

He related to her that he started at the bottom at Palmetto Fidelity as a rookie teller. "I was determined to work my way up, and I have so far. Hopefully, I can move on to something more challenging in the next year or two."

Little did Trent realize he spoke precisely to her point during their phone conversation from a week ago.

"How can you get where you want if you are not meeting

the right people?" she queried him.

"A lot of that is luck, I suppose."

"Trent, I think I can help you."

"How?"

"You already started."

Trent stared at Alcione while he continued chewing on the top sirloin cuts. He then took a long sip from a glass of white wine. This couldn't be a case of asking that he become a corporate gigolo in order to attain some kind of accomplishment, he wondered.

If not, then what was it?

After they finished eating, Alcione led Trent by the hand through the crowd, stopping close to the makeshift stage. Aña Carvalho Malhieros had begun her second of two sets, marking the final part of the grand opening event.

Over the course of the evening, Trent was already hanging closer to Alcione, and she did not shy away from it. She repeatedly rubbed up against him while they listened to Aña's cover of "*Samba de Verão*"—it triggered a flashback of them standing naked while peering out at the beach back in the hotel suite.

She turned quickly to him, saying, "My family's restaurant is important. But you are a big reason why I came back to the States this year." She gave him a quick peck on the cheek.

"That's only because I owed you a favor."

"No. I wanted to see you again even if you did not owe me anything."

"What if my wife and I were not separated?"

She shook her head. "It would not matter." Then she turned around and resumed listening to the performance.

"What if my wife and I were not separated?"

"Do you still love her?" She turned sharply toward him, expecting a response.

"She is still my wife. She is the mother of my son."

"Are you happy with her?"

He became contemplative. Then he seemed to bristle at the thought. Finally, he shook his head as if he wanted to dismiss the entire question. She nodded and then smiled knowingly.

Chapter 35

Trent's hands were clasped behind his head while lying in the bed next to Alcione. It had been an eventful past sixteen hours.

Arguably, Trent was a fulfilled man beyond his wildest imagination. Alcione was the real deal both publicly and privately. He mused at the thought maybe he should have taken a video as a reminder of some of the things they did after returning from the grand opening. He'd almost forgotten what it was like to experience unbridled sexual feelings and be able to express them without wondering if he first needed to negotiate his release out of the Dog House Inn.

Humph, he'd given recidivism a bad name, anyway, for all the times he'd spent there dealing with Sonia.

Last night was one for the ages. After returning from Fogo de Janiero, they took a stroll around the complex. They also strolled along the beach, going as far as the pier before returning. They joked of having sex on the beach under the moonlight—that was about the only thing they didn't do. But they made up for it by exploring a few positions out on the balcony before finishing in the bedroom.

Without any warning, Alcione had turned over and kissed him on the cheek.

"Good morning," she said; there was no mistaking about her natural, exotic beauty.

"What is good morning in Portuguese?" he asked.

"*Bom-dia.*"

He repeated it to her.

She smiled back at him. "If you can learn samba, you can learn Portuguese."

Then something dawned upon him as he sat up in bed. "Alcione, do I really know you? Do you really know me?"

Surprisingly, she did not have an answer.

Humph, the more he thought about it, what he did with Alcione was slightly atypical. He actually took time to find out personal, intimate things about the other women before he made any moves—it was his way of being careful, regardless of whether it was justifiable or not.

"Do you realize in all the time we've been around each other, you've never asked me any serious questions?" he said. "You've never asked me anything that might help you know me any better?"

It was as if the air was sucked out of the hotel suite. Not that Alcione was a bad woman—for all he knew she could be an absolute gem—he also recognized that he was too set in his ways to change.

Perhaps sixteen years of his life woven in with Sonia had shaped his approach with women. Alcione was many things that Sonia wasn't. She may have been charismatic and exciting; she wasn't realistic for him. All he'd felt was a strong sexual attraction for her, and nothing more.

Alcione got out of the bed and strode toward the window, drawing back the curtains. She also yawned and stretched.

Mmmph, what a view!

She looked back over her shoulder. "Trent, why don't you give us some time?"

He leaned back against the head board. "I've given us some thought; that should have been the first thing I did."

"But you owed me." She then turned and faced him, presenting a view that triggered a morning erection on him that he tried ignoring.

"Yes, I owed you. But I was thinking, can we just be friends, if there is such a thing?" He attempted a wistful smile.

She turned around again and folded her arms across her breasts. She peered out of the window again. This time, she focused on specific things making short, measured movements with her head.

Maybe in a different era and in a different life, he would have joined her. He stunned her with the chortle he let out.

"Why are you laughing?"

"Nothing."

He eased out of bed and went directly to the bathroom. She glanced over her shoulder, admiring the mass of masculinity that had occupied space and time with her.

Upon exiting, he went over to the bathroom counter, brushed his teeth and combed his closely-cropped hair style. Alcione still had not put on any clothing. It was apparent that she was more than comfortable that way, whether it was cultural or simply the way she was.

Trent did not broach any conversation while he put on the beige slacks and black Polo shirt that he brought up from the car last night.

Meanwhile, Alcione continued peering out of the window.

"Take care, Trent. *Te cuida.*"

"You, too, Alcione."

He also attempted to repeat the phrase. Unlike his other attempts with the language and samba, he got it right the first time.

"*Te cuida.*"

She followed him into the main section of the suite. Before he grasped the door knob, he looked back at her and smiled— the gratuity and tab were paid in full.

Chapter 36

With a child-like gleam in her eyes, Tanya approached Sonia's cubicle eager to share her latest bright idea.

Sonia folded her arms and leaned back in her chair appearing suspicious.

"Yes, Tanya. I know the wheels are turning up there in that noggin of yours."

"Is it that obvious, Ms. Sonia?"

Tanya sucked the inside of her mouth and proceeded as if it didn't matter what Sonia said. "I was thinking maybe we can have a Friday potluck with Charlotte's team . . . We haven't done anything like that in a while. Don't you miss having them?"

She nodded her head, soliciting Sonia's approval; she merely shrugged. "I hear Alvantrae makes a mean potato salad and chili."

"I miss your cheesecake," Tanya raved. "You have to bring a

couple of them."

Tanya had piqued Sonia's interest by smooth stroking her ego. Her cheesecakes were popular with virtually everyone that she knew. Her favorites to make were cherry and blueberry.

It was a simple recipe that she used—handed down from her grandmother Esther—and the key ingredients were something she'd never divulged to outsiders.

Being open to the thought, Sonia also casually reached into her purse and placed her cell phone on her desk in clear view of Tanya. She quickly scrolled through her screens checking whether she had any messages.

Then she went ahead discussing some logistics with Tanya about having a Friday potluck, pending Phyllis' approval. In the midst of their conversation, Tanya noticed something different about her cell phone screen saver, which was a slide show of various pictures.

"When did you add that one?" Tanya queried.

People can be so nosey around here. They don't know how to mind their own business.

With maternal patience, Sonia answered, "This past weekend."

"Who's in that picture?"

"My sister."

Tanya attempted adding to the conversation that she was more than willing to bring plastic silverware and Styrofoam cups and plates, as well as a crock pot, if needed. But she could not resist returning to what previously piqued her curiosity.

"I wouldn't mind knowing who's in that picture with your sister?" Her eyes were like headlights at nighttime and she had another of her silly grins.

Sonia returned a side-eyed glare. "That's her fiancé. They're getting married in a few weeks." She then put away her phone.

Tanya acted as if she couldn't quite place Shonna and her fiancé in her memory. Then she snapped her finger.

"Hey, isn't that who I think it is?"

"What are you talking about?"

"That man with your sister looks like Lance!" She was careful not to announce his name as if it was over a public address system.

A dozen training classes of new temps had come through contract services since his quiet departure, yet there were still some phone reps who had been there long enough to remember him.

"When did that happen? Tanya asked.

Sonia waved her off. "Things happen. Sometimes you never know when and where it will happen."

"Yes, lawd. You got that right! I wish them the best."

"I'm happy for her because she's happy," Sonia said. "That's the most important thing."

And just like that, Tanya had a deliciously mischievous thought she wanted to act upon. That also meant she had things to do and people to approach regarding the Friday potluck.

Vicki left contract services just as she declared she would at the beginning of June. She famously left on break on a Wednesday afternoon and never returned. She e-mailed her resignation a couple of hours later. Charlotte was asked double as team supervisor and over the unit for incoming appeals until a permanent hire was made.

Tanya approached Charlotte with the same child-like enthusiasm as she did with Sonia about a Friday potluck.

"As long as it's okay with Sonia and it's okay with Phyllis, I don't see it being a problem," Charlotte said, glancing at her new desk that was partially adorned with her personal items.

In her next move, Tanya shouted over at Alvantrae, who

barely stuffed his Louis Vuitton handbag in the desk drawer to his right. He'd just returned from lunch.

"We're planning on having another Friday potluck, and you have to bring some of that potato salad and chili that you make."

Alvantrae craned his neck slightly to the left and acknowledged with a nod. "You know game recognizes game." He then rolled his eyes and proceeded to log onto his computer.

Turning her attention back to Charlotte, Tanya said, "I already have Ms. Sonia bringing a couple of those cheesecakes that she makes—"

"And you better leave them for the rest of us this time!" Alvantrae yell from behind.

Two-thirds of Sonia's cherry cheesecake was already eaten before it was placed out on the table for the last Friday potluck; the blueberry cheesecake was untouched.

"Hey, I got a little carried away. I was having a stressful day with Shabu and the rest of his buddies, and Ms. Sonia's cheesecake hit the spot and helped settle me," she said, looking back at him.

"Humph, a real deep spot!"

"You just mind your business and bring that potato salad and chili!"

Tanya was now on a roll. She figured while she was at it, she would be remiss if she didn't divulge the tidbit of information that she learned from Sonia.

"You wouldn't believe who I just saw in a picture today?" she quizzed Charlotte, who didn't seem eager to know.

She was busy with accessing screens to monitor her phone reps' call patterns.

"I'll tell you who I saw," Tanya said, still hoping to draw her into the conversation.

Charlotte stopped and glanced upward.

"Lance is getting married." Tanya's eyebrows were raised and she had clenched fists as if she were reacting to it for the first time.

"Huh?"

"Yeah!"

It took Charlotte eight visits to a counselor spanning six months and a prescription of Prozac for anxiety to help her come to grips with Lance's abrupt departure out of her life. She also found more constructive ways of dealing with her fear of loneliness by attending church and taking advanced piano lessons. Playing music helped soothe her soul when it was troubled.

Tanya spoke slowly with the details. "You wouldn't believe who he's marrying—"

Charlotte hunched her shoulders.

"He's marrying Sonia's sister!"

Alvantrae, whose ears was like antennae, butted into the conversation.

"Well, ain't that special!" He returned to typing in notes from his previous call.

"Yeah, ain't it?" Charlotte muttered; a numb feeling quickly moved throughout her.

Tanya figured she'd said enough. She sashayed off to her desk while Charlotte stared blankly at her computer screen for several moments.

Chapter 37

Charlotte glanced over to her right at Sonia, who was on the phone. She sucked her teeth in defiance thinking of her.

How dare her freakin' sister find happiness with that SOB, she fumed; her fiancé was the reason why she needed all that help. Neither he nor her sister deserved to be happy. And Sonia was just as guilty by relation.

After Sonia got off the phone, she happened to have looked over to her left and waved at Charlotte.

"Hey, Charlotte!"

Humph!

"Hi."

Charlotte was still of the opinion that Lance was a world-class coward for passing up on her sexy, brilliant womanhood for the sister of a calculating, shallow and snooty work colleague of hers.

There had to be some logic to the insanity.

Charlotte had difficulty coping after Tanya dropped that gossip bomb on her. She stopped her routine of taking her medication and the anxiety attacks returned with a vengeance especially when she was alone in her new apartment located about a half-mile away from the new hospital being built in the Harbison subdivision.

Although she tried playing the piano as a catharsis, she was frustrated by her inability to concentrate. She was too embarrassed to contact her counselor. And she was unwilling to speak with anyone at church because she didn't want to hear any packaged advice about forgiving Lance even as she'd already been forgiven for the sin committed in her life.

No, that god blasted punk deserved death even if it was merely symbolic.

While passing Sonia's cubicle one afternoon, Charlotte overheard her mentioning that her sister's name was Shonna Chandler and she was the station manager at WNPW. She grabbed her cell phone as soon as she returned to her cubicle and accessed the station's Web site. There were no page links with Shonna's name on the site. But under the station's photo gallery, she came across an event picture that had a caption with Shonna being credited as station manager.

Later that week, Charlotte arranged to take off a half day. She used that time to make an unscheduled trip over to the radio station.

Charlotte looked the part—at least in her opinion—pretending to be a businesswoman looking for a station that would air her community service-oriented talk show. Standing nearly six feet tall without heels, she wore her hair down and parted down the middle, an ivory jacket, white blouse with a black dot pattern, and black slacks.

"I need to speak with someone about bringing a weekend

talk show to this station," she said.

The receptionist replied, "The person you need to ask is our station manager Ms. Chandler, and she's in a meeting right now."

"I can wait. I have only a few questions to ask."

The receptionist remained professional with her demeanor, but it was obvious she was everyone's body guard. "Lots of people come by here wanting to take up only a few minutes to ask a couple questions.

"Ms. Chandler wouldn't be able to get anything done if she stopped to answer everyone's questions."

Charlotte felt tension quickly rising up from her neck to the base of her skull. If it were left up to her, she would have snatched the receptionist out of her chair and pummeled her onto the carpet.

She lucked out, however. She glanced to her right and spotted Ted Jenkins, who was the afternoon DJ. He froze in midstep once he recognized her.

"What are you doing over here?" he reacted.

"TJ, how long has it been?"

They rushed to hug each other. Charlotte and Ted were college classmates. They had mutual acquaintances and hung out together at one time.

"TJ, you're looking good!" she said. "I'm going to have to get your number before you leave."

"Sure." He reached into his pocket for his wallet. "My cell phone number's on here." He also looked her up and down.

"You know you were always my favorite." He even went as far as sucking his teeth and nodding his head.

Charlotte lowered her voice. "Can you do me a big favor?"

"What [do] you need?"

"I'd like to ask your station manager a couple of questions for an idea that I've been thinking of putting into action. But your receptionist over there—"

Ted held up his hand, assuring her it would not be any problem. "Let me get a couple of things from my office, and I'll be right back."

Charlotte stood in the same spot waiting for him to return. She never bothered to look back at the receptionist, who was busy answering the phones and checking her fingernails.

Moments later, Ted returned with Shonna. At first glance, she recognized that she was about average height, which was similar to Sonia, and they bore a strong resemblance. She also looked for any rings on her left hand.

Ugh!

There was something glittering from her third finger. She almost lost it right there.

"Hi, I'm Shonna Chandler," she said, extending her right hand out toward Charlotte. "TJ says you two were partners in mischief at one time."

Charlotte glanced over at Ted and smirked. "If he says so, and it looks like he still is getting into mischief."

"Well, TJ says you had something to ask me. I've got a couple of minutes."

"Thanks." She also mouthed the same to Ted, who quietly walked off to one of the studios.

The next thing that Charlotte noticed about Shonna was her seemingly youthful and energetic appearance, but that she was nonetheless older. She also wore her hair styled similar to Sonia, long and straight down past her shoulders.

So he's into collecting antiques? Humph!

Charlotte's only concern coming to the station was whether it might come back to haunt her in the form of Sonia bringing their meeting to her attention. So, she stuck to her script and asked well thought-out questions as if she was serious about looking for a station to broadcast her show.

"This may sound like I'm putting you off, but I'm not," Shonna explained. "I would want something different and refreshing. Something that would make me say, 'Hmmm, I like that and I'll get up every weekend to listen to it myself.'

"Do you understand where I'm going with that?"

"I do. But I thought money was more of a factor."

"It is, in the final analysis. But we'd still like something that will catch our attention."

"I see. Well, I'd like to sit down and talk to you in more detail one day very soon."

"Sure. Just arrange something through our receptionist Kareatha up front."

Yeah, right, Charlotte hissed to herself. *I'll arrange something with her!*

Out in the parking lot, Charlotte still could not believe what she saw on Shonna's hand. She spent several moments inside her car taking deep breaths and calming herself so that she might be able to focus on the road while driving.

She still needed further proof before driving off. She scrambled for her cell phone and did a public records search through the Richland County government Web site. And there it was, in capital letters, a bride listed as Shonna Chandler and Lance Miles as the groom; the application date was a recent addition to the database.

Seething first as she backed out of the parking space, then cursing as she peeled rubber out of the parking lot, Charlotte didn't bother to wipe away the tears that also streamed down her cheeks.

Chapter 38

Whate's all this talk about having a bridal shower? Shonna reacted to Sonia's question, with her hands on her waist.

"I still had to ask you," Sonia said. "Some women do have them, you know—"

"I'm going on forty-five years old. It's not necessary. The wedding and reception will be enough for me."

"What about any wedding announcements?"

"Girl, please!" she hissed.

Shonna anticipated between fifty and one hundred people would be attending her wedding; therefore, she wasn't looking to make the society column of anyone's blog page or Web site.

"Are you sure now?" Sonia asked. "I can put one together just like that, you know . . . I don't want to hear you saying you wished that you had a bridal shower."

The wedding was less than four weeks away. Shonna had

already secured a chapel on the campus of the large university in downtown Columbia where she's an alumna. She once attended a wedding ceremony there several years ago and always thought it would be a cool place to have one.

"We need to get in contact with someone who's going to do the music and singing," Sonia suggested. "I think I know someone at the church where I'm now attending whom you might like."

Shonna stared at Sonia.

"What's wrong?"

"I don't want any pomp and circumstance," Shonna said. "Save that for someone else's wedding."

Sonia tossed her pen on her note pad. "Why don't you and Lance just go to City Hall and be on your merry way?"

She then walked over to the refrigerator and gestured if she wanted something to drink; she held up her hand, indicating that she didn't.

"I would, but I don't think your parents would ever live that down. Your mother would be calling me a heathen, doing exactly what the world does." She sighed, continuing, "What's wrong with something plain and simple?"

Sonia jerked her head back and smirked. "You're already on your way since you're not having any singers and musicians. And what are you going to do about a rehearsal?"

"We don't need any rehearsal. You'll just tell everyone what they need to do, where they need to stand, and everything should be over in less than a half-hour."

"Yeah, and then you and Lance will then be knocking everyone over to get on with your honeymoon," Sonia quipped.

Shonna wiggled in her chair. "And what's wrong with that? Me and my husband will be naked and not ashamed. Whatever we do will be honorable before all," she added, rolling her neck, "and none of you prudes and holier-than-thou cynics who say we shouldn't be married in the first place can say it would be defiled —well, maybe a little kinky."

After being put in her place about not having a bridal shower and any wedding announcements, Sonia suggested that Shonna handled all the arrangements by herself.

"You've shot down everything else. But I might as well ask it. What about floral and candle lighting arrangements and catering for the reception?"

"Candles and flowers?" she reacted. "If I'm not going with the pomp and circumstance with the music—and you'd think that I would being that I run a radio station—then I'm certainly not going to trouble myself with any flowers."

"What about a bridal corsage or bouquet? You know, something to toss over your shoulder at the reception?"

Shonna shrugged her shoulders. "Okay, I'll do that. But that's about all I'm going to do."

"My lord, something!" Sonia was quick to write herself a note about getting a bridal corsage for the wedding. She then snapped her finger.

"That reminds me. I need to contact Trent and arrange a day to get Taylor fitted for his tux."

"You two still aren't speaking?"

Sonia looked at Shonna. Slowly inhaling through her nostrils, she went on to reply, "I'm beginning to wonder if Trent likes it this way. He can do his thing and still say he's married."

"Maybe you need to go ahead and finish what you started?"

"I'm still praying that I won't have to. But I'm not going to continue sitting and waiting, either. We've now been separated five months."

"Well, whenever you speak to him, tell Trent that he's invited to the wedding. I'd still invite him even if Taylor wasn't in it as an usher."

Shonna turned serious for a moment. She held back the thought and observation that's been on her mind long enough.

"Do you know why couples have great sex?"

Sonia looked at Shonna as if she had no right asking her the question. "It's because the man understands what the woman needs, and he listens to her."

"That's only part of it." Shonna crossed her left leg over her right.

"Well, that's been the problem with me and Trent. Unfortunately for him, that was one of the things that Milner had also recognized."

Sonia closed her eyes and contemplated her comment. She offered up a quick prayer seeking forgiveness.

Shonna remained patient with Sonia. "The reason why couples have great sex is because they also have great communication. Think about it."

"I've thought about a lot of things, and I can't tell you how many times I pleaded with Trent about listening to me. That can turn a woman off, and then she doesn't care any more."

"Sis, it goes both ways. You've wanted Trent to listen to you. But did you ever try listening to him?"

"Why? He never listened to me!"

"I'm sure Trent has his faults."

Sonia sucked her teeth. "You got that right!" She then looked away, staring at the sweep hand on the kitchen clock make its circuit.

"Sis, I'm not going to sit here and argue with you," Shonna said. "It talks about examining yourself. Sometimes it's hard to do that. But if you and Trent ever talk about why things deteriorated the way they did, ask him if he thought you ever listened to him. Okay?"

Sonia sighed then hissed. "Yeah, right. I've heard that one, too. Hopefully, I'll remember it."

* * *

Sonia arranged to pick Taylor up from the bank and take him to be fitted for his tux. It was the first time they had a mother-and-son moment since she moved out. She'd never been separated from him for this long. But she hoped this might be the start to them reconnecting.

It was incredulous to think that she birthed him into this world, but in a span of a few months it was as if she had never seen him before. While he was being fitted at the Men's Warehouse, she could not help but stare at him and study his mannerisms and features. Her boy was making a fast transition to manhood. It was like yesterday she remembered buying his school clothes for the first time.

"Will there be any problems with the legs?" she asked the salesman. "As you can tell he has thick thighs. His father has had problems with pants splitting along the inseam."

"He shouldn't have any problem. We are just talking about him participating in a wedding, is that correct?"

"That's right. He's going to be an usher."

"I don't see the need for him wearing a larger size in the waist. This should work."

"Okay, if you say so—I don't want to be coming back here as the angry mom."

"Yes, ma'am. I guarantee you. This will work."

Afterward, Sonia and Taylor went over to the food court in the Columbiana Mall. Taylor apprised her that his grades were okay, but they could have been better.

"I passed all my classes last semester with at least a 'C,'" he said. "My lowest grade was an eighty, which was in Computers. My highest grade was a ninety-five, which was English."

Sonia stared at Taylor. She wondered if any of the blame

should be placed on Trent since he was so boastful about his parenting skills.

"You know you can't be doing that in the tenth grade," she said.

"I know. But last year was not easy."

"You mean the classes?"

"No. You know what I mean."

Sonia breathed loudly. He didn't have to go any further. At least progress could be measured in Taylor's willingness to spend part of the afternoon with her.

He looked at her again.

"I think Dad misses you," he said. "He won't tell me that."

"Do you miss me?"

"I guess. I mean, it's been hard."

Sonia was quick to tell Taylor that she regretted her behavior and the embarrassment of being seen with another man. She also mentioned that she was no longer involved with Milner, although she did not divulge his name.

"Can you forgive me?" she asked.

Taylor hunched his shoulders. "I was told that's what I'm supposed to do, huh?"

"I can't make you do that, but it would be nice."

Taylor brushed the topic to the side and began talking about him practicing with his school's junior varsity basketball team. He figured it was better playing basketball in tenth grade after he had a year to acclimate himself to high school.

Sonia reminded him that Trent ran track in high school. "Have you ever thought about doing that?"

He shook his head. "I've played basketball a long time. I think I'm pretty good at it. I think I have a chance to see a lot of playing time. And they say I'm one of the fastest guys on the basketball court, which is good for the transition game and breaking down press defenses."

Sonia reached out and grasped Taylor's hand. "I bet Trent would be proud if you did give track a try."

"It is after basketball season. I'll think about it."

Chapter 39

After sending her e-mail that reminded Phyllis about taking Thursday and Friday off, Sonia was anxious about the response she might receive.

She was prepared to march down to Phyllis' office if there was any questioning of the validity or any hedging of her request.

There was none.

She better not have....

> Why didn't you tell me any sooner? I would have taken up a collection for a wedding gift. There will be one waiting for you to give her when you return. Have a great time!

At least Phyllis had enough sense not to mess with her, Sonia mused. Now she needed to handle a final order of business before leaving late Wednesday evening. She stopped by Charlotte's cubicle apprising her that she'd be gone for the rest of the week.

"If it's okay with you, I'm going to have my phone reps to sign in and out at your desk tomorrow and Friday," she told her. "I won't be back until Monday."

Charlotte was surprised. "That's not like you taking any time off. You'll come in when it's snowing."

"I know. But my sister's getting married. I'm helping her with everything."

Sonia, having tucked her purse under her arm, waved good-bye to Charlotte, who went from simmering to boiling and spilling over.

This flippin' thing is going to happen. To her, the news was worse than being insulted and a bunch of people huddled around laughing in her face.

Since she worked the late shift among supervisors, Charlotte waited a few minutes ensuring that Sonia was gone before she tipped out the workplace for a few minutes. The call volume was slow, and there were only experienced phone reps still working; she reasoned they should be able to handle most calling situations.

"TJ, I was thinking of setting up an appointment with Ms. Chandler. Do you think you can help me with another favor?"

"You might want to wait a while. She's getting married this weekend, and she's going to be gone for about two weeks," Ted said.

"Really?"

"Yeah, she's marrying some dude much younger than her. I mean, to each is own, you know—"

Charlotte was stuck between gritting her teeth, looking for a wall to kick or punch, or simply wanting to shout so loud that it broke glass.

"I guess I'll have to wait, huh?"

"Yeah, but I'd give it a couple of weeks."

"Are any of you glad for her?"

"Yeah, we are. And we're going to show our support. She's good people. She really is."

"Do you know where she's getting married?"

"A chapel at the university on Saturday."

Charlotte did her best to play off the information. "I'm not getting married at anyone's chapel. I don't care if I were in Las Vegas. If and when it happens, I'm getting married in a church!"

"I know that's right." Ted then chortled and sucked his teeth.

"Why haven't you gotten married?"

She hissed at the question. "Some men don't know what they're missing, I guess; I'm happy living a stress-free life. There are lots of people who aren't."

"Well, you know you've always been one of my favorites."

"Is that right?"

"Maybe we can talk about that some time—"

"I might have to take you up on that." She alerted Ted that she was at work and needed to get back to her cubicle. Ted wasn't a bad person to consider, she thought, once she got past his gap-tooth smile à la former football player and current TV show host Michael Strahan. Maybe that was why she never went too far with him while they were in college. But now he had a name for himself and fame and fortune was soon coming his way: In a month, WNPW would be the flagship station for the debut of his nationally syndicated show.

"When is a good time to call you?"

"Any time. But, so you know, I'm like a moving target." He added a laugh to his comment.

"I'm not worried about that. I know how to stop you in your tracks."

"You do that. Bye!"

* * *

On the day of the wedding, Sonia had Trent to drop Taylor off at her parents' home since she already picked up his tux.

She actually went out to Trent's car and greeted him.

"Taylor did tell you that you were invited to the wedding?"

He nodded. "I sent a gift along with him."

While Sonia was still bent over peering inside his car, Trent caught a view of her cleavage. She was coy about not making any issue of it even as he tried looking elsewhere.

At least some things hadn't changed about him—he always seemed to break for a set of breasts or buttocks. Besides, he was still legally entitled to gawking at hers. All he had to do was ask, and she might have been bold to show him more.

"Would you rather that I drop him back off here, or you'll come and pick him up after the reception?" she asked.

"Just call me. We can talk about it then. It's nice that he'll be spending some time with you," he said. "I'm sure he's sick of hanging around me."

"All right. The wedding is at four o'clock. We figure the wedding and reception will probably take all of ninety-minutes to a couple of hours—I'll just call you." Sonia also seemed to also cast a longing stare at him. He also played it coy with her.

"I better get back inside,' she said. "Shonna's not the most punctual of people. And I know she can be a mess on days like these."

"Okay. Tell her again I said congratulations."

Sonia was slow at turning around and walking toward her parents' home. Although she didn't go out of her way enticing him, her round hips had a natural sway to them. She suspected that he'd be checking her out—and she was right.

He didn't put his car into DRIVE until she reached the steps. And even then, he didn't peel off, but eased away, which brought a smile to her face.

* * *

Before leaving her parents' home, Sonia went over her checklist with Shonna. The catering and wedding cake was being done by Nadine DeLoach, who owned a bakery and restaurant in the Boozer shopping plaza on Broad River Road. They prepared for a reception in upwards of one hundred guests.

Lance had only his middle sister Charmaine and Derek, his classmate from college, attending the wedding. Derek was also standing as his best man. His mother and oldest sister Lauren refused to come because they didn't like him marrying a woman sixteen years his senior. His youngest sister Sherece was unable to attend because of a prior cheerleading commitment with his niece, Stefanie.

"Are you nervous?" Sonia asked.

She managed a wistful smile. "I think I'm doing fine under the circumstances."

"Are you sure this is what you want?"

"Yes." She swallowed softly.

Sonia gave her a hug. "Sisters always. I love you."

"I love you, too." Shonna separated and wiped a tear from the corner of her eye.

Prentiss came from her bedroom and informed them that she and Tillman would be following them to the university. Then she stared at Shonna as if a replay of her life went before her eyes. Meanwhile, Sonia had returned to her room, checking in on Taylor.

"Mom, is there anything wrong?"

"I was curious," she said. "Did you and Lance have any premarital counseling?"

Shonna sucked her teeth. "No we didn't, Mom. We feel good about what we're doing."

"Oh-kay—"

Prentiss went out of her way to remain stoic. But once she was back in her bedroom, she hissed and rolled her eyes and ranted to Tillman that she still felt Shonna was making a bad decision.

"There's only one way of finding out," he said. "That's the scary part of it all. We're only her parents. We can't live her life."

"I know." She walked over and hugged him.

"Yep. Maybe they'll prove us wrong."

Sonia, Shonna, and Taylor arrived at the university's chapel around 3:15 p.m. The chapel was empty except for a mainte-nance person who waited impatiently for someone to show up. Prentiss and Tillman arrived about ten minutes later, but they decided on waiting a few minutes before committing to going inside the chapel.

About 3:35 p.m., Lance arrived with Derek and Charmaine. The first people he saw were the Chandlers walking toward the chapel.

"Good afternoon, y'all!"

"Hey, Lance," Tillman replied. "Are you nervous?"

He chortled and then hunched his shoulders. He was al-ready dressed in a new, solid black Ralph Lauren two-button suit, crisp white long-sleeved shirt and black tie; he wore a matching black pair of Calvin Klein slip-ons.

Prentiss was more than impressed—there was a first time for everything.

"You look like you really want to marry my daughter," she said; she then motioned with her head toward the chapel.

"She's inside doing the last touches."

"Thanks," he answered, before looking off to his right. "Mrs. Chandler, this is my friend Derek; he's going to be my best man today."

He smiled and extended his hand out to Tillman first then Prentiss, respectively.

"I guess you'll be next, huh?" she said.

Derek chortled. "I don't know about that. I'm still hoping I can hold out until I'm thirty-five. At least that's what Lance and I had always talked about. But it's obvious that Shonna's a special woman. She's all that he's talked about for the past year."

She raised her eyebrows, somewhat surprised. Maybe he was serious the entire time, and it wasn't any fantasy game for him.

Lance then introduced Charmaine to his soon-to-be in-laws, to which Prentiss complimented her on her beauty. Tillman, who shook her hand, merely was a silent observer and admirer.

The guests started filtering into the chapel shortly before four o'clock. Initially, it was a smattering. Then it became a steady stream of people.

Back in one of the offices, Sonia had pulled Lance off to the side for a brief chat.

"All I ask you, Lance, is to treat my sister right," she said, looking up at him. "She's waited all this time to marry. Don't be a disappointment to her—."

"I promise."

She left the office and addressed the gathering that the wedding would be starting in about fifteen minutes. She instructed Derek all he had to do was stand to Lance's right and hand the wedding rings over to Pastor Anthony Ethridge when asked. Meanwhile, she would be standing to Shonna's left. And her father would stand with Shonna until he's asked who would be giving away the bride.

"This should go without any real hitches," she said. "We don't have to worry about any musician or singers, or any processions down the aisle."

She left Lance and Derek and checked on Taylor. He was busy escorting female attendees to the pews upon their initial entry into the chapel.

Upon his return to his post by the last row, he noticed Sonia and gestured with his head, implying if he was doing fine. She flipped him a thumbs-up.

Sonia's last stop was with Dana Foreman, Shonna's friend from college, and her husband Nick, who offered to do the video.

She suggested, "If you can stand at an angle catching everyone, I think that will work fine. You wouldn't believe how much I had to convince Shonna into having someone doing a video of her wedding."

Nick waved Sonia off, assuring her that he was as ready as he could be. He was more than proud to display a near-professional quality camera, with a stereo microphone adorned with a rabbit's tail to muffle any extra noise; an extended handle for extra stabilization; two extra battery packs, and an external light.

Shonna shook her head. "Nick, this isn't any Hollywood production."

"I know. But I believe in doing things right." He went on to mention that he's got state-of-the-art video editing software to aid in the post-production.

"Don't worry about Nick," Dana assured Sonia. "He's done dozens of weddings, and everyone loves what he does with them."

"Okay, if you say so—"

* * *

Charlotte, who did not sleep the night before, sat nervously in her car waiting for the top of the hour. She felt she had cried out all the tears that she was capable of crying. And she was tired of taking ibuprofen for the headache that had lingered all day.

Although time had distorted some of her memory, there were some things that still remained vivid with her about Lance: their first date, which resulted in them getting a room at the Hampton Inn not far from her apartment; the day that she confronted him at UCP about avoiding her, and him unceremoniously dumping her.

Shonna was merely collateral damage. The hussy who seemed ageless, although that was debatable, simply didn't know the kind of shallow, sad statement for a man she was marrying.

As when she visited Shonna unannounced, Charlotte figured on a commanding presence. She wore a peacock colored evening gown that had a solid short slip with a sweetheart neckline, sheer chiffon overlay with synching at the center bodice detailed with an open back. She wore black Guess brand sandals with an open toe.

She was equally determined to offer Lance a visual reminder of what he forfeited.

"Are you here for the wedding, too?" asked a man who appeared extremely enamored by her appearance outside the chapel.

"Yes, I am. Is it about to start?"

He excused himself for a moment, promising that he'd be right back. "It looks like they're about to start." He grunted and shook his head. "I sure wish I was the one standing in front of everyone with you!"

"Excuse me, I better stop by the ladies' room," she replied before walking away.

He let out another grunt. "Lawd, they don't make 'em like that every day!"

* * *

The gathering of nearly eighty people quickly hushed once they saw Sonia, Lance, and Derek take their places in front of the altar. That was also Taylor's cue to take his seat next to his grandmother.

The next person to stand at the altar was Pastor Ethridge. Then Tillman came from a side entrance along with Shonna, who decided on an elegant ivory colored jacket and long skirt with a split on the side. Both the jacket and skirt were adorned with pearls and lace. She also wore black open-toe sandals. She wore her hair long and straight, which stopped at her shoulders.

At that moment, everyone's attention was now on Pastor Ethridge. Charlotte's timing couldn't be any better as she eased into the chapel and sat two rows behind the last people seated.

From her vantage point, she also noticed Ted. He sat in a row with about a eight people, all of whom she presumed were from the radio station.

Pastor Ethridge greeted and thanked everyone for coming. He spoke briefly about marriage being the second most important relationship on earth after one's relationship with God, as well as the second most important confession one could ever make.

"Lance, have you acknowledged a relationship with your savior?"

He nodded.

"And Shonna, have you acknowledged a relationship with your savior?"

She also nodded.

Pastor Ethridge smiled. "What has been brought together in heaven shall not be loosed on earth."

Then he looked directly at Tillman and asked, "Who gives this bride away?"

Tillman cleared his throat. "Her mother and I." He gave Shonna a hug and took a seat next to Prentiss on her right. Lance took over where her father stood.

Pastor Ethridge then went according to tradition, asking, "If there is anyone among us today who opposes these two joining together in matrimony, speak now or forever hold your peace?"

Charlotte took a deep breath, exhaled loudly, and stood up. "I do!"

Pastor Ethridge did a double-take, as did most of the audience which reacted to her voice. Everyone's attention was now upon Charlotte, whose eyes were slits, cheeks were flushed, eyebrows that were closer and with her arms folded.

She now slid over toward the middle aisle. "That's right. I object to these two marrying."

"For what?" Lance reacted.

Shonna, who was agape, turned to him suspiciously. It was as if she had to hear this exchange before reacting the way she felt like reacting. Sonia was astounded that Charlotte knew where the wedding was taking place especially since she wasn't invited and there were no announcements.

Ted, who had unknowingly given Charlotte all the pertinent information, shook his head and buried it in his hands.

"It's obvious that dogs like you think you can mess over people and decide on marrying old tricks like her," she said, pointing at Shonna. "I just want you to see what you missed out on, and I also want everyone in this place to see it!"

Lance turned slowly toward Shonna. His expression was apologetic, yet conveying at the same time had no knowledge of Charlotte showing up, or that he had no dealings with her since he decided on a relationship with her.

"If I were you, Shonna Chandler, I'd think twice about becoming the laughing stock of Columbia," Charlotte continued. "Everyone on your job have been laughing behind your back—even TJ, who's sitting right over there!"

She scanned the chapel before focusing just ahead to her right.

"Charlotte get out of here, now!" Lance yelled. "You have serious problems!"

She looked herself over and disagreed. "You're the one with the problems. You might have lots of stamina—I'll give you that much—but it looks like she'll have to catch her breath before both of you find any rhythm.

"Hey, but if that's what you want, more power to you!" She then snapped her finger.

Shonna, who looked over at Sonia, finally identified Charlotte for herself. "She came to the station talking to me about starting a talk show—"

Sonia stared at Shonna. Then she glared at Charlotte, who appeared to take additional steps closer to the altar.

"You better leave now!" Sonia snarled at her.

"Huh, like, what you're going to do?" Charlotte retorted. "You're the last person in Columbia who can tell anyone what to do.

"Uh-huh, and don't think Phyllis hadn't told me about you whoring around in Sumter—"

That witch!

Sonia marched toward Charlotte and squared off face-to-face with her.

"Did you think I was going to let him and your sister get off that easy?" Charlotte then placed her hands on her waist, staring down at Sonia, whom she enjoyed more than a six-inch height advantage.

That was a bad move. Sonia reacted by connecting a hard right-handed slap to Charlotte's cheek. That was followed by a sharp, short left jab to her chin, causing her to stagger backward into an empty pew. Then she charged Charlotte and slapped her again.

"I'll stomp your eyes out of your head!" she said, standing over Charlotte.

Taylor sprinted over to the fracas and pulled Sonia away.

"Mom, what's gotten into you?"

"Yeah, you better pull your mother away from me!"

Sonia lunged at Charlotte again amid Taylor restraining her. "Don't talk to my son that way!"

"Mom, don't worry about it!" He finally led her away.

Charlotte, who was partially disheveled, laughed heartily. "That's all right, skank. This is far from over!"

It was apparent that Charlotte had no back-up plan. Her sole intention was to disrupt Shonna and Lance's wedding, and she accomplished just that. Nobody bothered to offer her any help.

Feeling no shame, she straightened herself, stopped by the pew where she sat and picked up her purse. And as she sashayed to the door, she snapped her finger prior to opening it, and slammed it behind her.

She did not bother to inspect herself until reaching her car. There, she noticed that she had a bright red hand print on her left cheek and on her both sides of neck. She chortled and drove away from the campus.

Sonia sat with Taylor not far from where she accosted

Charlotte. She checked her fingernails and noticed that she cracked one on her left hand and two on her right hand.

Her moves may not have been as smooth as Laila Ali's or her punches as powerful as Ann Wolfe, whose claim to fame was flooring Vonda Ward; a former NCAA basketball All-America and undefeated world boxing champion at the time she lost to Wolfe. But they were effective and memorable.

"You don't know how much time I spent working on these nails only to take only a couple of minutes to mess them up," she told Taylor.

He was a boy. A woman's work on her fingernails meant nothing to him.

"Mom, I didn't know you got mad like that?"

She touched his cheek and chortled. "It's obvious that I don't like anyone embarrassing my family."

That struck a chord with Taylor. "Yeah, I get it." He smiled at her.

"I forgive you, Mom."

"Thanks."

They moved to hug each other.

Nick, who had his camera running throughout the commotion, rushed over to Dana and asked the obvious with her. She nodded, indicating that she took a cell phone video of Sonia's skirmish with Charlotte. She was five rows away from all the action.

This was no doubt a YouTube moment and Nick was incredulous. He also began thinking through some of the post-production possibilities he could exploit if the video came out the way he hoped it would.

Meanwhile, Pastor Ethridge was visibly embarrassed for the nuptials. He apologized to them, but Shonna and Lance told him that it was not his fault.

"What I can tell you is when a person objects to a couple

marrying, it doesn't really affect anything," he said. "The only times there are issues are if someone has accused someone of bigamy or if the bride or groom might be too closely related.

"Otherwise, the saying is really true, one monkey don't stop no show."

* * *

Amid the loud rumbling of conversation, of which many joked about or attempted to recount what happened, Ted, fellow DJ Preston Coffey, and producer Quetari Simpson were among five from WNPW's staff that tipped out of the chapel along with four other couples.

Prentiss nudged Tillman often about leaving, as well, but he refused to bail out on his daughter; she was visibly uncomfortable about remaining.

Beyond her nails, Sonia required only some reapplication of her makeup and there were surprisingly no tears or rips in her champagne colored sequined gown. Her biggest concern, however, were Shonna and Lance.

Charlotte's questionable behavior was enough to convince Shonna that Lance knew or had nothing to do with her in the time they'd been dating seriously leading up their wedding day.

"You don't have to tell me anything else," she told him. "I'd seen enough for myself."

"Now you see why I never mentioned her?" Lance said. "What she did at work that day was nothing compared to today."

Sonia, who joined the nuptials, overheard only the end of Lance's comment about Charlotte's disruption. She also agreed.

"Two completely different incidents, but the same crazy

person." She did not elaborate any further.

Pastor Ethridge simply mentioned that he'd heard stories like these but this was the first time he experienced anything like it. He was tepid asking Shonna and Lance if they still wanted to continue with the ceremony.

Besides, he'd already received a $200 gratuity from Sonia as soon as he arrived.

"I would completely understand if the two of you would rather do this another day—"

They looked at him.

"Man, you better do your job!" Lance said.

Shonna added, "You better earn your money!"

"Well, amen—"

Pastor Ethridge announced the wedding ceremony would continue, which was met by a polite applause among most of the remaining audience. He was quick with getting to the exchanging of vows and rings.

"By the power vested in me by this state and that which is ordained by God, I declare you, Lance and Shonna, husband and wife." He paused to look at both of them individually before adding, "You may embrace and, uh, amen—"

And so it was done.

Shonna and Lance glowed. They managed to accomplish something in the face of much cynicism and adversity. Pastor Ethridge suggested that they went ahead with signing their wedding license in case anything else arose beyond their control. In addition to Ethridge's signature, Sonia signed as the other witness.

"I'll personally mail this as soon as I leave here, which," he said while looking at his watch, "will be right about now."

"You're not going to stay for the reception?" Shonna asked.

"I've got a service to get ready for in the morning."

Afterward, a visibly relieved Sonia was the first to congratulate the nuptials. "I can no longer tease you about how un-comfortable you were as my matron of honor."

"When Lance and I host our first gathering at our place, we're going to make sure that you're the bouncer," Shonna joked back at her.

The reception was held in a two-story dining room that administrators and faculty used during the regular school week. About twenty-five minutes into the chatter, eating and drinking, and taking of pictures, Sonia noticed a couple of Richland County officers near the entrance.

She was accompanied by Taylor when approaching them.

"Is there anything I can help you with? This is a wedding reception."

The taller of the two officers answered, "We're looking for Sonia Buckner."

"I'm Sonia Buckner."

"Will you please come outside?" the other officer asked.

"She looked back at Taylor. "If anything happens, call your father. My purse and keys are with your grandparents."

The taller officer identified himself as Officer Willis and ap-prised Sonia that a simple assault complaint was filed against her. Standing in the immediate distance was Charlotte, who convinced the officers to accompany her back to the univer-sity after showing off her bruises—she still had redness on her face and neck.

"Officer, that's the woman who slapped, punched and tried choking me. I want to press charges right now!"

Sonia glared to her left. "I should have done more than that to you!"

"Ms. Buckner, will you please face away from the building and place your hands—"

"How do you explain slapping someone who tried disrupting her sister's wedding as an assault?" Sonia reacted.

"It is what it is," Officer Willis answered. "We don't make the laws. We only uphold them."

Sonia looked back over at the dining hall.

"Taylor, call your father and tell him what's happen! And tell your grandparents not to worry, okay?"

Sonia was noticeably awkward in her movements while adhering to the officers' instructions as they placed handcuffs on her.

"You've never done this before?" Officer Willis asked.

She shook her head.

Meanwhile, Charlotte gloated and antagonized Sonia once the officers began escorting her away. "I told you this was far from being over!" She shifted her purse from her right shoulder to her left shoulder and walked back to her car.

Damn, what a year! Sonia sulked.

* * *

Trent had just returned from the bathroom when he passed by his cell phone. The number was familiar; its entry was among his contacts.

"Taylor?"

"Yeah, it's me."

"Do I need to pick you up from the wedding?"

Trent suspected one of two things might be the reason for Taylor calling. The first was him being so disgusted with Sonia that he preferred calling him. The other was along the lines that it seemed uncharacteristic if Sonia herself didn't call informing him that she was on her way.

"Yeah, I need you to pick me up because Mom's just been arrested." Taylor was more than calm informing his father of the news.

Trent's face contorted. "For what?"

"It was so cool. I had to pull Mom off of the woman—"

"All right, man. Can you at least tell me what actually happened?"

Taylor started laughing. "Mom punched out some crazy woman who tried spoiling Aunt Shonna's wedding, and she had her arrested. You should have seen Mom. The woman was much taller, but Mom walked up and slapped her and knocked her down and threatened to stomp her eyes out of her head!"

A son and wife with propensities to fight? As if he needed any reminders, fresh in his memory was the way she insulted and threatened Alcione when he prevailed at saving his marriage.

"Son, there are a lot of things you don't know about your mother," he said. "And fighting might be one of them."

He went on to ask Taylor if anyone else knew yet that she was arrested.

"You're the first person I called. I haven't gone back inside. I'm sure someone's probably asking where Mom is—"

"Do you know what officers arrested her?"

"Richland County."

Chapter 40

On her way being taken to the county jail facility, Sonia noticed Officer Willis drove in the same general direction as WNPW, which was east of the I-77 freeway.

She seethed at being arrested. Forty years as a law abiding citizen, including the last dozen in which she hadn't as much as been issued a parking ticket, was being trumped by this incident.

"Walk through that door straight ahead," Officer Willis said once they arrived, "and take a seat in one of the chairs."

Sonia proceeded as directed by Officer Willis, but stared at him the entire time. Humph, he did what he had to do, and she did as well: She slapped Charlotte aside her head, punched her in the face, and then tried to choking her. If necessary, she'd do it again, doggone it.

"Please remove all your jewelry and place the items in this bag, ma'am," the next person told her. "Once, you're finished sign right here."

It took the better part of an hour being processed by the jail administrative staff. After her mug shot was taken, she was directed to sit in a waiting area until further notice.

As she surveyed her surroundings, many of the women made repeated trips to the two black phones that were on the wall.

"I thought we were allowed only one phone call?" she asked the woman who plopped onto the plastic bench chair to the left of her.

The woman returned a surprise look at Sonia. "You ain't never been here?"

"First time ever."

She sucked her teeth—what was left of them "It ain't like in the movies any more. They give you ten minutes each call you make, but it has to be a local call or collect. You better hurry up; you never know when you'll be taken inside."

"Thanks."

Sonia got up and waited her turn. A young lady who appeared to be no more than half her age gestured that she could come after her. Sonia acknowledged with a nod.

Closing her eyes, and then letting out a long breath, she dialed Tillman's cell phone and hoped that he would answer. She leaned against the wall once she heard his voice.

"Dad, this is Sonia; I don't have long to talk."

"I figured you'd get around to calling us," he said. "Where are you?"

"Somewhere off Bluff Road; it's past the football stadium."

"Taylor told me what happened," he said, pausing to chuckle. "You're a trip, girl."

"Yeah, right."

"Your mother's worried sick about you."

"Tell her I'm all right. I'm just mad that I'm here."

Tillman mentioned to Sonia that he had already looked into

getting her out of jail. But he couldn't do anything until she appeared for a bond hearing. That wouldn't be until nine o'clock in the morning.

"You mean to tell me I've got to stay in this god awful place until tomorrow?" She hissed and stomped her foot on the concrete, which stung her heel.

"It doesn't sound right, but they say that's their schedule," he answered. "Do you know what they brought you in on?"

"Simple assault."

He shook his head. "Taylor says the woman you decked was crazy."

"That's saying it nice." She described quickly Charlotte and Lance's dubious history to Tillman, including how it affected Shonna in the beginning.

He asked, "Are you all right?"

"I guess. I mean, how am I supposed to feel when this is your first time being arrested?"

"Don't worry. We'll get you out." He sighed, looking over at Prentiss. "Your mother wants to talk."

"Sonia?" Prentiss said, looking upward and giving thanks; the phone's system apprised Sonia that she had three minutes.

"Mom, I don't have long. Sorry about making a scene. But I'd seen and heard enough from Charlotte."

"That's here name, Charlotte?"

"Uh-huh."

"Taylor's with us right now. We told him to tell Trent that he can come by the house later and pick him up."

"That's fine."

Prentiss rushed to tell Sonia that everyone at the reception had no idea that she was arrested until Taylor informed Shonna and Lance. Then Shonna informed her and Tillman.

After conferring with them, Shonna agreed that they would

go on with the reception as if Sonia had to leave due to an emergency.

"They'll probably find out the real story, but we didn't feel it was our place to tell anyone," Prentiss said. "At least you were able to take some pictures with Shonna and Lance right after the wedding; they did look real nice together."

"It was nice until that hussy disrupted things."

Prentiss' maternal instincts wanted to chide Sonia for taking things to the extreme by accosting Charlotte. Her righteous inclinations were along the lines of consoling Sonia that vengeance was not hers.

Then there was another part—the one which Sonia inherited many of her traits.

"Lord, forgive me for saying this, I know we're supposed to pursue peace with everyone, but I was ready to join you hitting her," she said, looking over at Tillman. "She's lucky that Tillman held me back."

Tillman jerked his head to the right. "I knew Sonia had it under control after she got in the first punch."

"Granddad, she got in all the punches!" Taylor butted in from the back seat.

The system now indicated Sonia had less than a minute. "Let me speak with Taylor—"

"Mom, guess what I'll be posting on my Twitter timeline?"

Sonia was reduced to smirking. "Boy, I've got less than a minute. Come on now."

"Hash tag beat down," he said, laughing. "I love you!"

"I love you. Make sure your grandparents get me out of here."

The system disconnected the call.

* * *

Sonia spent the night in a cell block used for detainees before being placed into the facility's population. The area had more than fifty cells each on both the upstairs and downstairs levels. Around eleven o'clock the next morning, she was summoned by an officer who stood near the watch desk.

"Get your stuff," he said.

"What for?"

"You're ATW."

"What does that mean?"

"All the way. You're leaving. Someone has posted your bail." Sonia was stoic. She'd been that way after being issued the facility's standard clothing—a faded dark blue top and baggy bottoms—along with a pair of cheap plastic shower shoes; she was not allowed to wear her Badgley Mischka evening pumps inside the jail.

Without delaying, she returned to her cell and stuffed the mesh laundry bag with the thin bath towel, face cloth, and blanket that was issued; she also stuffed the tooth brush that was about the size of her pinky and tube of tasteless toothpaste.

Minutes later, she followed the officer along a series of corridors back to the administrative intake area. She was more than glad to be reacquainted with her pumps, jewelry and the strapless chiffon gown with lace and pearls that she wore in the wedding. Her hair could have used a good brushing.

Her makeup was partially smeared and she had not yet taken a shower. At least she would be able to take care of all that and sleep in an actual bed instead of lying atop of a plastic platform with a thin foam pad for a mattress.

After pulling her hair back and tying it in a knot, she approached the jail attendant, who then had her escorted to the release area. Her stride shortened once she passed through the metal detector.

"Trent?"

He turned around. She walked guardedly toward him. His arms were still folded while waiting on her.

"I was expecting my parents to come for me."

He nodded. He had a lengthy conversation with the Chandlers after picking up Taylor. They wanted to know his side of the story why he and Sonia were separated. There was no animosity or discord.

The Chandlers offered to post Sonia's bail, but Trent said it was his duty to pay the $100 fine plus an additional $100 in court costs.

"They were okay with me coming here."

She joined him walking out of the facility. "Can you take me to where my car is parked?"

"Yeah, I can. Taylor's out in the car waiting on us."

"I'm really glad to be out of that place," she said. "For all the taxes we pay, you should see what's off in there. It's a joke. The food, well, that wasn't even food. Geez!"

"I can only imagine."

Sonia stopped once they reached the parking lot.

"What's up?" he asked.

For the first time all weekend, Sonia's emotions were getting to her. Tears began welling up in her eyes.

"Trent, I really miss you. Words can't explain how much I've missed you."

"That's nice to hear."

"I'm also sorry for causing all of this. Life's too short to be holding grudges and doing things out of retaliation," she said. "Will you forgive me for cheating on you?"

Trent glanced at her. "I'd already forgiven you even if you never asked."

They resumed walking toward his car. Sonia felt impressed to say that she was also wrong for not listening to him despite her nagging that he listened to her.

"Where did you receive that revelation?" he reacted.

She withheld from retorting with a snide remark. "Sometimes you have to admit when you're wrong. I've had to do a lot of that lately."

"I see." Taking a deep breath, he went on to add, "Your car is parked in the driveway in Chapin. We'll get your clothes later."

Her eyes widened, and she moved to hold hands with him, which he didn't refuse.

"Trent—"

He resumed looking straight ahead. "We've got a lot of things to talk about."

"Yes we do."

He clicked open the car, stunning Taylor. He bolted out of the car and rushed to hug Sonia.

"Mom!"

"Baby, I'm so glad to see you and your father." She kissed him on the cheek.

Taylor blurted about there being a video on YouTube of her accosting Charlotte. There were already more than four hundred thousand views of it, making it an instant rave. He also mentioned posting its link on his Facebook timeline.

"It's about ten minutes long. Definitely hash tag shots been fired!"

Sonia corrected him. "Taylor, there were no shots fired."

"Mom, I know. But that's what we say."

She teased Trent by giving him a familiar stare that implied Taylor was solely his son. He returned the same stare, which shifted the blame solely on her. The bantering brought a smile to their faces as it once did during better times.

As Trent drove away from the facility, he asked, "How was the wedding?"

"I wish you were there to see it," Sonia said before pursing her lips. "Other than that fool showing up, it was a beautiful wedding. Shonna and Lance looked so happy at the alter it had me thinking about us."

Trent reacted with a side-eyed glare. Then he glanced into the rear-view mirror checking on what Taylor was doing. He appeared to be listening to music and interacting on his social networks from his cell phone.

"You and me?"

Sonia reclined back in the passenger seat. "Yeah, us. I was thinking maybe we could renew our vows."

"Me? The one who forgot when your birthday was?"

"The same one."

She smiled knowing that her heart was purged of the disappointment long ago. "You don't realize how much you mean to me—I need to tell you that more."

"Make sure you say that when we're renewing our vows."

"I will."

Trent looked over at Sonia again. "We've got a lot of things to talk about, don't we?"

"We sure do."

She folded her arms and stretched her legs while savoring the possibilities. It was about as complete of a feeling she had in quite a while.

About the Author

 Since the age of 13, N. Wood Lane has dabbled in and out of writing. Lane once aspired to live in Brazil and start a newspaper in Rio de Janiero. The closest Lane has ever visited the Southern Hemisphere destination point was by renting videos from Blockbuster featuring actress Sonia Braga. Lane's affinity for Brazil also includes rooting for the country during soccer's World Cup and its music—but to this day still does not know Portuguese.

Back in the mid-1990s, Lane aspired to write a novel after reading Connie Briscoe's *Sisters and Lovers* and Terry McMillan's *Waiting to Exhale*. That aspiration never became a reality until Lane was well past age 40.

These days, Lane considers writing a way of remaining mentally engaged since attaining AARP membership eligibility.

Lane currently resides in South Carolina and has been in the insurance industry since 2001, and is at work on a third fiction novel.

Suggested Reading Group Guide Questions

1. Was Sonia right for having an affair with Wharton Milner after the disappointments she previously had with Trent?

2. Did you have a favorable or less-than-favorable impression of Sonia? Did she redeem herself at all in *The Bed I Made*?

3. Did you have a favorable or less-than-favorable impression of Trent? Would you consider him a good husband? A good father? Or both?

4. Who was your favorite or least favorite character in *The Bed I Made*?

5. What was your favorite or least favorite scene in *The Bed I Made*?

6. Did you think the title *The Bed I Made* was appropriate as the sequel to *Do It to My Mind*?

7. There were several subplots in *The Bed I Made*. One of them involved a May-December relationship between Shonna handler and Lance Miles. Did Shonna and Lance make the right decision?

8. What was the largest age difference in a relationship you've had? What is an acceptable age difference?

9. In *Do It to My Mind*, one of Sonia's arguments was that Trent hardly listened to her. Do you believe it's important that wives also listen to their husbands?

10. How can wives better show respect to their husbands?

Suggested Reading Group Guide Questions (cont.)

11. How can husbands show a deeper love toward their wives?

12. Was Trent right for making good on the favor he owed Alcione? Could he have handled it differently?

13. How difficult is it to admit when you're wrong?

14. Were the characters believable? Was there a character who reminded you of somebody you already know?

15. Was the plot and subplots believable? Were they predictable?

16. Do you think the ending of *The Bed I Made* was the right ending? Should there been a different ending. If so, what would you have preferred?

Other Books from MavLit Publishing

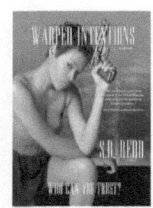

Warped Intentions
by S.B. Redd
9781937705121
$14.95

Love, Song & Dance
by Jevon L. Mack
9780983115205
$14.95

Do It to My Mind
by N.Wood Lane
9781937705190
$14.95

Thoughts of Life:
360 E. May St.
B.H., Michigan
by Birdman '313'
9781937705046
$14.95

Presumption of Paternity
by S.B. Redd
9780983115281
$14.95

MavLit Publishing
www.maverick-books.com